ALSO BY DOUGLAS HOBBIE

Boomfell

Douglas Hobbie

The Day

A John Macrae Book

Henry Holt and Company
New York

Henry Holt and Company, Inc.
Publishers since 1866
115 West 18th Street
New York, New York 10011

Henry Holt® *is a registered*
trademark of Henry Holt and Company, Inc.

Copyright © 1993 by Douglas Hobbie
All rights reserved.
Published in Canada by Fitzhenry & Whiteside Ltd.,
91 Granton Drive, Richmond Hill, Ontario L4B 2N5.

Library of Congress Cataloging-in-Publication Data
Hobbie, Douglas.
The day / Douglas Hobbie. — 1st ed.
p.   cm.
"A John Macrae book."
I. Title.
PS3558.O3364D38   1993   92-29076
813'.54—dc20   CIP
ISBN 0-8050-2519-7

First Edition—1993

Designed by Katy Riegel

Printed in the United States of America.
All first editions are printed on acid-free paper.∞

1   3   5   7   9   10   8   6   4   2

In memory of
my daughter
BRETT HOBBIE
January 11, 1965–October 14, 1992

B. HOBBIE '92

The
Day

*I*t would have been hard to choose a Camperdown elm over the more familiar and less expensive possibilities if there had not been the wonderful example of a mature tree rooted in their past and still living in their imaginations. The young tree was an erect stem, a head taller than Gwen, straight as a broomstick, which sprouted from its grafted head a half dozen haywire branches. The branches were hung with tissuey pale green clusters that looked artificial rather than organic: the Camperdown elm's comical flowers. They chose from a half dozen specimens, which stood, a lonely row of oddballs, among vigorous blooming *malus* and already shapely *acer* on the windy summit of the nursery's hundreds of planted acres. Gwen laughed, loved it for its endearing weirdness. They had halfheartedly planned to purchase such a tree for years, ever since they'd moved into their own house. It was to have been a housewarming gift from Gwen's sister Clare, who had sent a check from . . . was she in San Francisco then?— instructing them to buy a Camperdown elm. Clare had subsequently mentioned it over the phone and in writing, and Fletcher had assured her that they would get to it one day, but they had never followed through. Clare's death the preceding fall had prompted the May outing. They would plant the tree in her memory. As it turned out, a Camperdown elm wasn't nearly as difficult to locate as they'd imagined it would be.

They spent the rest of the morning browsing around budding things admiringly, sniffing flowers, learning new names. They exchanged smiles and nods with strangers. Everyone here seemed happy, milling among balled shrubs, concrete birdbaths, garden statues of saints and woodland animals like pilgrims who had arrived at their destination. They had soup and sandwiches at a little clapboard place ambitiously named The Golden Phoenix. It was cool for May, but sunny; the toasty interior of the car reminded them of a greenhouse, a particular greenhouse on a winter day. They decided, as long as they were so close, to visit the herb gardens at Coventry. As they drove south on the interstate, he now remembered vividly, after-lunch drowsy, the three o'clock sun slanting into their laps, and pleased with themselves at the moment, he suggested a little company to liven up the tedious drive, and Gwen, reclined in her bucket seat, watching the road through heavy-lidded eyes, suddenly reached over, as if his humorous hit-or-miss suggestion had triggered a powerful chemical reaction in the willing part of her brain, and unfastened the front of his corduroy pants, warning him to keep his eyes on the road. The sensational flattery of her unexpected interest. He signaled and changed lanes and slowed to the speed limit, his happy cock a naked monstrosity in the front seat. In turn she permitted him to work his hand into her pleated khaki pants. Scouting fingers pressed beneath cotton underpants and found a wife, yes, whose stream of thought was warmly confluent with his own. Unbuttoning her pants for him, she said, There should be a law against this. It had to be the sun, she explained, the sun felt so good. He felt more like an awkward teenager than a man who had been with this woman for more than fifteen years. Ordinary people sped by in cars and trucks at heedless speeds, oblivious to the Fletchers, who cruised along in their secret life of the moment, insular as aliens. A yellow school bus passed, the children waved, a bunch of goofy faces in the window, and the Fletchers waved back, the outrageousness of their undone pants hastily concealed under sweaters. Even the sight of innocent children didn't discourage them. They were animals. His agreeable wife stretched out her legs and closed her eyes, biting her lip as if in a corny movie, turning her face to the window, the unflattering sun, her brow crinkled with concentration. The earnest pleasure written all over her unguarded face seemed proof that women had it better than men. She drew up her knees and grabbed his tensed wrist with both hands. Jesus, stop!

D o you remember the last time we were at Penny's?" Gwen asked, interrupting his pleasing memory of the last time they'd driven this same highway. "Christmas we had your family at our house, so we must have been at Penny's last Thanksgiving, too. Do you remember?"

"We were." Sifting through his notebook the night before, reviewing the past year—where had the time gone?—he had come upon his ungenerous entry for Thanksgiving: With Gwen's family at Pen's—eating proves the highlight of the day.

"I don't remember one detail of that memorable

occasion," she said. "Isn't that rotten of me? We haven't seen them since then, the whole year. Christ."

"Mother, I want to enjoy myself today." Kate in the backseat. "I've been looking forward to it for weeks."

"I'd love to enjoy myself today, believe me." She turned to Fletcher. "What's funny? Why are you smiling?"

"I was thinking about the last time we were on this road, the day we drove to Coventry. May, remember? The day we bought the Camperdown elm. That little adventure."

"Don't remind me."

"What adventure?" Kate asked, enunciating the word—*adventure*—as though it could hardly describe a day in her parents' life.

"I must have been out of my mind."

"You must have been." Someone altogether different from the woman sitting here now, a wreck of anticipation.

"Mind telling me what we're talking about?"

"Just a funny time your father and I had last spring."

"Fine," Kate said, annoyed with them.

"Today is the anniversary of Clare's death." He wanted that out on the table, a matter that had not been broached lately, autumn all but past, trees bare again, the holiday approaching. "It occurred to me, reading my notebook last night."

"Thanksgiving?" Her tone was indignant. "Not Thanksgiving, Jack."

"The date, not the day. The twenty-eighth. Thanksgiving was the twenty-second last year."

"A year. It seems longer than that, doesn't it? It seems ages ago. Oh God . . ."

"What?"

"I hope Mother has her head screwed on today. I'm dreading this."

"I remember her from San Francisco," Kate said. "I thought she was great."

"Do we know what she did that Thanksgiving?" he asked. "Was she with anyone or alone . . . ?"

"I don't know and I'm not going to spend the rest of the day thinking about it. I don't want to think about Clare. Whoever Clare was."

Each morning for months he'd awakened to the realization of Clare's death, which came over him like nausea, as if remembering too late something important he'd forgotten to do. Only recently, yet sooner than he'd expected, anger and guilt gave way to near-acceptance, her death lost its everyday jolt and became Clare's story—what had happened to someone he knew. Today, though, he'd awakened again with gut-wrenching dread.

"I hope our little tree makes it through winter." Gwen had changed her tone, relenting. "It lost its leaves so early."

"We did our part. One third peat moss, one third manure. Watered it faithfully. The Camperdown elm is very hardy, isn't that what the nursery man said?"

They had planted it in the east corner of Gwen's garden on the south side, sheltered by the house and set off by the hemlock hedge. The original Camperdown elm had stood against a towering wall of evergreens. In winter it looked craggy and ancient as a Rackham drawing, a tree with feeling (Gwen's observation). In full leaf its dense pendulous branches almost reached to the ground so that walking underneath was like entering a green cave. Whenever young Fletcher visited Gwen

Wells at her school, they paid their respects to the Camperdown elm. One spring evening they went so far as to make love (an apt name for it then) under the tree, lying down with their clothes on, Gwen in a cotton dress, her underpants in Jack's back pocket. A dog came along, followed by an elderly couple reciting the names of flowers to one another. That had happened only once, which may have been why the moment was still so present, an unusual instance of ripe youth, in Fletcher's mind. The story had been known to Clare, and he tended to believe that's what had inspired her gift. In her time, Clare had also had an abiding affection for that particular tree on campus—over there by the Victorian greenhouse, where everyone liked to get warm and breathe humid earth after an hour skating on the frozen pond across the street. If the Camperdown elm at the college was as old as the century, as they liked to believe, then it was over sixty years old when Clare graduated from the school, and it had stood there for over seventy years by the time Gwen took her degree. Art history. Now the tree was in its nineties, still discovered each spring by newcomers, you assumed, venerable shelter for helter-skelter romance. When she came east, Clare had written, she expected to see her gift to the Fletchers thriving in their backyard. She never came.

"I think it's going to make it," he said.

Gwen reached over and touched the back of his head sympathetically. "Poor Clare." A moment later she said, "The cars! You'd think there was a mass migration going on."

"Mirrored migrations."

Everyone dressed up more or less, bearing the bounty of legendary recipes wrapped in tinfoil, bearing mixed feelings toward those loved ones who that very moment eagerly and uneasily awaited them—drive carefully!—this most heavily trafficked day of the year. A turkey roasted, you figured, for every car.

"The people!" she exclaimed. "All these people. It's unbelievable, isn't it? Clare, I mean. It's still unbelievable."

Coventry: one mile. Which made the exit after that theirs.

*P*enny's stately white house, center hall 1700 something, set against the slope of silver woods like that, with low winter clouds blowing behind it, casting dramatic light across the still-green lawn, reminded him of one of Gwen's old watercolors, a picture she had done when they were living in two rooms on Commonwealth Avenue, waiting for Kate to be born, just kids themselves it seemed from here. The painting now hung in their kitchen, acquiring significance with the passage of time, a symbol of Gwen's native gifts, or the leveling sadness of life, or the costly sacrifice of selfless motherhood. Fletcher had been the household genius, and his girlfriend's ambitions, because she was pregnant, had taken a backseat for both of them to his work. Fledgling architect. In Boston in 1975 that meant long hours doing as you were told for less than a thousand a month. Now there was little way of knowing what might have been possible for either of them. Change a single detail, he would tell her over a bottle of wine, and everything changed. Fifteen years later it was practically impossible to imagine that anything—everything—could have been otherwise. Thanks to Peter, Penny had gone on to inhabit her younger sister's youthful vision, call it, of life as it might have been.

That old saw. He'd never perceived it before, the likeness between his sister-in-law's place and Gwen's imagined idea of home.

"This always reminds me of my grandmother's," she said. "It has that feeling. Those trees."

The sugar maples along the road had a storybook grandeur. Without their leaves they stood like the souls of trees, hoary, wracked, enduring. Rock maples to Peter, the woodsman. He had cabled them and fed them, a new liquid injection system like something intravenous for trees, and taken out the dead wood. They seemed to be doing all right. Fletcher turned up the long drive, newly resurfaced with oil and stone. He missed the old, narrower road with its spine of grass. The sight of his in-laws' car, for example—clean, gray, like new—it represented them too clearly, like their tidy dwelling on the coast, the undisturbed living room, the magazines on the coffee table, certain colors. Don't be unkind, Jack, that's them. That was his wife talking. You could imagine them, the Wellses, as they pulled into the driveway today, two silent figures behind the windshield. Curly, for example, a tall, stooped figure, a giant really, obediently bearing the basket of baked goods from the immaculate trunk of the car. He would be wearing what his wife had told him to wear—that was a family joke—as though from his orderly closet he could have chosen trousers that would offend us. You imagined hale, beaming Peter at the front door, the kids racing with shouts, the smiles that unexpectedly show up on everyone's face at the last minute. Penny would have waited in the wings, her kitchen, listening to the approach of her parents' lifelong voices, blunting the arrival of her mother with busyness. Pen was all right. Just now the family would be gathered around the island in the kitchen waiting for Gwen's family to show up. The weather, how nice you looked, how you were feeling. It was as though you saw them too clearly, these people.

"Who's here?" Gwen asked with impatience. "Has Penny invited someone else?"

An unfamiliar car, something sporty, was parked in front of her parents' car.

"Jesus, Gwen, he's finally got it on the road. His classic."

For years he and Peter had never failed to make their way to the barn—Thanksgivings, Christmases, Easters—to inspect Peter's dismantled treasure, a canary-yellow Jaguar convertible of some important vintage. He'd never expected to see the car in one piece. Here it stood: restored. There was a recession going on.

"What's Peter, fifty? Evidently his passion for cars struck deep enough in adolescence to last a lifetime."

Sam, who had slept most of the way, came to life in the backseat. "Dad, that's excellent."

Kate asked, "What's wrong with it? It's only a car." She now used against him the habit of mind Fletcher had taught her: question everything.

With the soft tip of her fourth finger, Gwen applied gloss to her lower lip and asked, "How's that?" Then answered, "I look like something the cat dragged in, I feel like shit."

"You look fine, Mother."

"You look fine, Gwen."

"I hate the way I look this morning."

Sam was to give his aunt the fancy bottle of extra virgin olive oil, Kate would give her grandmother the herbal wreath, Gwen would carry the basket of assorted breads. Banana nut bread, cranberry bread, lemon bread. She had spent the week preparing for today.

"Everyone be pleasant," she said, "please."

"No one knows how to be otherwise."

He saw someone in the living-room window, looking out, and imagined the sight of their familiar Saab, new five years ago, wobbling up the drive. The Fletchers are here. Abruptly, he set the emergency brake. "Okay, Sam, let's tear this place apart."

The oversized pumpkin on the front stoop, the cleanly raked lawn, the lamppost, for example, with the eighteenth-century-like copper fixture they'd spent a fortune on, or the large too-friendly dog wagging toward them, the dog's name, Buster: what was wrong with it? The trees, the sky, the children, this day. Relax.

The wide front door opened inward as they mounted the granite steps, and Gwen's family swept toward them, that was the feeling, a forceful wave of greeting that, receding, carried the newcomers into the house. Penny changing one thing or another every time you turned around. This time the wallpaper was gone, the walls of the spacious hallway all of a sudden off-white. And the piece of furniture there, a cupboard as old as the hills probably, beautifully beat to hell in its original blue-green paint, that was a new acquisition. Talk about it later. Following hugs for Kate and Sam, Patricia Wells turned toward him smiling emphatically with see-through teeth, she placed her hands on his shoulders, causing Jack to flinch, and offered him her pinkish fragrant cheek. He promptly kissed the woman. That hadn't happened in years as a matter of fact, not since the grandmother's funeral when, everyone distracted by grief, family feeling flowed freely, even toward Fletcher. He didn't believe her gesture for a moment.

"I don't want to hear any more about Clarence Thomas, Jack. We're no longer talking about Long Dong Silver."

"Clarence who?" was his baffled reply. "Wasn't that last month?"

Bo, Penny's youngest, wrapped himself around his uncle's right leg and began climbing to the top of Fletcher, grappling for handholds on his tweed jacket. Mary, their grown-up daughter, came up behind him and said, Hi, Jack, close to his ear. Peter, splendid in red suspenders, said, How's your pecker, and winked. Meaninglessly, Fletcher winked back. Gwen's father squarely positioned himself before his son-in-law, his feet two feet apart, as if stepping up to address the ball in his beloved game of golf. He took Jack up to the wrist in his two-handed grip and recited his part of the holiday catechism: What time had they left the house? What route had they taken to get there? How was the traffic? About ten, not too bad, the usual, were his son-in-law's out-of-order answers. Curly wanted to know—How about it, Jack?—if Fletcher was ready for a three-handed game of cribbage later on. Cribbage? Penny, different somehow, took her brother-in-law by the arm, Where did you get this hunk, Gwen? What was it? Her hair, yes, shorter, darker.

"I like it," he said. "The new Pen."

"It looked better last week."

Becky reached up for her hug hello and clung to his neck as Fletcher lifted her off the ground. Recognition gradually dawned on him as he squeezed her sturdy little girl's body. Her dress, a bright floral print of rusts and oranges, greens and yellows and dark browns, had belonged to Kate. At nine? Ten? When Kate had looked like Howdy Doody.

"I love this," he told her, nuzzling, breathing in Becky's clean smell. "I love this dress."

"She has two new outfits upstairs," said Penny. "She insisted on dragging this out."

"One of my favorite dresses in the world, Becky."

"Thanks, Uncle Jack."

His wife's family moved toward him, placed hands on him, took him in today, it seemed, as if Fletcher— son-in-law, uncle, brother-in-law—had won mega- bucks in the state lottery, gone out to lunch with a celebrity, as if he was one of them. Easy does it, every- one. His sense of ambush may have been apparent, for when he looked up he found a young woman, pre- sumably Mary's guest from college, grinning in his di- rection. Framed by the kitchen doorway, her hands in the pockets of her skirt, she appeared satisfied to be a disinterested bystander at this moment of family re- union, so fraught, as all such meetings were, with the implicit strain of blood ties. The stress, thought Fletcher, of endless relationships.

*P*eter's patchwork corduroy pants, his bow tie, the red suspenders again this year. "I thought Hallow- een was over, Peter."

"Twick or tweet, sweetie." The gay mimic. He handed Jack a crystal glass of whiskey. "This will blow your socks off, Fletch, the best single malt I've found for under thirty bucks."

"I told you Jack would say something about those pants," said Penny. "Peter bought them on Nantucket in the sixties."

"And they still fit you, Peter?" said his mother-in-law. "I think that's impressive."

"Screw Jack and my pants."

"You're perfect," said Fletcher. "I wouldn't change a thing."

"You turkey."

"Who said the magic word?" said Curly. He rubbed his long hands together briskly.

Peter held out a drink to his father-in-law as if proffering a magic potion. "If this doesn't put lead in your pencil, Dad, nothing will."

"That's not funny," said Penny.

"Pen, have you lost weight? Your face looks thinner, doesn't it, Mother?"

"That's stress, Gwen. Your ass gets bigger, but your head shrinks."

"You look wonderful today. Both of you do."

"I'm bleeding to death, like clockwork, you know, the very day of Thanksgiving."

"You should be used to that by now. How old are you, for heaven's sake?"

"Kindly don't tell me what I should be, Mother. I'm bleeding like a pig with its throat cut. Maybe it's my last period, that's what it feels like."

"I swear you look ten years younger, Pen. Maybe I should get mine cut. I'd probably look like Margaret Mead."

"I'm already sorry I did it."

With fingertips Gwen traced the edge of Penny's hair as it framed her face, a sister's touch, and Penny raised her hand to retrace. . . .

"It suits you perfectly. How would you like to be going bald?"

"Mother!" They laughed. "You're not going bald."

"Of course I am. You two have no idea, you're both at your peak, to hear you talk you'd think—"

"What do you think, Gwen, how's your peak?"

"I'm dizzy all the time, I can hardly breathe up here."

"Just wait. I actually was dizzy—for years. I thought I'd lose my mind. You'll soon discover—"

"I hope so, Mother. I hope I discover something, and, God, I hope it's soon. Anything, I'll discover anything."

"Hold still, you're coming apart." She attended to the zipper on her daughter's skirt, slipping fingers into the waistband. They're different, he thought, than men, their familiarity, this touching. "If you've put on weight, you'd never know it in this skirt. It fits better than ever."

Penny dressed like her mother—the soft off-white sweater with taupe skirt, plus pearls, clear nail polish, a light-handed layer of makeup intended to soften and smooth—and wore her mother's habitual expression of vague anxiety, or impatience, always busy anticipating difficulties. The likeness between them was the source of their impatience with one another. Never more than a fifty-fifty chance of getting along at any given moment. A wrong word, a momentary frown, could throw them off for days. Their thin-skinned strife would last a lifetime. Penny complained about her mother's repetitive stream of complaint, yet talked to her on the phone every day of the week. Mother is driving me crazy, she'd tell Gwen, and in the next breath she'd be off to spend the weekend with the woman, drive each other crazy face-to-face. He liked to think that Gwen, as the youngest, had gotten away, although it was probably too soon to tell. Nothing had seemed clearer than

Clare's escape from the world of Patricia Wells. Would they succeed in getting through the day without the unwelcome subject of Clare intruding? That wasn't right.

Penny's bristling efficiency—arranging appetizers just now on a Canton platter—her inattentive smile, her new haircut: on Thanksgiving in her own home, in the swell bosom of loved ones, she couldn't relax, not for a minute. The same emotions were replayed each year like a theme song. Headache by the end of the day, if not sooner. Her highstrung honeymoon of migraines was family lore. Screwing was the only thing that spelled relief. Did that mean her honeymoon had been happy? Over twenty years ago. You never knew. If you were Fletcher, you doubted it. Penny had toed the line, and life, she seemed to convey now, had been one disappointment after another from first date and top of the class to marriage, house on the hill, new haircut . . . till death us do . . . Twenty years from now she'd follow her mother's example, count grandchildren as her last hurrah, live from one gift-giving occasion to the next, and settle, complaints notwithstanding, for her lot.

Don't be so fucking glib, Jack, you're no different.

Just now, of the three, Gwen's smile was the only one to be believed, willing to enjoy this, given half a chance.

They swapped recent points of interest concerning their children: Becky's experimental ant colony, Bo's fainting career as an acolyte, Kate's piano recital, Sam's memorable remark in answer to his father's question about great authors. I've heard of Shakespeare, Dad, but I never heard of Toadstool.

"Isn't he something?"

Penny's rosemary, four feet tall, stood in the south

window of the kitchen. From May until October the
fragrant plant lived in her garden on the east side of
the house. Each fall, for the last ten years, he guessed,
she put it in its giant clay pot and brought it inside.
For the first time he noticed pale lavender-blue flowers,
the color nearly of Gwen's blouse. He gently stroked
the evergreen branch and smelled his perfumed hand.
Rosemary.

"Penny, I didn't know rosemary flowered."

"Everything flowers, Jack, especially plants."

"Where have the other two gone?" Gwen's mother
asked.

"I beg your pardon. I meant, I have never seen
rosemary flowering before."

"You said, 'I didn't know rosemary flowered.' "

"Mary's friend seems pleasant," said Patricia Wells.

"Her mother lives in California and her father lives
in Switzerland or something civilized like that. I think
he's an architect, Jack, if I'm not mistaken. He restores
chateaux for rock stars, something mundane and deca-
dent. She seems unspoiled by whatever privileged hard-
ships—"

"There you go, Jack, there's a contact for you," said
the mother. "At least she speaks to you. So many of
these kids today are so . . . bored. And she's not dressed
in black from head to foot. All they wear is black, what
can that whole generation be in mourning about?"

"She's hardly a kid, Mother. She's considerably
older than Mary, although you'd never know it."

Gwen glanced toward the doorway, then asked, "Is
this the friend that got raped last spring?"

"God, no, that wasn't a friend of Mary's. Just a girl
in the dorm."

"I didn't hear anything about a rape last spring," her mother said. "A girl was raped?"

"I'm sure I mentioned it to you, Mother."

"Just a girl in the dorm, Pen? You mean rape is less disturbing if the victim is not a friend of Mary's?" That was Jack putting his foot in it. No, Clare was far from mind at the moment, otherwise the topic wouldn't have come up.

"Are you still here?" Penny asked him.

"Come on, Jack," his wife said, "go solve the world's problems with Dad and Peter."

Patricia Wells would like Mary's friend less if she had been the victim of rape last spring. That was to be held against the woman. Her timidity, her avoidance. Concern for others rarely extended beyond the limits of her family. What happened outside the closed circle of her Thanksgiving was not her worry.

"They must be looking at Peter's new toy," said Penny.

"Jack knows it's more interesting in here with us."

"Isn't that the truth?" Gwen sampled a smidgen of pâté and hummed her approval. "Good-bye, Jack."

"I'm off to see the toy that will solve the world's problems," said Fletcher cheerfully.

T here is nothing like rape to get your head together. . . . Such boldness could be offensive, hardly the tone a victim was expected to take when speaking of the crime against her.

We let her die. She's dead, and we let her die.

Peter and Curly, a head taller than his bearish son-in-law, stood by the white board fence that surrounded the pool, covered now with blue plastic until May. "I want to see you in there next year, Jack. Where were you all summer?"

Fletcher didn't know where the summer went, just busy, they'd missed it.

"That hot Fourth of July weekend, I was like a damn seal, wasn't I, Peter? I spent the whole day in there." Gwen's father extended his hand as if bestowing a blessing on the scene of that summer's day.

"I would have said walrus, Dad. Have you seen that recent *Den of Thieves* book, Jack? We were just saying, Jesus, it's never been quite this bad before, has it, outright bandits like Boesky and Milken, this whole S and L mess, steal and lie, take their money, we'll figure it out later. That's the philosophy—fuck 'em, they're stupid, do what you want. What's the latest estimate, Dad, seven hundred billion including interest, for Christ's sake? Most people can't even afford sneakers for their kids anymore."

"I wouldn't know a junk bond if I slipped on one and went ass over teakettle," said Curly amiably. "We don't hear more about it because people can't grasp it. These Wall Street fellows might as well be on Mars for all some poor slob in Iowa thinks."

"Who was that Chinese kid who blew away the whole damn physics department because he didn't win best term paper? There went half the scientific gene pool in Iowa, how are we going to conquer outer space that way, Dad? Wasn't he an astronomer? A Chinese astronomer in Iowa, can you figure it out?"

"A crying shame," said Curly soberly. "Was it twenty-three dead in Killeen, Texas, the week before?"

"Then he shot himself," said Peter. "Why didn't he think of that first?"

"That's an idea, Peter, why didn't he?" Curly asked.

Penny's garden plot, largely fallow now, had been enclosed by a neat picket fence already weathered to a rustic gray. They were still getting spinach, kale, brussels sprouts, believe it or not. "But they had peppers this year, didn't you, Peter, there must have been six different kinds of peppers, all colors, you never tasted anything like it, fried up with onions and that homemade Pekarski's sausage fresh from right down the street." Curly raised his head and closed his eyes, remembering. "Out of this world, positively."

"They let you eat the sausage, did they?" said Fletcher.

"Out of this world," Curly repeated.

The slate roof on the north side of the one-and-a-half-story ell had been replaced with red cedar shingles. An old house was never done. The raised paddleball court, now half-concealed by overgrown sumac, looked like a large cage formerly inhabited by some pacing animal. It must have been damn near ten years since he and Peter had gone at it, often stripped to the waist, and always a close battle although Peter had ten years on him and smoked two packs a day back then. Into the pool afterward, bareass that one time, no one else around, surprised to see that Peter was uncircumcised, for example. Not to have known such a basic fact about your brother-in-law said something, didn't it? No one played paddleball anymore.

Out front they huddled over the low roof of the Jaguar like conspirators, Fletcher considered, with secrets to impart.

"I might have liked a little job like this once," said the father-in-law. "In my youth," he added.

"Famine, AIDS, environmental devastation, what's

a toy like this have to do with world problems, Peter?"

"Listen to this guy, Dad, he sounds like a Democrat running for President, those poor clowns. Quayle is all set to run in 'ninety-six. They asked him if he thought the anti-abortion vote would still be significant. True story, Dad. He said he'd always cast his vote for the unborn and he hoped the unborn would always vote for Dan Quayle."

Curly smiled agreeably, not to offend. Had they heard the one about the upset mother who complained about the neighbor's boy pissing his name in the snow behind the barn? A clear drop of water dangled on the tip of Curly's impressive nose. On the heels of the punch line—I know my daughter's handwriting when I see it—he turned toward the house. Leave them laughing. The nose and ears kept growing, seemed like, while the rest of you gradually diminished. But Curly was still a handsome man.

Peter watched him lumber toward the front door. "He's a great guy, isn't he? Goddamnit, Jack, he really is."

The perfection of Peter's impeccable peppery mustache, the neatly groomed hair graying handsomely around the ears like that. Starched shirt cuffs tidily rolled back, his woodsman's strong wrists. The businessman's manicured spatulate fingers. Hands out of *Where the Wild Things Are.* You became what you did. Peter hadn't changed one bit since he'd known him, as far as Fletcher was concerned, but he had only achieved thorough mastery of his appearance recently, once his actual age had caught up with the self he'd been fashioning since he was twenty-one probably: grown-up mover of his time and place. On Peter the wedding band made perfect sense, for instance, and the watch, super-duper damn watch worth more than Fletcher's car at this point, considerably more.

"As for thieves," he said, "the IRS is all over me for that J. D. Realty tax bite, Peter, and now I have Gigley on my back to boot. I'll never forgive you for that, you bastard."

There had been a couple of years in the eighties when Fletcher, for the first time in his life, had made money. Ingari, Itzkoff, and Fletcher, in a series of windfall breaks starting with the Maloney School condominium conversion, had done the Orchard condominium development, the new Pioneer Bank in the center of town, and half a dozen large houses for Jeff Black, one of the area's prominent landowners, to name the young firm's major projects. Itzkoff, who had graduated with Fletcher (RISD '73), had teamed up with Ingari, a Yale architect more than ten years his senior, in the heart of Massachusetts, and persuaded Fletcher, who had nothing to lose, to move to what appeared to be an evolving region of New England at the time. Ingari, a savvy operator, had established vital ties with banks, contractors, prominent citizens. They already had work, they needed another partner. Confined to junior status in the Boston company, Fletcher took the chance. The Valley, as Itzkoff described it, was an enlightened place, a kind of rural city, so along with bookstores, good bread, okay restaurants, and constant concerts, readings, performances, exhibits, etc., you got fields and streams instead of fear and trembling. New Avon particularly, the former mill town with its Veterans' Hospital, state mental hospital, and famous college, had grown significantly even since Gwen's college years there, becoming a mecca for artsy, politically correct, entrepreneurial, environmentalist types, and so Gwen didn't mind returning. Within five years of Fletcher's arrival, IIF had several noteworthy projects to its name, had extended its reputation north to Vermont, eastward almost as far as Boston, and moved its operation, with ten full-time employees, to ten thousand square feet of a former brass works factory, which they had ingeniously renovated to suit their needs. When IIF's growth was eventually reflected in Fletcher's income, his brother-in-law, the financial wizard, was on hand to shelter it.

There was a natural gas deal, an apartment building in Texas and another in Southern California. Five years later all three investments had been lost. Gas had been discovered in five out of six wells, but was never produced, and the enterprise finally folded, thieves picked it up for nothing when a handful of major investors decided to get out, humble limited partners like Fletcher be damned. More disturbing, when Congress shut down shelters in '86 or '87, must have been '87, Fletcher was required to pay taxes on roughly one hundred and fifty thousand dollars he hadn't earned, the tax bite from which he had not yet recovered. Gigley Inc., meanwhile, in a tax-deferred exchange, had traded its Oak Towers for the James-Tech office building in Marina del Rey, places Fletcher had never laid eyes on. Thanks to the recession, two of James-Tech's primo clients, occupying forty thousand square feet of the building, had decided not to renew their leases. James-Tech was to be foreclosed, the last investment lost, and one of the consequences to schmucks like Jack Fletcher was to be a capital gain, on paper only, of one hundred and sixty thousand dollars, which he would owe taxes on in '92. The thought of it made his head spin with bad feeling for Peter, his brother-in-law, who had sold him this crippling anxiety, this further undoing in the midst of an already treacherous recession. He had called Peter to holler; the additional tax liability was bound to sink the whole family of Fletcher. He was ashamed to tell Gwen about it. Peter was cool. Everyone had known the shelters involved a roll of the dice. Duped Fletcher suffered while the likes of Peter West simply walked away. That wasn't right.

"Those deals were good," Peter insisted now, an edge of indignation in his voice, "run by good people, then the Rule of 78's got knocked out—on December 30, for Christ's sake, bang, you're dead—then this fucking recession, office buildings all over the country going down the tubes. Those were uncontrollable events, Fletch. We won't let you die. Don't worry, all right? Trust me."

"You plan to pay the taxes?"

"We'll work it out. I can probably make a deal with the IRS. Would I ever let you down, for Christ's sake? We'll take care of it."

That was a lie, of course, a practice endemic to Peter's profession. The government would take every spare dollar for the next few years. As it was, they were barely holding on.

"How's Frank Lloyd Wright these days, anyway?" Peter asked pleasantly. "Anything cooking out there?"

Ingari, Itzkoff, and Fletcher had two main prospects. A hilltown to the west was going forward, despite the economic climate, with a badly needed grammar school, backed by federal funding and increased town taxes. They were working on their presentation. Fletcher's own town was undertaking a new building to house the police department and assorted public offices. Ingari was pulling all the stops to land the contract. Otherwise, Fletcher was following a couple of private leads. An orthopedic surgeon wanted a two-hundred-thousand-dollar addition, including new kitchen and family room. A local restaurateur hoped to convert a nineteenth-century cylindrical brick gasworks into his dreamspace, if he could persuade the bank to buy it. Fletcher was also talking to a veterinarian about transforming a Victorian monstrosity into a hospital for cats and dogs. Things were bad out there. The end of the present downturn didn't seem to be in sight.

Peter placed his hand on Fletcher's shoulder, avuncular, and advised him to be patient. "The world isn't going anywhere, Fletch. We needed the correction. All that high-roller garbage had gotten out of hand. Good times will be back, baby. I met a couple from Russia, Sonia and Vladimir, a client of mine is trying to work out a deal on contemporary Russian art, whatever that is. He can buy it for practically nothing, turn around and sell it in New York, Washington, Chicago, that's the plan. He's been going back to Leningrad and Moscow with cigarettes and toilet paper since before the Wall came down. He comes home with fur hats and army watches. So he brought Boris and his wife over just for kicks, his main contact. We went to dinner with them one night. They have nothing over there, Fletch, nothing. The USSR is over, kaput. The poor woman cried at the sight of food on the table, they each gained twenty pounds in three weeks. People stand in lines all day and live in one room at night. Be happy we live in Bush Country. The fuss about health insurance, right, you get sick over there, you die, period. Chaos. Remind me to tell you about Kamchatka, Fletch. This is a potential gold mine, paradise. If you come into some money, let me know, will you, I'd like to see you in this one." He paused. "The endodontists are the real thieves, cost me two grand by the time he got done with that sucker." He pointed to a gold-capped molar in his lower jaw. "Hey, the man in the street is a little anxious right now, but there's still piles of money out there. You have to spin your web of connections, then every day is a fresh kill, I learned that thirty years ago trading antique guns while I was at school. Money grows like mold, recession or not. Hey, Jack." He gestured to his house, the surrounding landscape. "Who would have believed this would be me? I don't even know how to spell. I was always a shitty speller."

"So was John Cheever, I hear, the original country husband." A tidbit Fletcher had picked up browsing in the bookstore, the writer's sad recent journals—a secret life.

Peter was confident enough now to boast about former shortcomings, money being the sole measure of a man's worth. Such success bespoke a stupid world was another way of looking at it. Don't kid yourself, Jack, Peter is nobody's fool. Gwen's view.

"Your average Joe used to support the whole family for a year on the cost of Mary's tuition for one semester. Not that long ago, Fletch. Recession, right? We couldn't get a room at the Plaza for a weekend in December, imagine that, hundreds of bucks a night, no vacancies." They would stay at the Westbury with the polo players instead.

"Did Gwen tell me you were in Chicago or Texas or . . . ?"

Peter had been to Florida to check out a property a couple of weeks ago. The night before last he'd returned from holding a recent widow's hand in California, figuring out what to do with the deceased's life insurance. "She's going to be fine, Fletch, but right now she doesn't think she can live without the guy. He made a fortune in asphalt, moved to La Jolla, his doctor missed the colon cancer, totally treatable today, they missed it, went to the liver, dead within months. The horrible truth, he was an asshole, pardon the pun, she's better off without him. Most of these guys taking up space in the Plaza, waltzing around town like they have the world by the tail, they're dumbbells, including the low-life sleaze that owns the place. Determined thick-skinned mediocrity wins the day. They've stumbled into the big time, the current is bearing them along, they don't even know what happened. This Andy in California, he had an oil company twelve years ago, which went under, apartment buildings to kingdom come, half of them empty today, a newspaper some-where, ranches, now he's producing a lousy movie. On location in Italy or Spain, Andy's artistic period. He owns mansions in three countries. He has a neck on him like this, ex–football player. He can't read, Fletch. That's only a slight exaggeration. If I can't spell, Andy can't read. That's who's running the show. Schmucks who don't realize that never get into it, never know how it works. They think the world is for other people, not them. You follow me?"

"No."

"Why let the assholes have all the fun?"

They continued around the house to the backyard again. A dense arbor of honeysuckle, its stubborn green leaves curled by cold, framed the entrance to Penny's herb garden.

Switching gears then, intended to provoke, Fletcher said, "Can you remember the last time Clare was here with the rest of us? I was trying to figure that out. It was a Christmas maybe."

Peter stepped nimbly, positioning himself between Jack and the house. He raised his arms as though this was one-on-one and his brother-in-law had the ball. "For Christ's sake, do us a favor, Fletch, don't mention Clare. That's all we need today, no one's said a god-damn word about Clare. All I want to do is get through the next twelve hours or so without Clare. Bring that up and Mom will go into a tailspin, guaranteed, she'll come down on Penny, the day will be shot to hell." Peter placed a hand on Fletcher's shoulder and fixed him with his dark bloodhoundish eyes. "Is that too much to ask?"

"No one's mentioned her?"

"You got it, so far so good, everybody's happy."

"Today is the anniversary of her death, did you know that, the twenty-eighth? Not Thanksgiving," he added, "the date."

Peter had taken Jack's arm to usher him out of the garden.

"We hadn't seen her for ten years at least, I never expected to see her again, Clare the loon had flown the coop, then we find out she's dead and gone, Fletch, what are we supposed to do? I can't get this through Penny's head. She'd written us off, damnit. We didn't walk away from her, she walked away from us. The truth is I liked Clare, I didn't have a problem with Clare personally, that's the truth, but she wasn't an easy person to deal with, she was difficult. I don't know what the hell she'd been into for the past ten years, but it didn't involve us, she was through with us. We weren't the reason what happened happened. I keep telling Penny that."

"Gwen and I heard from her occasionally."

"Hey, I never knew what the fuss was about in the first place. The grandmother's funeral, that's when I drew the line. She didn't even show for Gram Wells's funeral, for Christ's sake."

"She wasn't informed, was she? No one told her about it."

"Is that how you remember it? That's pretty damn forgiving of you, Fletch. I remember she wasn't there, that's what I remember."

"We all knew how Clare felt about her grand-mother. She should have been told."

"Even though she hadn't seen the ancient old biddy for years, right? Never visited her in the hospital, never once went to the nursing home in, what, three years?"

"I called her that weekend before the funeral, I couldn't reach her. She went through the roof when she finally heard, she couldn't believe no one had no-tified her."

"And Dad's heart attack, that was the other thing. His own daughter, could you believe that shit?"

"It's complicated."

"Clare and I go way back, Fletch. I knew her before I knew Penny. She was out of control way back then. The freedom fighter. That's long before your time, 1963 maybe, we'd just graduated from college, Clare turns out to be one of these SNCC people. What was that, student nonviolent something, she went to Mis-sissippi that summer while my buddy and I were tend-ing bar on Nantucket. SNCC was the beginning of the end with the family, I'm sure. Your little girl right out of school going down there where they're still hanging them in trees. Imagine Mary going off . . ." Peter shook his head, pouting grimly, to think. . . . "Clare Wells, my pal met her on a sailboat, I think. A few years later I meet someone called Penny Wells on John James's front lawn—fate, is that what you call it? Even back then Clare was never around, maybe one holiday a year at best, too busy with her high-minded life on earth. The whole family lives on the East Coast, but she had to be at Berkeley continuing her radicalization, her liberation, her self-actualization, whatever you want to call it. She had the kid by then. No husband, just a kid. Peace, love, was that still before your time, Fletch? That march on Washington, the poor people's shantytown they set up on the mall, Clare was right there, fucking the system. Remember her Vietnam vet? She was in her thirties then and her soldier was still in diapers. I bet she was balling the boy. How about the Florida eight or ten or twelve or whatever they were, her charismatic Scott, high on the FBI's harassment list, she had one of them holed up with her for months apparently, sanctuary at Clare's place. Then what, the trailer on the godforsaken vineyard, if that's what it was."

"In Missouri," said Fletcher. "We were there once."

"She was a little bit out there, our Clare. Far out. While we're all coping with Dad's heart and Gram Wells, she was in India or Indonesia. Poof, gone for years. The next thing we know she's back in San Francisco, was that it? Did she have AIDS? Was she homeless? We didn't know what she was."

"Not homeless, Peter, she was running a church program to help—"

"Gwen would call every so often to upset Penny with something she'd heard about Clare, that's all I knew about it. Don't get me wrong, Fletch, I liked Clare. We liked nothing better than insulting each other all day long. She was a good egg, she was beautiful, I loved listening to her one hundred percent crackpot version of reality. She was smart as a whip, smarter than Penny probably, which is going a ways. For years I tried to get along with her, I didn't really give a shit whether she thought Nixon should be tried for war crimes or I should turn this place into a summer camp for inner-city kids. The whole secret to our relationship: she didn't like me. The kid, what was his name . . . ?"

"Noah."

"An impossible little prick, I couldn't stand the sight of him, but I haven't seen him for ten years or more either, maybe he turned out all right."

"He's followed in his mother's footsteps apparently. I bet he's an impressive character."

"I better get back to the house, Fletch. Penny will be down my throat."

"What's up in New York? You didn't say."

"A holiday for the kids—not Mary, the little guys. Stroll down Fifth, look at windows, a fancy dinner by city light, a pillow fight in the hotel, some play probably for an arm and a leg. Bo wants to bring his skates and cut a figure eight in Rockefeller Plaza."

"Sounds like life is a struggle, Peter."

"Listen!" His brother-in-law pointed up. Overhead, behind clouds, the distinctive honking of Canada geese. "I love that." He listened. "Those fellows are late this year. Hey, we should get back inside, they'll be looking for us."

"Go ahead, Peter, I want to visit your bees."

*H*er revolutionaries, misfits, sad cases. Her pet project one year was the release of a young man who had been locked up since he was eighteen for killing two Vietnamese civilians following the land mine death of his best friend. As Fletcher understood the story, the vet's dependency backfired into abuse, he laid all his unquenchable frustrations in Clare's lap. One afternoon he borrowed her car and never returned. Had she been balling her soldier? Had she screwed the charismatic Florida eight or ten or twelve? One of her heroes was vigilant I. F. Stone, dogged true believer in the just society. For years she waged a losing battle with the IRS, at every opportunity withholding payments that she regarded as taxation without representation, refusing to support wars or weapons. Her motive was to be a nuisance, to remind someone out there that they were dealing with an individual who came to her own conclusions. Clare was scrappy, spunky, fun, or she was difficult, as Peter put it, depending on who you were.

In Florida checking out a property, in California holding the hand of one of asphalt's fortunate widows. Money grew like mold, smothering former dreams and desires, corroding worried souls green with greed. Meanwhile poor schmucks believed the world was not for them, no longer for them, if ever it had been. Guys waltzed around the Plaza together: assholes.

You remembered the time Peter submitted to Gwen's funny urge to make him up, his darkened eyes powerfully, steamily, female, his reddened lips puckered like a sore obscenity, a ring of fire. Gwen got out an old wig from somewhere, she painted a birthmark on Peter's prominent cheekbone. In the end Penny refused to come in to dinner until he washed his face. Her husband had taken to the part too enthusiastically for her taste. That slapstick, even innocent, fun, Peter's last moment in drag, went back to their Commonwealth apartment. Those days were gone. Their charade of fellow-feeling. How did you have so little to say to one another after five, ten, fifteen years, a lifetime? Less, it seemed, as the years went by. Everyone set in so-called ways, all figured out, don't waste your breath. To Peter, Clare had become a lonesome, desperate diehard for whom private life had been reduced to proclaiming public causes. That was blind, like Fletcher insisting the real Peter West was a repressed transvestite. Encased in delusions and deceptions, like a turtle in its shell, the man was impenetrable. You'd never break through.

The first time Peter visited them on Commonwealth, he walked over to Fletcher's two shelves of books, mostly paperbacks, and asked, with cheerful irony, Is this your personal library, Jack? You might remember that for the rest of your life if you were Fletcher. Even then Peter wore pinstripe suits, highly polished grown-up shoes, and could afford to take his sister-in-law and her would-be architect to an expensive French restaurant. Pretentious frog's legs at Joseph's. Why would you remember that unmemorable occasion when you couldn't recall what you had for supper two nights ago? You didn't realize Peter had never read *Ulysses*, for example, didn't know Manet from Monet, hardly knew a cornice from a cupola. His hands, mustache, the content shape of his belly, frog's legs: details that came to represent the person you had come to know, practically all you knew even after fifteen years, like you're driving to the store for beer and hear an old song that puts you in mind of the summer you shared a cottage on the Cape together, so you come home with Anchor Steam beer, Peter's beer that season. The connoisseur. Your personal hoard of gradually accumulated detail, with its private meaning, was what you meant by knowing someone, even love, the items memory had selected to preserve for reasons too seemingly arbitrary to ever figure out.

W hen he first met Gwen Wells—students abroad in Florence, she a junior and he biding his time with graduate courses on the Renaissance—her older sister Clare was the brilliant radical of the family whose exploits made Gwen herself, she seemed to assume, that much more interesting. In fact, twelve years younger than Clare, Gwen had had little to do with her big sister growing up. That freedom summer of '63, for example, when Clare, fresh out of college and ripe with idealism, had gone south in pigtails to register black voters (he'd seen a black-and-white picture of her from those years that might have been titled "Passionate Youth"), Gwen would have been ten. Two years passed—Clare missed the family occasion of Gwen's graduation—before he finally met the oldest sister. That would have been Thanksgiving of '75, he surmised. He had seen pictures, but pictures had not conveyed her in-the-flesh appeal. In her mid-thirties, she was to him an older woman with a thin athletic body, a hiker of the Sierra Nevadas, a copy of Rexroth in her backpack. She had the enticing good fortune of thin arms and large breasts, blondish hair with naturally occurring glints of reds and darker colors, and out-of-control curls that must have sprung from her father's side of the family. I'm Clare, stuck in his mind, the bored way she said it, as if she was tired of being Clare, or was regrettably aware of the way her reputation had undoubtedly preceded her. She didn't seem all that interested in who he was, the man Gwen

33

met in Italy, and skipped the politely interrogative routine concerning his past, present, future. He thought her smile bordered on condescending at one point, as though anyone who had voluntarily thrown in with this bunch—her family—couldn't possibly be of interest. Her son, Noah, must have been ten or so, about Sam's age now, blond hair to his shoulders, moody, he'd brought his guitar and wouldn't talk. The tension between Clare and her mother was obvious even to Fletcher, who had never seen them together before. The two women never looked each other in the eye.

He felt rudely excluded as he watched the three sisters walk down the drive in fading afternoon light. On the way back they were holding hands, Clare, the tallest, in the middle. He'd just about decided he didn't care for the big sister after all—she'd ignored him most of the day—when the woman buttonholed him at the kitchen sink. She hadn't realized he was an architect person, she said. Look, she had a little project in mind, a faculty friend, who happened to own a whole small island in Maine, had invited her to build something there for herself for summering. Frankly, he was a much older guy who had adopted her as daughter-disciple after she turned down his sweet, wacky proposal of marriage. She was a member of the history department at a university in St. Louis back then, her period was the Civil War, her much older guy was the last word on slavery. So look, and here this Clare took hold of young Fletcher's tie and gave it a gentle tug, do I need an architect to build a simple getaway Thoreau-type dwelling? She couldn't afford to hire people, she wanted to do it herself, she just needed someone to get her started. So how about it, she tugged his tie, think about it. The idea was that he and Gwen would get to use the place too, whenever. . . . She had an outdoor face, nice crow's feet as distinct as tribal markings, teeth not perfect. When she kissed him good-bye, along with everyone else, he thought her kiss was slightly more open to possibility than might have been deemed appropriate under the circumstances, unless that was the wine talking, or a spontaneous warmth occasioned by the accumulated mellowness of the afternoon. He wasn't sure.

Almost two years later, stopping in Boston on her way up the coast, she was at last determined to make a start on her island shack. Noah was in California for the summer with his father. Fletcher had already given notice to leave the disappointing Boston job—he'd spent most of the preceding year constructing models of malls—and join Itzkoff and his Yale mentor in the western part of the state come September. He was through at the end of June, he and Gwen had to find a place to live, they would have to do a U-Haul number and make the move, but it was feasible that he'd find a couple of weekends to drive to Maine and lend Clare a hand.

Gwen and little Kate, born the previous year, July 4, 1976, at the Boston Lying-in, out of wedlock, went along the first time. Weir Harbor, an hour north of Ellsworth, and an interminable seven hours from Boston the day they made the trip, was a far cry from vacationland Maine. There were no sailboats in the harbor, no nifty little street of shops calculated to ensnare tourists. The place was poor, unadorned, yet pristine-seeming, as picturesque as a trumped-up still life arranged for Sunday painters in straw hats. A fleet of freshly painted lobster boats pointed the tide. Lobster pots were stacked on piled piers along with piles of lobster buoys in primary colors. Sea gulls stood single file on the ridges of steeply pitched gray-shingled houses with white trim. There was the native hierarchy of wormer, clammer, lobsterman, that was man's work. Local women worked in the sardine cannery in a neighboring town. An odd cluster of retired people, couples mostly, had gathered together in the past few years on a narrow peninsula divvied into building lots by Weir Harbor's sole developer, a fat man with a name like Hatch. Clare's friend, Pierce, had acquired his quaint uninsulated house, situated on the east side of the harbor, for practically nothing in the early sixties, and along with it, for an additional one thousand dollars, he'd purchased the island that stood just beyond the mouth of the harbor. In recent years he'd come to Maine less, and it had become clear, as age sapped his energy, that he was never going to create anything on his island as he'd once imagined doing. Clare's at-first-sight infatuation with the place led to his open-handed offer, he'd like knowing she was out there making the most of it. That summer Pierce was out of the country and Clare had his house—a wonderful west-facing porch, a wood-burning stove in the linoleumed main room, three tiny wallpapered bedrooms upstairs—to herself.

When they arrived, she was in the thick of her ongoing oral history opus, which she referred to as "The Tapes." Evidently she was always getting on tape the true story of some poor wretch, a great person, whose story needed to be told. Her portable filing cabinet, several cardboard beer boxes, was stashed with interviews that told of hard-luck lives, most often sagas of gross injustice, that Clare had recorded over the years, going back to the sixties in some cases: her treasure chest of human voices that someday would be heard. The majority of interviews were with black people of all kinds, north and south, trapped in racist America. Civil rights was where Clare had put down her activist roots. She'd done hundreds of hours with Vietnam vets of every stripe, chronicling that episode of U.S. history, another civil war. Prisons represented a new window on wrongs perpetrated against the individual in the name of society. Her next planned category of forgotten lives would be women. Eventually she hoped it would all add up to some kind of a book. Preoccupied as she was with the lives of others, Clare seldom made herself the subject of her engaging and provocative talk.

Did we therefore imagine, he now considered, that you had everything under control, everything you needed? Stubbornly cheerful, despite the sort of repeated setbacks bound to plague so-called counterculture advocates, and always busy, she seemed to him exceptionally self-sufficient, as if she needed less of everything than other people. She had her son, her friends in need, her books and projects, the sick society to overcome. He gradually gained the impression that she had few longtime friends, she spent a lot of time alone. As far as he knew, no one visited Clare that summer in Maine apart from Gwen and him. That seemed a strange way for an attractive woman in the prime of life to live. Why would anyone want to cut themselves off like that on an uninhabited island? At the time that pretty obvious question had not occurred to him, Weir Harbor seemed so wonderful. You could still dig a bucket of clams at Nelson's Cove in an hour back then. Succulent mussels, largely ignored by the locals, existed in old-world plentitude. And Clare herself represented another sort of person altogether, not as pretty or cleverly creative as her youngest sister, not as polished or seeming-sophisticated as Penny, but eccentric maybe, forceful, freer, on her own, news to a straight arrow like Fletcher, important news.

F rom shore the island looked small, a humpback shape slightly elevated in the center and tapering symmetrically at each end. Conifers, spruce and balsam, stood like erectile spores on the back of a submerged beast. In good weather it took less than half an hour to row out there in Pierce's wooden dory, which typically took on several coffee tins of water each trip. Vertical granite, topped by trees, rose from the water on the lee side, as impenetrable, Gwen observed, as a medieval walled city. A small stone beach on the west afforded the most convenient access. What made only a modest impression from a distance became, as you stepped ashore, a multilayered, unknown world, and as you entered it, parting branches and up to your shins in undergrowth, the place acquired greater mystery and dimension. Blueberry, bayberry, and juniper densely clutched the spongy ground where taller trees didn't inhibit their growth. There were scented ferns and plush mosses. Outcroppings of lichened granite created several small clearings. Vivid wildflowers bloomed in narrow rock crevices. The interior of the island was peaceably quiet, then you stepped out of woods onto a bright expanse of pinkish granite, great geometric blocks and slabs, and rounded smooth surfaces over which waves broke and receded, and beyond that nothing but ocean. Tide pools sparkled, if the sun was out, with jeweled forms of life. Surf, agitated to white foam, pounded thunderously into a shallow cave. They explored the island, exclaiming its wonders, like ten-year-olds who had found the perfect headquarters for their secret society. Gwen's big sister had stumbled into fantastic luck, as far as Fletcher was concerned. He liked this family.

He and Clare spent the afternoon weighing the pros and cons of possible building sites. Gwen and their real-life cherub discovered snails and welks and purplish starfish in limpid pools. The search for perfect sea urchin shells with their geometric designs reminded Gwen of an Easter egg hunt. She loved the whole thing as much as he did. The wind came up before they returned, though, the water turned slate-gray, choppy, Fletcher and Clare each pulled an oar, sitting side by side, and Gwen, holding Kate with one arm while she fisted the gunwale with whitened fingers to keep her balance—My goddamn Raynaud's—became afraid for her baby. She didn't return to the island during the few remaining days. She did sketches of the harbor from Pierce's porch, and one watercolor, an evocative portrait of the island partially shrouded in fog, which made her time there feel worthwhile. Meanwhile, he and Clare, having chosen the most advantageous site, began to plan the thing to be built on it. She went around in green wellies, baggy khaki pants that tended to hang off her hips, a cotton turtleneck, a handmade cable-stitch sweater by Patricia Wells exactly like sweaters made for Gwen and Penny, in fact, but pretty dirty in Clare's case, well worn, and a green felt fedora she'd picked up in Freeport.

Opaque fog moved in the last day and discouraged them from going out, but by then they had a crude vision of things and Fletcher worked late into their last night translating his penciled scheme into the building materials necessary to bring it about. Each night he climbed the narrow stairs to the small peach-papered bedroom feeling completely bushed in a good way. The newness of the seacoast scene—gulls, fog, damp salt air, plus the presence of a strange woman—was sexually energizing. He and Gwen enjoyed mutually determined lovemaking every night they spent in the iron double bed, which sank in the center hammock-like, Kate barricaded in the closet on blankets. Since the baby had been born, Gwen hadn't been interested in sex much. The trip to Maine seemed to have dramatically restored her desire. His horniness persisted once they were back in Boston, but Gwen promptly lost interest again, desire squelched by the impending move, the noise outside, the humid city air, the asexual associations of their familiar bed. Reasons for what you didn't want weren't hard to find.

Although she'd enjoyed the Weir Harbor visit, especially shooting the breeze with her sister for an hour each morning over coffee for really the first time in her life, Gwen decided not to make the long trip the second time, knowing she'd be alone with the baby most days while Jack and her sister worked on the island. Instead she seized the opportunity to be in Wellfleet, where Penny and Peter had taken a cottage for the month of August. She would need the car, and so Fletcher flew to Maine the next time, Bar Harbor Airlines, his face pressed against the small oval window the whole journey, observing the archipelagic coastline.

F rom here the house seemed still, although you knew it was a hotbed. . . . Buster was curled up on the stone stoop at the kitchen door of the one-and-a-half-story ell, which bordered one side of the garden, eavesdropping, so to speak, on the humans within.

Sam hadn't been to the Big Apple yet. The Salvation Army blowing its brains out from a platform above the thronged avenue would be something he'd remember. "Joy to the World" was more thrilling to a child than geese above clouds. Concerning Peter, to take another example, you never forgot the time they'd all gone to New York together after Christmas. Fletcher looked back to see if he and Gwen had lost the other two. Atlas towered overhead. Out of step with the prevailing crowd, Peter strolled down the middle of the sidewalk like a lord, like a full-throated Maurice Chevalier, say, his mighty trenchcoat draped over his broad shoulders like a cape, and his hands clasped—no less!—behind his back. What was he thinking! The throng streamed around him as around a blind man with a cup of pencils. Loyal Penny, chafing at the bit, clung to his arm. Gwen cried, He's crazy!

Peter!

Heading back uptown, they stopped at Cartier. Peter wanted a link added to the gold band of his new watch. Fletcher glanced into the glass case: the likes of Peter's watch cost as much as Jack's car. That made the New York trip five years ago. Really? Sporting a watch like royalty. Could the man even spell Manhattan? Fletcher's black plastic digital watch, his jogger's watch, said 12:24. That was just about what he'd paid for it.

The truth is I liked Clare, she'd written us off, we weren't the reason what happened happened. If you were Peter, you believed as you pleased. Tell yourself lies all day long so the lies you sell ring like the real thing in your own tin ears. Peter had clients throughout the Northeast, Florida, the Southwest, California, he had associates all over the country. Most of the time you had no idea what he was up to, how he sold a client or what he sold a client, how he sold himself or how much of himself.

He stepped behind a black birch to piss, that's what three cups of coffee will do, no tingling rumor of desire, wee chum good for nothing but a leak. A girl's hand writing your name with it in the snow, that would be more than a laugh. That would put lead in your pencil. Peter's massive hands, fingers like cow udders, led Gwen to believe, as she had confided to Fletcher over the years, an ongoing fascination, that the man's prick had to be a baseball bat. Penny would tease, but she wouldn't tell.

He climbed the plank stairs to the paddleball court. From here you looked down on a cozy scene: house and garden. At the least, the Wests had all this. Stone walls, gray woods, smoke from a chimney, a fabulous sky. To Clare, Penny's life was a prison, period. Soul for sale. Was that any closer to the truth about Penny than Peter's equally narrow view of Clare the loon?

Freedom fighter. No one grew more bored, more sick and tired of the so-called struggle, her high-minded life on Earth, than Clare herself. Who could be bothered with always getting to the bottom of things? She was a little bit out there, our Clare, fucking the system, balling the vet. Nothing like rape. . . . Was she homeless? We didn't know what she was. Our Clare! Don't mention her, so far so good, everybody's happy.

They stopped in Ellsworth for boxes of nails, a good level, a crowbar, chain oil for Pierce's saw, miscellaneous necessities. He had the list, she had the money. They stopped at George's market and loaded several bags of groceries into the back of her faded

green wagon, a ten-year-old Volvo. They had a funny
time buying groceries, deciding what to eat, who was
who in the food department. The hour's drive to Weir
Harbor she talked nonstop, a side to her he hadn't seen
before, regaling him with tales of Weir Harbor incest
and alcoholism and weird child-raising practices, which
she'd picked up from Meg, the lady who ran the P.O.
She'd already persuaded the Colby twins to transport
the load of lumber, bags of cement, and asphalt shingles
to the island on their lobster boat, the *Brenda Lee*. They
refused to take anything for it. She'd done well on the
lumber, which had been delivered from an inland saw-
mill. Out of sheer excitement she'd already dragged half
the stuff to the proposed site, carving a path through the
thick undergrowth in the process. She hadn't informed
the town of her plan to build on the island and she
didn't intend to. If they came after her for a permit,
she'd plead ignorance. They drank gin on the porch,
watching the sunset reflected in friendly August clouds.
The island grew black. I'm glad you finally got here, she
said, this place could make you crazy.

They rowed Pierce's red wheelbarrow to the island
in the blue and white dory. He smiled to recall that
scene. Choosing a site, they'd decided to sacrifice an
ocean view for an open area of ledge that was sheltered,
invisible to anyone passing the island, and required the
removal of only a few scrub pines. They toted water
from a sinkhole fifty feet away to mix concrete, and
poured three cylindrical footings, digging down until
rock stopped them. The ledge would support the fourth
corner of the building, with rocks piled beneath the
centers of the sills. Her backpacking days had made her
sturdy, good at donkey work like getting down on
hands and knees to clean out the bottom of a hole, her

nice breasts weightily pendulous in her soiled white T-shirt. The first day on the job, she declared ordinary modesty one of the first casualties of outdoor life, and squatted behind a boulder only yards away to take a leak. Rowing back at dusk, they were dirty and hungry, but also exhilarated, like a pair of desperadoes who had spent the day digging under the prison wall to freedom. To Fletcher, who had never done anything like this before, the footings alone felt like a major accomplishment. You mean Jack the architect has never mixed concrete before?

One recurrent image turned out to be her face in a hooded sweatshirt, the memory of a photograph taken on the island—the background was fog, her color rosily heightened and escaped curls dampened darker by moist air—a picture he deleted from the pack of Maine pictures he later showed Gwen because of what seemed obvious to him in the older sister's amused, impatient expression.

Each day began with a set goal and ended when the goal was accomplished. The sills were composed of two two-by-tens nailed together. Two-by-fours nailed the length of the sills supported two-by-six joists. The floor was cheap-grade tongue and groove pine boards. Clare measured and marked while he cut, using Pierce's chain saw for the most part. The Colby twins had offered the use of a small generator along with a power saw, but she didn't want to become too involved with a pair of Weir Harbor red-faced bachelors already too attentive to Clay-a, as they hailed her on sight from the deck of the *Brenda Lee*. They both nailed, and got blisters in the same places, Fletcher's refined hands no more accustomed to the work than hers. By the end of the third day, they had a pretty damn level platform fifteen by eleven feet, a piece of work more satisfying to Jack the architect than anything he'd done yet in his chosen profession. Clare stomped on the boards, she threw her head back. This is a floor, Jack. That was another snapshot in his visual record of the project—Clare standing on the new pine boards with upflung arms as though she was on top of the world. This is going to be home, she said. I'm talking home here.

The island menu consisted of crackers, cheese, sardines, peanut butter, blueberries by the fistful picked from dense low bushes, making for bowel movements as blue as a bear's. All shitting shall take place below the tide line, thank you.

Most mornings they rowed through low fog, then shed layers of clothes as the day progressed. His shoulders burned as usual. The hottest day yet, Clare dropped her cut-offs and T-shirt and settled down in the largest tide pool—Don't mind me, Jack—then stretched out in the sun on warm granite as though nothing could be further from her mind than the fact that she was a big juicy woman, basically, and Fletcher was an excitable young man. She was at home in her skin, something she'd picked up on the West Coast, he imagined, in her liberated youth. He was doing fine, the way art students spontaneously adapt to flesh and blood in life-drawing class (he'd taken one once), until he also stepped out of his jeans to enter the island swing of things and found himself—uh-oh—getting hard, breezing up, despite his grasp of the situation. He splashed, hollering and clowning, into the scrotum-tightening sea (he'd spent half his time in Italy reading Joyce's book), certain an erection would be enormously uncool with this laid-back member of Gwen's family innocently being herself. His penis nudged his pant's front now, as he stood in Peter's paddleball court, aroused more by sudden nostalgia for that boyishly irrepressible stiffness than the vaguely remembered first sight of her long, relaxed, able body.

The studding was typical stick construction, two-by-sixes rather than two-by-fours, nailing three together for corner posts and bracing the posts to the floor. They framed for a half dozen small double-hung windows selected from an Andersen catalog. By the end of the first week, the studding was largely complete. That was the week both Groucho Marx and Elvis died, he was bound to remember, because those famous deaths remained details in the subsequent retelling of his time on the island. Carter was President with what's-his-name . . . Mondale. Brzezinski, unearthed from some so-called think tank to comment on Bush's war last year, was Carter's Kissinger. The brother, Billy, provided the clownish human touch. Dead now. Politics rarely came up during the island project, except South Africa, come to think of it, yes, Carter was the human-rights President, Clare's passionate speech one morning gesticulating in the stern of the boat as he rowed, then that fall the martyrdom of Biko. And the death of Robert Lowell. He was able to place that passing in time, too, because it was Clare who had introduced him to the poet's work that summer, once reading aloud poems about Maine, that skunk one, while sitting on Pierce's porch with citronella candles. Fletcher had purchased his last book, *Day by Day*, and that had connected him to Clare a little longer, he felt, once the island interlude, call it, was over. Chaos in South Africa still prevailed; he hadn't read a Lowell poem in ten years.

He made the pitch of the roof steep enough to allow for a sleeping loft someday, but not so steep that the rafters were more than they could handle. Rafters and collars were two-by-sixes, too. They knocked together two crude ladders to raise them. The small building took on its final shape. Set amidst dark evergreen trees, the new lumber of the frame glowed golden—It's so beautiful, she said—nothing less than a work of art in the eyes of Jack the architect. There was the impression of her body, in the brief congratulatory hug between them, placed flat against him from head to foot, an offering, but he assumed he was mistaken.

The neighborly Colbys dropped off a thirty-inch striped bass, Fletcher cleaned and filleted it on Pierce's dock by flashlight, they cooked it with onions, tomatoes, garlic, white wine. Clare dug out a pipe's worth of marijuana that she'd been saving to heighten a special occasion. They had a small fire with the stove door open to take the chill out. She wanted to know why he and Gwen hadn't gotten married yet. Answer: the baby was her decision, they decided to go through that together, Kate was theirs, but that didn't make marriage something they needed to do. She said, You're my little sister's boyfriend, for Christ's sake, I'm ten years older than you are. She said, I haven't thought about anyone sexually for a long time, I haven't fantasized about anyone, I haven't been excited sexually since I don't know when, I forgot how it feels. She had moved from her chair and stood leaning against the table, facing Fletcher, who remained seated. She was wearing, he recalled beyond a shadow of a doubt, a blue-and-white-striped cotton skirt, which he liked the look of her in. Earlier he'd said something about how nice it was of her to have put on a skirt. She said, I want you to feel how good it feels, and guided his hand under her skirt with both of hers, laughing, happy, I'm as wet as Juliet.

The roofing boards and the asphalt shingles, intended to simulate weathered wood (Clare's budget balked at cedar shingles), went up quickly. Once they had a roof, they wanted to try living there, but that proved premature, more like camping out, and took too much time. Being there at night, sea, stars, utter eerie seclusion, was a rush, initially, then they missed Pierce's double bed, where they could pursue their more recent Maine project—sexual abandon—more thoroughly. The bitterly cold ocean didn't cut it where feminine hygiene was concerned. A woman can't have intercourse three times a day and live, she said, without hot water. As August progressed and time closed in on them, they began working twelve-hour days on the island house. He had allotted himself two weeks in Weir Harbor, come what may, but at the end of that time they had barely begun sheathing the small building. Gwen, who had their Commonwealth apartment all but packed and ready to go by then, was exasperated—We're supposed to be moving to a new place, Jack—yet she was also sympathetic, she wanted them to finish what they'd started, and she was happy Clare and Fletcher had become friends, believing maybe that their friendship would ultimately bring Gwen closer to her older sister, someone she'd always longed to know better.

It took most of a week to nail up the board and batten siding. They made a door and hung it on wrought-iron strap hinges purchased from a blacksmith in a nearby town, who complained about the cost of advertising in *Yankee* magazine. They made shutters for two windows and boarded up the rest. The Andersen windows would have to wait until next year, along with the cistern, the outhouse, the wood-burning stove, maybe a brick chimney if they got ambitious. Next year she'd hit the secondhand shops and tag sales for household stuff, although it would be fun to build the table, shelves, bookcases. Next year she'd paint the place with wood preservative. They spent a day cleaning up the site, carting back tools and unused materials. That night they had a pretty good-sized bonfire of scrap lumber on the ocean side of the island. Quoting Thoreau, another of her heroes, Clare said, You can always see a face in the fire, a line that had stayed with him. He rarely beheld an open fire without recalling the words, and the face that usually emerged was hers. The last night in Pierce's house they cooked their favorite Maine meal, mussels with olive oil and plenty of garlic over pasta. He wanted to talk about Gwen, what had been going on here, where everything went from here. She said something like she loved the cabin, she loved building it, she loved being with him, everything, now she had to return to St. Louis and resume her life there, he had to go become an architect and take care of his family. She said, Don't ruin it.

T he first night in their rented apartment—the spacious first floor of a sprawling Victorian—in the town where both Gwen and Clare, in different decades, had gone to college, he sat in the kitchen surrounded by cartons Gwen had packed and labeled, each designated for the appropriate room in their new life. He had loaded them into the U-Haul truck, driven from Boston, and laboriously unloaded them only hours before. Gwen had gone to bed with Kate. They were asleep. He poured himself a drink, Jack Daniels in those days. The color of the ten-foot-tall kitchen walls, an institutional green, had to go, beginning tomorrow. Beyond the dark living room, cluttered with more boxes and lumps of random furniture, its uncurtained windows blackly glaring, he contemplated a narrow corridor of his new neighborhood. The wide front door stood open to admit cool night air. There was a streetlamp across the way illuminating the vacant sidewalk. A sparky little mutt, the unmistakable silhouette of a Scottish terrier, in fact, passed across his field of vision. The rasp of a cicada started up again. He didn't want to paint these tall wretched walls beginning tomorrow, he didn't want to unpack the stuff these boxes contained, he didn't want to meet whoever lived next door or his dog. He was in the wrong house with the wrong woman. That was what a few weeks in Maine with Clare Wells had wrought.

W hen he saw her again, around Christmastime, it was in the midst of Gwen's family. She stuck close to her sisters, and gave him no clue that anything had transpired between them. When he brought up the island, as if to demand some flicker of recognition from her, she chatted amiably about her Maine plans for the summer, but she wouldn't indicate, by word or gesture, that her plans involved him. At the end of the day, offended Fletcher followed her to her car to voice his complaint. Her son, Noah, was present. Now when she looked at him—she was puffed up with goose down, a bright-colored wool ski hat pulled down around her ears—the veneer of propriety was gone. Look, she said firmly, that felt right last summer; now it feels wrong. She certainly hoped he would visit the island again, but—I have to be completely straight with you,

Jack—he was only welcome if Gwen and Kate were with him. In fact, none of them returned to Weir Harbor or its small island. Clare was denied tenure in St. Louis, ostensibly to do with budget cuts and the fact that she had not yet finished her dissertation (Civil War women). She insisted it was departmental politics, pure and simple. ABD meant Anti-establishment Bitches Die, she wrote Gwen, another phrase that stuck with him. Rather than work a final year, she quit that spring with no prospects anyone knew about. Whatever the understanding had been with her colleague, Pierce, the island was lost with the job; whether the old guy withdrew his offer or she refused any longer to accept it was never clear to Fletcher.

S he entered her vineyard phase. It was there, the one and only time her parents paid a visit, that the final falling-out between mother and daughter occurred, just at a time of life when they both should have been able to do each other some good. As far as Fletcher knew at the time, the actual incident had been a typically trivial everyday blowup. Patricia Wells had been critical of her daughter's decision to live in a trailer in the godforsaken Ozarks, and Clare had told her parents to clear out. Peter had said ten years, but it was more like eleven or twelve. Surely neither mother nor daughter, despite the history of their at-odds relationship, imagined that they would never see each other again. In fact, Clare never made another appearance at a family gathering. Peter and Penny, for that matter, never saw her again. To the children, Aunt Clare was the name, rarely mentioned, of someone never quite real. Noah, from that point on, grew up without family on his mother's side, for all intents and purposes. For the next decade it was Gwen who represented Clare's fragile contact with her family, and that most often took the form of notes and letters. Possibly Gwen was just young enough to have escaped association with the rest of them from Clare's vantage point. And maybe Fletcher, he speculated, was a factor in her willingness to stay in touch. En route to the wonders of the west the summer following Clare's evident break with her family—she had missed a full year of holidays, birthdays, anniversaries—they stopped in on her.

The Ark Vineyard was a friend's Missouri experiment situated at the top of a steep dirt road at the end of a hot hilly journey. Clare came toward them carrying a basket of fresh vegetables. God, it's great to see you two. She was thin and weathered. Noah, a tall, handsome teenager all of a sudden with shoulder-length hair, ragged jeans, bare feet, hardly spoke to them for three days. From September to June he boarded at a prep school in St. Louis. There were plenty of people around, largely young, who had arrived with all their worldly goods on their backs to hang out until the harvest began. Friends, and friends of friends, turned up on weekends. The Ark Vineyard was an event. There were ponytails, guitars, recorders, Frisbees, mongrel dogs, free hugs, plenty of friendly dope and wine. Fletcher met a woman from New Jersey who called herself Whispering Pines; her sons were Forest and River. A cluster of various multicolored tents stood at the edge of the woods. The prevailing mood of laid-back enlightenment, the communal feeling, gave him the willies. The onslaught, Clare explained, was temporary. I've taken up the simple life, she told them. I want to settle that question for myself once and for all.

Now most of her energy went into an organic garden almost an acre in size. She had cultivated strong, square hands with blunt fingernails. Her trailer, set back in the woods at the crest of the vineyard's southern slope, flew a Malaysian flag. They hiked to the highest point in the immediate area, toting beer and followed by a female goat. The back of Clare's blue T-shirt was black with sweat. She combed her fingers through her tousey hair, wild in the Missouri humidity, squinting against the light toward distant hazy hills. Where else would I want to be in this goddamn world?

Gwen eventually brought up the fabled year-old incident between Clare and their mother, posing as peacemaker. This was crazy, Mom was heartbroken, the silence had to stop before it was out of control. Clare became intense, and her tone was intimidating. Mother is a sick woman, she said. Nothing I've done since college has met with her approval. Clare had decided what she needed to do in order to have her own life was stay away from her mother, that's all there was to it. She refused to hear any more about it from Gwen, she didn't want Mother's crap ruining their weekend. The truth was there was more to the story than either the mother or Clare revealed at the time, but that only came out years later, once the damage was irreparable.

The hangover he had the morning they left the vineyard, too dazed and numb to talk, was, to date, Fletcher's worst hangover ever. They promised to stay in touch. Clare promised herself a trip to New England, maybe after Noah was back in school, to catch the foliage.

With satisfaction Fletcher recovered the goat's name ten years later: Corrina. Goat cheese was intended to be a by-product of the vineyard life. To his knowledge, goat cheese never happened. Tousey: one of the old grandmother's words to describe a granddaughter's unruly hair.

For the next few years, according to her periodic cards and letters, the vineyard worked well for her. She undertook a series of essays on the simple life, inner and outer, for which she hoped to find a publisher eventually. She had a friend at . . . North Point Press rang a bell for some reason. Each time they heard from her she was planning to come east—to check out the ocean, hike through Vermont hills, strap on cross-country skis, to attend a class reunion at her college to see who was still alive and doing what. In one letter she enclosed a check, three hundred dollars, with specific instructions to the Fletchers to purchase a Camperdown elm. But that was later, only after they'd bought the house, he reflected, after they'd gotten married. She'd left Missouri by then. For possibly two years she was in Indochina with the AFSC. They received a letter describing Cambodian refugee camps, a nightmare. The next time they heard from her she was in Bali, which was paradise. The gulf between Clare and the family, even the Fletchers, widened. She had returned to San Francisco when Curly's heart attack hit. Gwen was elected to notify her, and for a while Gwen provided reports from the front lines, but the family crisis didn't provoke Clare to fly back to see her ailing and frightened father. She never called, as Gwen believed she would, to comfort or console her mother. Sometime later when Gwen confronted her sister—What if Dad had died? How could you live with that?—Clare didn't turn sentimental. There was no last-minute reconciliation scene in her current fantasy life. Gwen and Penny continued going back and forth to their parents' house for months to play the part of loyal loving daughters. By the time life was more or less back to normal, Gwen's sympathy for her childhood idol, the big sister, had significantly eroded. When Gram Wells died the following year, age ninety-three, after several years in a nursing home, no one informed Clare until weeks after the funeral. The absurd separation, which they believed with each new year couldn't possibly go on for yet another year, now began to seem permanent, unbridgeable. Too much time had passed.

She had turned her back, as Peter said, and yet they let her go without ever getting to the bottom of what was wrong, if that had ever been a possibility. All their self-congratulatory holidays went on without her. Fletcher had become one of them, that's how it must have looked to her. Jack the architect. She had no family, that's what it came down to. There was a long silence. Eventually they heard through the grapevine—a cousin who happened to be a male nurse at San Francisco General, if he remembered right—that she was working with AIDS patients or IV drug users, unwed mothers or battered women, some forsaken disenfranchised group.

Finally, at his instigation, the Fletchers, all four of them, made a weekend visit to San Francisco, the last stop on a three-week vacation to California, which had begun in La Jolla. It had been seven years, as he calculated subsequently, since they had last seen Clare, since the days of her Ozark interlude. She had long since forsaken the so-called simple life for the more desperate vagaries of city life. Gwen was anxious, even reluctant, to face her unforgiving and unrepentant sister after so long—Clare had never laid eyes on their son, for instance—but their brief stay was a success. Clare was welcoming, warm, easy. Apart from the most superficial updating, they skipped the family routine. They didn't attempt to fill in their disparate pasts, they settled for the day, like eager dinner guests determined to make the most of an evening that could easily go either way. Kate, tall, thin, eleven, fell in love at first sight, and blushingly smiled in her aunt's presence all weekend, a tulip in full sun. The two sisters and their daughter/niece sauntered through the park arm in arm, leaned against one another to stay warm, laughing, breezily intimate. Watching them from behind, Sam in hand, as they strolled among giant exotic plants, beneath strange vast trees—eucalyptus, sequoia—Fletcher briefly felt as if they had landed on another planet, a happier place than Earth, where all flora and fauna effortlessly thrived. In fact, whatever the emotional stress of her work in San Francisco, another topic they didn't dwell on, the city seemed to have rejuvenated Clare since they had visited her, sunburned, sinewy, up to her elbows in cow manure, in rural Missouri. Now in her mid-forties, short wavy hair still blond, she could have passed for a woman ten years younger. Partly inspired by his daughter's good instincts, Fletcher was as infatuated again, at least for a night, as he had been ten years before. Gwen's report from California—Our black sheep is in great form—only pissed Penny off, reinforcing her view that their do-gooder sister had always managed to look out for number one, leaving the saps back home, bogged down in the family swamp, to stew. But Gwen was happy to have connected again. Saying good-bye, she and Clare hugged each other hard, both became momentarily tearful and vowed to plan regular visits at least twice a year.

G wen's father opened the back door and, bending from the waist, gave a bit of something to Buster, bit of brie for Buster. Curly always had a soft spot, bit of kindness, for cats and dogs. If he'd ever looked at me the way he used to look at Willy, Gwen said, I'd probably feel differently about a lot of things, including men in general, sex, her mother, herself. To some extent she knew where Clare was coming from. Give these girls the wholehearted hands-on affection their father lavished on the family mutt, they'd have a different story to tell. Instead, he'd left all that up to his wife.

Dad. Fletcher had never called him that, never called him Carlton or Curly either. In all the years he'd been with Gwen, he'd never called her mother Patricia, Pat, Mom. The ongoing people in your life. Peter was his watch, his *Popular Mechanics* mentality, his Jag, certain phrases like "I know exactly what you mean," "Trust me," the raincoat over the shoulder, his hands, the fact that after so many years of family get-togethers he and Fletch had so little to say to one another.

Penny, for instance, was fixed in Fletcher's mind with her kitchen, her haircut now, the way her eyes avoided you, an argument over a book once. You forgot what book, and remembered that she didn't give a toot for what you thought. Brighter than her provider. One time she parted her lips when he kissed her against the refrigerator on her birthday. Her tongue like sticking her hand in fire—that quick. She said, That feels incestuous. One kiss in a lifetime. Could they have done each other more good if they'd met once a year to make love, say, rather than to stuff themselves silly? You never knew.

Brilliant bittersweet, a voracious climber, covered

one end of the fenced paddleball court, a twisted and tangled mass laden with flame-colored berries, which had turned back their golden shells.

We're dying, you'd think that would make a difference. You imagined there was always time to write, to call, to get in touch. Clare was there, waiting in the wings, waiting to pay her visit to the Fletchers sooner or later. That had seemed enough. You assumed she had long adapted to living without the ordinary comforts and everyday supports with which most people padded their lives. Like the scene before him, featuring Patricia and Carlton Wells, the West family, the Fletchers. Clare had never had much use for the conventional mode, or maybe that just wasn't in the cards for her. Yet seeking your own alternatives, increasingly urgent as alternatives became harder to find, you felt life become a lonely battle for survival, a survivor's lonely battle, rather than the manageable business of day by day with its routine ups and downs. You don't say, was an expression she used ironically. She was not the sort of person you worried about, she could take care of herself. For months he wanted to pick up the phone, a visceral impulse, and ask, What's this I hear? What's going on? He wanted to hear it from her. He missed her now more than he had missed her while she was alive.

This time when he looked up at the sound, a wide far-flung V of flapping Canada geese emerged from moving clouds into clear sky. They had changed direction.

Gwen stepped outside, leaving the back door open behind her, a glass of wine in her hand. She looked up, and gestured to others behind her: hurry. Her father, Kate, and Mary's friend came out into Penny's garden.

They all held their faces up to the sky. When Fletcher looked again, the geese had vanished, re-vanished, behind clouds.

It was a show.

Wasn't that enough?

Gwen remained in the garden after the others went back inside. She stooped and touched the ground and brought her hand to her face—thyme probably—reminding him again of their visit to Coventry last spring. She sipped from her glass. At the opposite corner of the garden she stooped again and this time tasted whatever she'd found. Her slim and scented dressed-up figure.

My life, he thought. They'd been enjoying slow, stuporous, finger-lined fucking lately. Something they needed like dreaming. Like dreams, these blind warm encounters beneath sheets and blankets didn't make much difference to the days. Or, like dreams, it was difficult to know what difference they made once day broke. Sleep was another story. It had become hard to imagine sleeping without her body asleep beside him.

She looked in the direction of the barn.

"Jack." She walked toward the apple tree and called his name again, then looked directly at the paddleball court, but evidently didn't notice him standing inside. "Hey, you," she hollered, "come on in." As she strolled back to the house, she raised her arms over her head, one hand holding the empty wineglass, the other opened as if reaching. At the door, Gwen turned back to the yard and called, "Everyone's waiting for you."

C oventry that afternoon. . . . A robust robin made a fuss in an old stone birdbath. Warblers and finches darted from shrubs. A Maypole streaming festive pastel ribbons stood before a red barn. Lilacs were in bloom, one of Fletcher's favorite smells. And quince. Western light shone through newly budded trees, a gauzy luminosity. Gwen toured the herbal beds bent over, as if searching for something lost. She called things by name just for the pleasure of naming. She took his arm. Don't you love it here? Everything feels so—she paused for the word—peaceful.

They had the place to themselves, except for a red-haired young woman and, he guessed, her mother, who were seated on a wooden bench beneath a shagback hickory whose buds had not yet popped. The girl seemed to observe them as they sauntered from the Monastic garden (parsley, sage . . . mugwort, marjoram, savory) to the Gray garden (Artemesia, Gwen muttered, lamb's ears, lavender; the veronica incana was incredible). When they passed near the young woman, she fairly beamed at them, attracted, he thought, to one idea of the possible future. Attracted to Gwen, a grown-up woman, a wife, who seemed happy. Gwen smiled back like a gracious celebrity deigning to conquer a shy adoring fan. Good afternoon, she almost sang.

Would the carnal X-rated scene in the front seat of the car have seemed to the girl an appropriate act for the couple she now saw enjoying the gardens? An act of love? That unexpected sexual exchange would hold them, he knew, for two weeks, three weeks, depending on children, work, a chance word, the weather, wine, money, the moon, memory. That made fucking seem more important than it was.

A swallowtail, black with indigo, alighted on blue Canada phlox. He was able to identify butterfly and flower thanks to Gwen. Thanks to Gwen, he knew woolly thyme when he saw it, he knew gypsophila, digitalis, bee balm, silver mound. Thanks to Gwen, he knew a Camperdown elm when he saw one, a gold-finch, bittersweet.

He lingered in the Shakespeare garden, edged with boxwood, and read small metal labels stuck in the ground. Rosemary, rue, wormwood, bay, columbine. For example. The same plants. The same planet. Iago's words were written in white paint on a slab of slate: Our bodies are our gardens; To which our wills are gardeners. . . . So if you plant nettles or lettuce, kill maple trees or drop bombs, polish cars or sentences . . . sterile with idleness or hellbent with industry: the power and authority lies in our wills. Today people perfected their bodies while they lost control of their lives . . . while the real garden, the same planet, was imperiled on all sides, the will serving the Iago in us as often as not. The quaint disorder of the present garden, like Shake-speare for that matter, was lost to the world for the most part. Clare's will, even Clare's will, had brought death to the garden.

Gwen had gone on to the Knot garden, her hands clasped behind her back, browsing. She could be thrilled by a healthy border of nepeta. She squatted again to inspect a plant. A figure in a garden.

Inside the gold-green cave (arrows of western light streaming through dense branches) of the Camperdown elm a lifetime ago—young Fletcher inside Gwen Wells for the one and only time under the circumstances—they held still as the elderly couple passed the tree. Too late to do anything else. In a forthright dignified voice the woman was talking about the flowers—Oh, look, dear—and the old gent was grunting his assent: Oh yes; yes, yes. Their voices drifted on. Gwen held her boyfriend tighter. Later, at dusk, young love in the persons of Gwen and Fletcher sat on a wooden bench, given in memory of someone or other, as the old pair returned from their walk. Thin, white, tidy. They both held canes. Good evening, they chimed in bright old voices, smiling like ambassadors of goodwill from their time of life. To which the momentarily sated sex maniacs chirped their reply.

It took guts, as Clare would say, to grow old. It took will and imagination to walk out and enjoy the garden leaning on a stick stronger than your bones, wobbling down the path yet another time, mustering a smile for the new blood.

He had come up behind his wife where she stood in the center of the Colonial garden. A sundial stood on a granite pedestal. Count none but sunny hours.

What's wrong?

Nothing. I was just . . . thinking.

You're crying. Are you crying?

My own sister, Gwen said. Clare, she pleaded, our sister. I didn't know.

I know, he said, I know how you feel. We hadn't seen her for a long time, we didn't know what her life was like.

Gwen's voice was point-blank. She's dead, she said. And we let her die.

T he beehive, two white boxes, seemed dormant, although you knew it was a hotbed of activity. Last Christmas they received a five-pound jar of West's Best Honey. Becky's marvelous label pictured a house on a hill.

Clare had mentioned bees in one of her vineyard

letters, a detail that hadn't registered, not concretely, until Peter had acquired his hive and Fletcher, one summer day, had inspected it with him. Peter in bee hat and veil, armed with his smoker, taking out the honeycombed frames to examine the brood and, for Fletcher's edification, locate the queen. Clare had promised them honey. Before she had harvested it, a black bear discovered her hive—a wild moment she was privileged to witness while gathering kindling at the edge of her woods. She was indignant, she wrote, losing the hive before it had yielded a drop, and losing her beautiful bees after seeing them through a full round of seasons. On the other hand, she added, she wouldn't have missed the sight of that gorgeous bear exuberantly shattering the hive to pieces for the world.

Thanks to Peter, Fletcher had been able to imagine his island friend in her beekeeper's veil, tending her hive. Alone on the vineyard, living in her own eyes alone.

Sitting on his haunches, he placed his ear to the side of the top box as against a dying man's chest. Listen: a distant drone.

*H*e paused outside the ell's large bay window, which looked in on the kitchen. Gwen's tall father frowned over the platter of appetizers, his hands behind his back. Patricia Wells, pleasantly plumpish in her blue apron, averted her face from the heat as she peered into the oven. Penny had come to a standstill before the refrigerator, momentarily stalled, a hand raised to her brow, the new haircut. Peter held his stout index finger to his lips as he passed Fletch's daughter a glass of white wine. Kate's look was mischievous, her tongue in her cheek.

It was a show. Every corner of the canvas or screen or page brimmed for Fletcher with resonant detail. And this was free? Get in there, Fletcher. Hasten.

"There he is."

"Here you are."

"Where were you, Jack?"

Now listen, Richard, just hold on a minute, I know what's at stake, just let me worry about it, all right? The letter you received yesterday, disregard it, the man is a fool, he always was, that never should have been written. Do you understand? I don't know what it means, we'll have to find out, but that guy has his head up his ass, he should be sued for distributing that kind of misinformation. Schneider is one of the biggest growers in Hawaii, he's for real, there's no reason in the world for him to participate in out-and-out fraud. He's a businessman, no different than you are, Richard, he's got a wife, a couple of kids, the whole thing. Now I'm telling you there's no way in hell I'm going to let that go down the drain, I can't believe we're even talking like this. It's a solid investment, Richard, I never would have put you in it in the first place if it wasn't one of the best . . ."

"Who in the world is Peter talking to?" asked Patricia Wells. "He sounds distraught."

Penny closed the oven door, her face flushed, a vertical vein visible on her forehead. She reached for a paper towel above the sink. "God knows, Mother, some desperate client or . . . I never know who he's talking to."

"On Thanksgiving? At home? That takes some nerve, doesn't it?"

Fletcher tapped Peter's shoulder, showed him his empty glass—if he could reach around him into the freezer here for a second.

"Jack, I could use a cube or two while you're at it," said Curly.

"Really," Gwen said, "what can't wait until tomorrow?"

"Peter lives on the phone, you know that. He's on the phone sixteen hours a day. Peter's world doesn't take holidays, weekends . . . money, money, money, remember that song from . . . ? Haven't you ever seen the mark behind his ear—like what violinists get on their necks? Look." Stepping over to Peter, causing him to switch the phone to his right hand, she twisted the top of his left ear to show them, her mother peering over her shoulder to see. "See that mark, that's from . . . the phone is Peter's instrument, he's the Isaac Stern of the telephone. Isn't it like he's been branded or something?"

"For Christ's sake . . . just a second, Richard." He held the phone to his broad chest. "For Christ's sake, Penny, get your hand away from . . . can I have a little fucking, excuse me, Mom, but can I have a little quiet for two seconds, this happens to be awfully important. Richard? Goddamnit, I'm right in the middle of the kitchen with the whole damn family. I don't know what to tell you right this minute. I wish I could be more helpful, all right? I'm going to get on it first thing in the morning. Of course, it would be disastrous, that's why it's not going to happen. Do me a favor, all right? Relax. Sit down, have a wonderful meal, pretend you never received that moron's letter in the first place. Can you do that for me? You just stick to the root canals and leave the driving to us. No, I'm glad you called, that's what I'm here for. Okay, we'll talk tomorrow. My best to the family, hello to Deirdre. You too, Richard. You too." He replaced the phone. "Jesus, Penny, honest to God, you see someone on the phone, you start picking at me like an orangutan. Did you see that, Dad? Fletch, pour me one while you're at it, will you? Not sherry, Scotch."

"Who was that, Peter? Doesn't he know you've got the whole family . . . ?"

He drank. "Jesus." He closed his eyes. "There, that's better." Another good swallow.

"Peter, do me a favor, will you? Relax." Fletcher grinning. "Trust me."

"Fletch, that's what you should have been—an endodontist. This guy sticks pins in your teeth—makes a fortune. Drives the biggest BMW they make, a castle in Ireland, a stable full of Arabian horses. The stable looks like a Holiday Inn. He sticks pins in toothaches. Why the hell didn't you think of that?"

Gwen said, "Can you see Jack in front of a castle on a horse?"

The small fry, Sam and Bo and Becky, had disappeared upstairs to toy with Peter's computer. Kate matched wits in the living room with her older cousin Mary and Mary's friend. Periodically Fletcher heard distinctly girlish giggling—there still was such a thing— and the piercing note of Kate's open laughter. Gwen and Penny and their mother coordinated the final preparations for the meal while the men loitered at the island with the pâté and cheese and Peter's best-buy Scotch. This anticipatory hour before the meal, he considered, with the fuss and stir of the cooking, the first buzz from the liquor, and everyone eager to seem happy, to seem energetic and animated and happy to be here, could easily prove the most festive hour of the day.

Let's skip the feast and go home with full hearts and empty stomachs. Heresy.

Gwen's mother reported an affair between the veterinarian in their town and the Episcopal minister's wife, who had decided to breed her Springer spaniel the year before. The woman looked like she had been reborn. "They walk around town hand-in-hand. You'd love him, Penny. What's wrong with being happy for a change?"

"You wouldn't be so broad-minded and charitable if it was one of us, would you?"

Penny said, "We're already as happy as pigs in swill, Gwen. Down-to-earth vets are for the repressed wives of roly-poly ministers."

"Your mother had the pick of the litter," said Curly. "But you know who would take care of it, don't you?" He snitched a piece of cheese. "When you walk a dog in our town, you have to take a little bag along with you. We're very neat."

"Get one," Gwen urged. Anything living, she believed, would be a positive addition to her parents' lives. Her mother disliked the untidiness of dogs, all cats in their feline ways, and the nuisance, the anxiety, of plants. "Springer spaniels are nice, aren't they?"

"All puppies are adorable," said Patricia Wells. "Your father knows I just want to give the young woman support."

"I thought it was the minister who needed support."

"I told your mother she could just put a studded collar on me," said Curly. "I already lead a dog's life."

Peter, who loved to inform, told them what he knew about Springer spaniels and the style of dog life best suited to the breed. "If you aren't going to hunt, Dad, it's pointless to have one."

"Christ, Peter, Dad doesn't know one end of a gun from the other. Hunt?"

"Unless that's what you call switching channels on that television set." Her husband's daily dose of TV had to be killing brain cells, otherwise how could he sit there and watch such . . .

"What I want to do at this juncture," said Curly, "is eat, play a few rounds of golf, and watch an occasional ball game on the tube. If that meets with everyone's approval." With that pronouncement he tipped up his glass with a flourish, his crooked pinkie extended.

"Doesn't he sound like a lot of fun?"

School photographs of Penny's two youngsters were taped to the refrigerator. Against a fake background of pale blue sky with hazy white clouds, as though he had gone to heaven, Bo stared ahead, a glazed look. The boy's smile appeared forced, but that did not detract from the charm of his missing teeth, or the crooked part in his dampened hair. Becky, posed before phony bookshelves, concealed her braces, and had not succeeded, this day, in taming her flyaway curls. Folk art, he thought. A serious moment for them, trying to look right.

"Pen, be sure and give me copies of these. They're fantastic."

"They're dreadful. The poor kids."

"This is Jack's idea of an accurate record," Gwen explained.

"No, I happen to think these pictures of Bo and Becky are very beautiful, in fact."

"Oh, Jack, you think that dump across the street is beautiful."

The sprawling ramshackle place across the street from Fletcher's house was a rental, inhabited by six to a dozen people at a time, depending. The paint had worn off for the most part, shutters dangled, the porch sagged. Yew and hemlock and rhododendron, long neglected, blocked the windows of the first floor. There were always a half-dozen cars parked on the front lawn—old vans, beat-up compacts, a faded Ford or Chevy—and two abandoned pickups out back. Grass grew knee-high around the cars in summer. The tenants brought a purple couch onto the porch in good weather. They stapled plastic over the windows in winter. Marijuana grew amid their stand of corn. The woodpile against the south side of the house was forty feet long. Here, with various transients, lived Denise, the social worker, Bruce, her boyfriend, Jimmy, a baker, Alexandra, part-time nurse and racquetball champ, Tom, the organist, Celia, the midwife, Gerty, the brown and white goat, two matched mongrels known as "the bookends," an assortment of cats, half of them strays. There were always comings and goings across the street, there was always music, there was always a light on. Its blighted presence on the street reduced property values, such as they were, by maybe ten percent. At least twice a year the police paid a call, answering someone's complaint, their blue lights alarming the neighbors' bedroom walls. Yes, to Fletcher, the dump across the street was beautiful, not from an architectural point of view.

"What's her name, with the goat? You know, the goat lady?"

"The goat lady?" asked Penny.

"Gwen," her mother said, "you shouldn't call someone—"

"The goat's terrific. You've seen her, Mother. She has the most beautiful delicate face. Sam is crazy about her. What's her name, Jack?"

"Gerty."

"The woman, not the goat. I know the goat's name is Gerty."

"Celia, I think. Yes, Celia."

"You know damn well it's Celia. No one over there has a last name, you know. Just Celia. Anyway, Jack thinks Celia is . . ." Instead of finishing her sentence, she sipped wine.

"What?"

Peter squeezed the back of his neck. "The goat lady, huh, partner?"

"Talk about dogs," Gwen said. "If those bookends of theirs . . . they let them run wild, I know one of them is going to get hit for sure, but if they shit in our yard again, I'm going to take Sam's slingshot, I swear, every morning there's a fresh pile of shit right smack—"

"Gwen, calm yourself," said her mother.

"Weren't you getting to know some neighbors once?" Penny asked. "They had a funny name, that old, old place at the other end of the street."

"I saw her in Stop and Shop recently, I think it was her, flying through the aisles like it was the end of the world. Their daughter must be in college already. They're attractive, at least from a distance. Maybe this Christmas I'll walk down with a fruit cake and introduce myself."

"You mean you're going to bring Fletch?" Peter said.

"Jack, didn't you talk to him about a renovation once?"

"Who?"

"The bearded man at the other end of the street, he used to be in real estate, didn't he?"

"I don't know who you're talking about, sorry."

"Of course you do. She's tallish, the brown cape near the end of the street. Maybe we'd like them. Bloomfell, is that their name?"

"We've been there for years," he said to Peter, "we still don't know half the people on the street. I'm not sure they still live there," he told his wife.

"Got that, Penny?" said Peter. "You complain about your horrible absolute isolation on our wonderful hill here, starved for company. Here's Gwen and Fletch surrounded by people they've never met. All you get from neighbors is their leaves and dogshit, right, Dad?"

"Speaking of the minister's wife," Penny said. "Our friends the Joys are having a terrible time these days."

"Let's not get started on the Joys," Peter put in.

Penny told them about Cora Joy's decision to return to Ireland right after Christmas. "She says she's wasting her life."

"Paul just bought her a house, Dad, can you beat that?" said Peter. "Terraces, gardens, views. They've been looking for three years, the minute they move in, Cora is packing back to the old country."

"Isn't that the way," said Curly pleasantly. He poured a dollop of whiskey into his empty glass, avoiding his wife's glance. His large ears rimmed red, Fletcher observed. If she uttered his name in a certain tone— Carlton!—he'd pour the drink down the sink.

"Cora and her friends go out to lunch all week," Peter said, "to get tipsy on sipped wine and swap sob stories, that's half the problem."

"What a pile of shit," Penny swore. She actually liked Paul half the time, she told them, but he mistook love for providing, or seemed to, as if a relationship was just a matter of dollars and cents. His backward attitudes were getting out of hand. The poor were not that poor, the spotted owl wasn't the end of the world, abortion was murder, hunger was beyond our control. "She doesn't like the way the man thinks. They haven't even shared the same bed since St. Patrick's Day or something."

Dolor and no sense, he thought: marriage.

Patricia Wells was frowning. This wrinkle in the cocktail hour was unwelcome. "For goodness' sake, Penny, who cares what your husband thinks about acid rain, or some poor people starving halfway around—"

"Stop right there, Mother."

"You know what's going to happen, Dad?" Peter studiously spread duck pâté on a heel of French bread. Thick. "Paul is going to take her to Martinique for a week right after Christmas, then he'll set her up in this Islamic antiquities business—isn't that the latest thing with Cora, Pen? He'll provide that, see, and then in the spring she'll be off to Ireland for a month and Cora will decide, hey, this isn't bad, after all, and the Joys will live as happily ever after as the rest of us."

"In a minute you're going to make me really mad," Penny warned.

"Gwen, do you know what's going on here?" Fletcher asked.

Gwen's mother declared, "I don't care about the Joys or the spotted owl."

"Really mad?" Peter crowed. He circled the island with sudden energy and grabbed his wife around the waist from behind. "The last thing I want to do is make this gorgeous woman really mad."

"All right, Peter, let go."

Funny thing was, for all his bluster, and despite his he-man success in the world, Peter lived right under old Pen's thumb to a large extent. Why? you wondered. Always seeking to please her, hoping to smooth the worried lines around her mouth, hold her next mood at bay. With so-called moods, Patricia Wells had subjugated Curly for forty years, the woman's insecurity smothering his good-natured outgoing appetites. One of Penny's major gripes concerning her mother—leaden, irony!—was the way the woman bullied her father.

"Let go. Now."

Fletcher had never met the Joys, yet he knew that Cora had been a redhead, a brunette, a blonde. In her youth she had toured Europe as an Irish folksinger with two other women. One midnight in a New York City hotel bar she burst into song, silencing everyone, winning smiles and applause, while her husband sulked out of sight. One night she got so drunk at Penny's that when she returned from the bathroom to rejoin the party she wasn't wearing her skirt. Her skirt had slipped her mind. He knew her door was always open to friends, or anyone else who found their way to it. On the basis of a photograph—Penny and her friend in turquoise bathing suits under a large palm frond—he could imagine encountering this friend of his sister-in-law's to discuss Irish life and literature, get drunk together, one song leading to another. He wished her the nerve to escape the future that Peter foresaw. She was right to want out of a life where money was mistaken for—of all things—love. According to Penny, Peter's friendship with Paul Joy was more stable, more satisfying and important to both men than either of their marriages. You assumed that was an exaggeration; it might have been an understatement.

"I went to Bermuda once twenty years ago," Curly was saying, "I'm ready to go again."

"Okay, Dad." Peter snapped his fingers. "That's your next birthday present. Plan on it."

"Peter, honestly, we're beyond Bermuda," said Curly's wife.

"I'm serious, Mom, plan on it."

Penny opened the oven. Steam escaped as she raised the sheet of aluminum foil to baste the browned turkey. "I hope someone's hungry."

Very funny Jim Gates—recently the poor man had half his stomach removed in Boston—told Gwen's mother a very cute joke at their Thursday-night bridge club, if anyone was in the mood for a joke.

"Go ahead, Mother, tell it."

Fletcher didn't want to hear, didn't care for the joke genre, the whole pathetic stand-up routine.

"Gwen, why don't you start the white sauce for the onions? Mother, could you keep one eye on the brussels sprouts while you're . . ." She opened the oven again and prodded an acorn squash, he saw, with a fork.

Patricia Wells told the one about the little Indian girl—Native American, you mean—who wanted to know how her father had come to name her brother and sister. "Well, the morning your brother was born, my child," she said in make-believe broken Indian, "I step outside our wigwam and see deer running across meadow, so I call him Running Deer."

"I hope Kevin Costner isn't listening to this," Gwen said. "That dumbbell."

"There's a good-looking goose," Curly whispered. Penny had taken the turkey out of the oven.

"Rolls," she whispered, pointing. Fletcher handed her a tray of rolls from the breakfast table. Into the oven they went.

"And what of my sister? asked the child. The evening your sister came into the world, little one, I step outside the wigwam and see the moon rising above the trees, so I name her Rising Moon." Patricia Wells paused. She frowned at Fletcher like an Indian father addressing his inquisitive little girl. "Why do you ask, Two Dogs Screwing?"

Only Peter laughed. "Jesus, I've got to remember that, Mom."

"The turkey, Peter. Here, Dad." Penny handed him a chrome-plated corkscrew.

"Everything's fine, Pen. Slow down." He carefully honed the edge of the long carving knife on a slate-gray stone.

"Jack, why don't you call everyone to the table. We're almost . . ."

Poor Jim Gates, Patricia Wells was saying in answer to Gwen's question, his poor wife was a basket case, her Alzheimer's seemed to accelerate week by week and now he couldn't possibly look after her any longer. "She sits there and looks at her hand without a clue. The poor thing can't tell hearts from clubs."

Three beautiful girls, he thought. They stood in long skirts by the French doors, which looked across the backyard to deciduous woods. Kate, lovely in her

mother's off-white silk blouse, and gold earrings that
dangled, a gift from her grandmother for her fifteenth
birthday, pointed outside.

This fall, as he sat in Judie's over a beer, he had been
startled by a young woman who stole up on him from
the rear and snatched his arm. Well, she said, Britishy,
fancy meeting you here. It was Kate. How long it
took—two seconds!—for that to register in surround-
ings which, to Fletcher's mind, had never involved his
daughter. There with girlfriends for soup and salad before an orchestra rehearsal. The girlfriends shyly approached to nod hello, then fled back to their corner as
if venturing from their table had been a bit of reckless
daring. Kate lingered, boldly standing at the bar. Her
drought in Africa paper, she reported, had received an
A. She was wearing his vast cableknit sweater from
Ireland over a pair of black tights. With Fletcher's last
five dollars in her narrow fist, she rejoined her friends.
He watched her walk through the barroom. She might
have been mistaken for a woman. When she sat down
again, he realized that he'd been observing this person
moments before, the back of her head, without recog-
nizing her. The incident, as if a turning point he'd been
anticipating had already occurred without his knowledge, disturbed him.

Mary had been blessed with Penny's eyes and her
tangled hair, Penny twenty years ago. His name for
Mary had been Mop. Today, in loose-fitting casual
clothes of dark earthy colors, she might have stepped
out of a Tweeds catalog, the source in recent years of
Kate's entire wardrobe.

Mary's friend was blond and wore a scoop-necked
sort of sweater-dress maybe, snug on top and full be-

low, Tweeds, too, probably, the color called heather green or Spanish moss or . . .

Peter's single-malt Scotch had made him light-headed, just pleasantly, and his manner open-handed.

"When forty winters shall besiege thy brow," he recited solemnly, "and dig deep trenches in thy beauty's field, thy youth's proud livery, so gazed on now"—he gestured toward them dismissively, limp-wristed—"will be a tattered weed of small worth held."

"Shit, Uncle Jack, thanks a lot."

"This is my dad," Kate said flatly. "He can't help himself."

The friend, Liz, pointed out the glass door. "We just saw a brilliant iridescent male pheasant. He strutted right across the lawn very pompously, then marched into the woods like little Lord Hotshot." When she smiled, thin faint lines, he saw, appeared around her eyes.

"Just released probably," said Fletcher. "Brave hunters can walk right up to them, the poor critters don't know enough to take off, they're used to being fed."

"This one is street-wise," said Mary. "He had the most beautiful turquoise feathers on his back."

"Don't be such a grim reaper," his daughter scolded.

"Kate, go call the little guys. Your mother is going to pieces out there, Mary. We're ready. Make haste," said Fletcher. "Make haste."

Observing them leave the room, he thought, Fletcher the fool.

. . . of small worth held. How did it go? Then asked . . . then being asked where all thy beauty . . . all the treasure of thy lusty days. Lust was a treasure itself, better believe it, gone whether you spent it or not, so . . . Deep-sunken eyes, all-eating shame. Tell us, wise friend. He had helped Kate learn some sonnets for school, was how he'd gotten into it, then as the long temperate fall wore on and he'd settled into work that was less than inspired, he found himself determined to commit to memory more of the bard's spine-tingling poems. For a time, for reasons not put into words exactly, he seldom ventured into the world without his chewed-up paperback copy, thin as a checkbook, in his jacket pocket. Ballast maybe. You kept it to yourself, rehearsing lines in your head the way a hurt friend or loved one rehearsed angry sentences, unanswerable ultimatums that would never get delivered, you knew, in the heat and confusion of the real confrontation, yet having a fistful of sonnets down by heart felt worthwhile, a weapon.

I was awakened, pinned to the bed. Where were your weapons then? Noah and his fucking inner-city legal clinic, he couldn't help being the person he was brought up to be. Nothing like rape to get your head together. Please write, for Christ's sake.

He was struck by the title of a paperback book on the small Queen Anne table by the door. *The Survival of Civilization*. God love us. Whose project was that? Mary's maybe. Graphs. CO_2. Ah, the ice age. Cometh. According to one graph, the game would be up before the year 2000, gather ye roses, Jack, that hardly gives us enough time to get Kate through college.

The bookmark, if that's what it was, was notepaper from the Woodstock Inn, Woodstock, Vermont. A list, legibly written in pencil by a hand unfamiliar to Fletcher.

Acorn squash
Onions and white sauce
Brussels sprouts
Stuffing/chestnuts
Potatoes
Yams
Cranberry relish
Garnishes
Cheese, pâté, liquor, wine
Rolls
Salad?
Something green?
Pies: pumpkin, mince
Ice

Dear Lord, he rehearsed, thank you for these thy gifts and the bounty we are about . . . Just want to say a word about the gathered family and the feelings, the feelings, the feelings, as each year we come together, observe time passing in young and old faces and voices, and the way somehow all this adds up to a life, your life here and now whether you know it or not, and the importance of the moment, the people in the moment, for better or worse, passing. The way it all adds up to an idea of love, if you will, although it's not easy. The way the same shit never ends. The way this somehow ends up being who you are, rooted in your lifetime, and therefore it behooves us . . . Let us pause for a moment now to think of those no longer . . . let us remember Clare this day, the best of us, how dare we not, she's dead and we let her die, our own sister, goddamnit. Just want to say something—high time a few words were in order—before icy winds cometh blowing off the massive shoulders of the glacial mass, or worse. We also want to welcome our newcomer and wish her luck getting through the day, she's going to need it. And the sky today, the drama of the sky, also plays an important part. . . . Amen. Cheers. Jesus, he was always an articulate devil. Somebody has to say something, we have to forgive and live, forgive to live, live to forgive, take your choice, I've had my say, you never know what will happen next.

*B*ittersweet branched from the Chinese vase in the center of the time-honored trestle table, the tangled centerpiece of this Thanksgiving. Mary moved it to the Welsh cupboard. She lit a match which fizzled, then another, and, reaching, lit the candles on the table. A woman all of a sudden, they could be proud of her, at least for the present. The three smaller children arranged themselves at their smaller table near the window. Sam into the pickles as he pulled up his chair, rubber snake in his back pocket, the hot shit. Bo had his awesome spacecraft at the table with him, fitting excellent space pilot into the hot seat, checking wing rockets, busy. Curly poured wine, red in one hand and white in the other, moving clockwise around the table from plate to plate, having already established who wanted what and who would sit where. He gave the bottle a neat twist after he poured. Each glass received an equal measure. He loved that, you figured, his allotted task, a sort of finishing touch of jeweled color, the moment brimming. At the tall carved blanket chest, eighteenth-century American, serving as sideboard today, Peter sliced white meat from the turkey and placed each piece on the blue Canton platter. He performed the task gravely, with the ceremonious air of a priest preparing Communion, God looking over his shoulder, his back to his expectant parishioners. "Pay attention, Jack, maybe you'll learn something."

Penny's china, white with an embossed border, went back to her wedding. Evidently she had hated the stuff for a while, disappeared it for several years, ended up liking it twenty-some years later, another treasure, these dishes out of all the possibilities just because . . . but if she'd thrown them away ten years ago, what would she have? The silver, which had been the grandmother's, had gone to Penny as the next in line once it was clear that Clare would never claim it. First come first served.

Kate brushed past, a covered silver dish held out before her with pot holders. "You're blocking the way, Dad." Sterling youth!

Back in the kitchen Gwen was saying, "They never actually said anything for years, they just suddenly sold the wonderful shop they'd sunk their lives into, then I'd run into them at an auction or a concert and you could tell something was wrong, Ted had gotten so thin and John, who had the dry sense of humor, just wasn't the same. It was still a shock, they were the two nicest men."

"Nothing surprises me anymore," said Penny. "Of course, if they put some money into AIDS research . . . when you think of Bush's stupid billion-dollar-a-day war last year, it makes you want to throw up, these idiotic men and their fucking smart weapons—"

"Penny, really!" said her mother.

"There were three hundred or more people at each of the memorial services, they'd made such a contribution to the orchestra and historic restoration. Anyway, what I meant to tell you—"

Jack asked. "Who are you talking about, Ted and John? Can't we leave them out of it?" He had called upon them concerning several projects over the years, enlisting their skills in the decorative arts. Just now it rubbed him the wrong way, Gwen dragging them into their hour of gossip along with everyone's divorces and adulteries and illnesses, more deep human interest to be smug about. Come off it, Jack, that's the way we all are.

Gwen ignored him, and went on to tell. . . . "They'd spent almost thirty years in this 1760s house which they'd saved from destruction, moving it across the river, and lovingly restored. The house was the love of their lives, really. Ted's memorial service was held there. John presided, looking handsome and gaunt and so sad. He held up this crock of yellow ware that Ted's father had given him long ago for his yellow ware collection and told us it now contained Ted's ashes."

"Cremains," said Patricia Wells, "isn't that an odd word?"

"After the service ended he asked us to step outside the tent—they'd put up a huge blue and white tent in the backyard—to witness the dispensation of ashes as Ted had requested. Is that what you call it? This is so Ted, John said. Everyone stood looking up while one of their friends climbed a ladder to the massive central chimney, carrying the yellow ware crock. John recited a poem, and then the crock containing, you know, was dropped down the chimney. That was an extraordinary moment, wasn't it, Jack? Can you think of a more perfect thing to do with your ashes, consigning them to the hearth, the heart of your house?"

"Are you in a maudlin mood today?" her mother asked.

"That's wonderful," Penny said.

"Just months later they did the same for John, so their ashes—"

Instead of biting his tongue, Fletcher said, "You tell a good story, Gwen, maybe you should send it to NPR."

"Can we forget everyone's problems for a moment," said Patricia Wells. "Let's be thankful we're all . . . " She left the room with her steaming bowl of onions. Her briskness, her efficiency, her pinkish hands. Don't be unkind.

Penny followed her, small crystal bowls of cranberry relish in each hand, surprised by nothing. "Oh, Jack, would you grab the rolls?"

Gwen glared as she passed him. "Fuck you. I'll talk about what I damn please."

Will you talk about your sister's ashes? That was a question too cruel to ask. None of them knew what had become of Clare's so-called cremains. None of them had been present—he still recoiled at the extraordinary fact—for her memorial service.

Someone was trying the stuck bathroom door from within. The stubborn door, trapping the uninitiated, was a family joke—a chore Peter had so long neglected that to set it right now would seem wrong. Applying sharper force, rapidly twisting the doorknob, Mary's friend Liz at last stepped out, grinning—Wow!—her color momentarily rosy.

"Yum," she hummed, and sniffed, and rolled her eyes, whites of her eyes clear as could be. "This is going to be fun."

Following, he thought, Fool. You fool, Fletcher. The rolls, forgetting the . . . you ass . . . rolls . . . hmm, smell them.

Patricia Wells had stopped before the long dining-room table, which gleamed white and silver, and shimmered, the length of it, with steaming dishes like . . . She held her hands pressed to her cheeks, surprised. Her eyes had filled with tears, her face contorted, mottled. Peter hurried to take the woman's arm. "Come on, Mom, we're with you," he said gently.

Fletcher did not believe these were tears of joy.

Peter stood, the picture of prosperous head-of-household, and raised his glass of wine, chin up, Rough Rider–type grin, live to be a hundred. "Come on, Pen, everyone get their glass up. You, too, Gwen, you're in on this."

"Cheers," said Fletcher, setting off echoes of that word around the table.

Becky asked, "Aren't we saying grace, Mom?" as if that was the children's due, then declined to do the honors when Penny asked her to.

"One of you older girls, then?"

"Don't ask me to say grace, Mother," Mary said. "I can't."

Fletcher—this was crazy—tensed. Lord, thank you for these thy . . . I would like to say . . . I want to say . . . Should the table turn to him, he was prepared to make phrases on behalf of all. I would like us to take a moment and recall . . . He scanned their faces: no takers.

"Carlton, there was a lovely simple prayer you always used to say for us, you must remember."

Curly, his hands folded before him, expectant, didn't speak.

When Peter called upon his son, the youngest present, to lead them in prayer, Bo bowed his head and mumbled thanks to a God who was great and good.

"Way to go, Bo." His father reached behind him to

tousle the boy's auburn head. "You're Vatican material, buddy."

The moment had passed.

With his ornate server's knife and fork, Peter extended toward the newcomer a good-sized slice of moist breast meat edged with crisped brown skin. "Here's a lovely piece."

Seated between Kate and Mary, Liz said, "None for me, thanks."

"Your religion got something against turkey?"

"Peter," his wife warned.

"Everything is wonderful," said Mary's friend. Unembarrassed, it would seem, she nonchalantly buttered her roll. Evidently in the habit, notice, of biting her fingernails, some of them. Long, thin fingers, a gold ring like a square knot, red gem on her pinkie, telltale callus on the first knuckle of her middle finger. Lead in your pencil.

Facing her, he spoke in headlines, "Charming vegetarian disarms meat-eater's holiday in rural Connecticut."

No response. His wife wouldn't look at him now, closed her eyes to count to ten. Silence was to be his punishment.

Gwen's father thrust his already heaping plate toward his son-in-law. "Put it right there like a good fellow."

"Hold it, Dad," adding to this pile of food a golden drumstick, which Curly had never failed to receive, not since Fletcher could remember, as if Curly's drumstick represented an upheld family tradition. Hate to see him go without it.

"Carlton, honestly, is that necessary?" his wife didn't fail to ask, her voice tinged with annoyance.

And Curly, who knew this routine as well as the Marx Brothers knew when to swing and fall and duck in *Duck Soup*, thoughtfully placed his knife and fork on the table and looked at his untouched food. The gesture commanded everyone's attention. He raised his wounded eyes. The face he now presented to his spouse, the face with which he had fended off a lifetime of scolding, was dumbfounded. With expert timing, the controlled voice smoldering, he asked, "Am I going to be able to enjoy my Thanksgiving dinner today"— he paused, this student of "The Honeymooners"—"or am I not?"

Fletcher met the visitor's glance and winked reassuringly.

"If you want to kill yourself, that's your business, I can't—"

"Mother, for crying out loud."

"Hey, Mom, Dad knows what's good for him."

Our bodies are our gardens. . . . Don't say it.

For all to hear, Kate declared, "Vegetarianism appeals to me."

"Don't get any ideas, young lady," her grandmother answered.

"And don't ever bring one home—an idea."

"Funny, Dad," she said.

"Or if you must bring one home, make sure it speaks English," said Mary.

"And wears pants," Liz added.

"With money in the pockets."

"Are these girls making fun?" asked the grandmother.

"You should have heard them this morning when I came downstairs in my sweatpants."

"Oh, yeah, Mom has taken up jogging, three whole miles with this little band around her head. I'm proud of you, Mom, you're so cute in that outfit."

"See what I mean?"

"That's why your eyes are so clear," Gwen said. "I can't run. After two minutes I have to pee."

"It might do something for your heart, but it will make your face haggard, mark my words, Penelope."

"It makes me feel good, Mother." Impatience flared in her face.

"Liz runs ten miles a day. She's as bad as you are, Jack."

"Maybe six, Mary, not ten."

"Well, there you go." Gwen turned to him. "You two can have a jog this afternoon and talk about the Zen of jogging."

"Our Mr. Foley, the minister, has become a jogger. He looks like such a sad sack in his sweatpants."

Curly looked up from his meal. "This squash, Penny, now that's something you could teach your mother, if the old girl could learn one more trick." He ate.

"No, I don't think there's anything I could teach Mother. Mother was born knowing just what's good for everyone."

"Pen, cool it," said Peter.

"All happy families have their runner. When everything's downhill, everyone runs."

"What's that mean?" his daughter asked.

"Yeah, Fletch, what the hell does that mean?"

"God, Peter, swallow before you blurt things in my face, if you don't mind."

"How about it, Jack," said Curly, "wouldn't you

like to give that Boston marathon a go? April, is it? They've got wheelchairs and every other damn thing running in it now."

"Maybe one of these years."

"We've heard that before," piped the mother-in-law. "No," she was quick to add, "I don't see how that can be good for anybody. When man was no better than an animal, he had brains enough not to run himself off his feet for hours on end."

"Was an animal, Gram?"

"You know, Flintstone man with his club, dragging his poor woman around by the hair."

"Those were the days," said Curly.

"No one runs anymore," said Kate. "That went out sometime in the eighties. There are just a few diehards left."

Peter held forth concerning the hazards of running for exercise, a whole list of risks from head to toe. He preferred to stay fit improving his woods. "Whenever I see someone my age hobbling down the street fit to burst, I think, that man's going to die healthy."

"It's stress management," said Liz. "Anything that makes me feel that good can't be bad."

"Look who's talking about stress," he said. "That's exactly how I feel, anything that makes me feel that bad can't be good."

"I'm sure that whatever makes you feel good is bad in one way or another and vice—"

"Oh, Penny, you and your pessimism."

"That's not pessimism, Mother, that's reality, and guess where I learned it?"

"Mom, this stuffing is amazing, what have you got in here?"

"Do you recognize it, Dad? Grama Wells's age-old recipe."

"Out of this world. Just absolutely—"

"What's in it?"

"Carlton, look where your sleeve is. A brand-new jacket and the sleeve . . . Isn't he impossible?"

"Chestnuts."

*L*ast year as they'd assumed their customary places at this long narrow table to partake of a meal practically identical to today's spread, right down to Patricia Wells's cranberry relish and Penny's dill pickles, and served up with similarly banal tabletalk, Clare had been in San Francisco, she had been alive. Our sister, he thought. How had she spent that day? One week later was too late to ask. He'd been sitting right here in this same damn chair, surrounded by these people, Clare's people, pass the stuffing, everything's wonderful, Pen, what's new anyway, while in San Francisco . . . How ridiculous, he thought, staring absently at the ample plate of food before him, how wrong. They all sat here now as if everything went on as before. What else could you do?

"Jack, why don't you ever take your wife to a movie?"

He had tuned out the movie talk, and missed Penny's praise for some recent hit. In Gwen's unbelieving eyes, however, he saw that Penny's recommendation would not be heeded. They had accepted the unalterable fact of their separate ways, these sisters, regarded one another's likes and dislikes with skepticism, and avoided futile confrontation.

Before he could respond, Gwen said, "Jack's afraid to go to the mall, he thinks stupidity is contagious."

"Of course it's contagious," Mary said.

Behind him he heard the three smaller children talking about movies they'd seen. Awesome, excellent, gross were the terms of their wholehearted appreciation. That was not to be interfered with—their keen short-lived enchantment.

Kate had introduced Jane Austen, eager to share her latest discovery, one of her mother's longtime attachments. He had missed the transition from movies to books. "Isn't *Pride and Prejudice* amazing?" she asked Mary's friend.

"I haven't read a novel in ages," Liz said. "I knew two professors who used them as . . . tools of seduction, if you know what I mean. I think that's what turned me off."

"It must be nice for our professors, flirting with stories all day while the rest of us are on the street slugging it out so we can pay their salaries."

"Now Peter's going to give us his thoughts on literature," said Penny. "Everyone pay attention."

"I get a kick out of these grown men pondering the innermost thoughts of a twenty-year-old girl who never left her backyard a hundred years ago, and getting paid for it. I mean, come on." He appealed to them with outstretched muscular arms.

"It's contagious," Mary said, "don't listen."

"You know, Dad," Peter cast his voice the length of the table, "the world will be on its last legs and these guys will be sitting on their thumbs with their noses—"

"Pondering the fine art of a mature genius, Peter, wondering at the scope of her sympathy and the accuracy of her observation, delighting in the texture and symmetry of her design. No one's too worried about innermosts. More like two hundred years ago, not one hundred."

"All right, Mom," Kate cheered, and Mary, laughing, clapped.

Peter's big shit-eating man-of-the-world grin all over his face. "Jesus, I get a kick out of you. You better keep an eye on her, Fletch."

Penny, as a matter of fact, had just finished Updike's last *Rabbit*. "I've read everything the man has written. That new sequel to *Gone with the Wind* is next on my list. Don't laugh, Jack, it might be fun, you should try it."

No longer vaguely apologetic about her insatiable appetite for the current hit list, piled in chain stores across the country like boxes of cereal. The way of the world behind her, the irresistible weight of it. "I don't read as fast as you do, Pen. You're a speed-reader, faster than the speed of sound." A book was like this day: get through it.

"Now, you know you could never mention a book that Jack approved of. He doesn't read what the rest of us do." Curly's tone was tolerant, not critical, as if offering an explanation.

"Of course, Peter spent his summer vacation re-reading his beloved Planty Pal," Penny told them. "Those are the only books he'll read."

Kate asked, "Planty who?"

"Everyone have a good laugh," said Peter. "There isn't a writer alive who can touch Trollope. My next book is going to be that *Whore's Ghost* by who, Penny? Clancy?"

"I've heard it's as dreadful as it's long," said Gwen. "Mailer, not Clancy."

Peter was in it for the CIA stuff. "I might have been a part of that," he explained. "I was approached by them my last year at college, did you know that, Fletch? Me and Bill Williams."

"That's nothing to be proud of, Dad," Mary said. "The CIA?" She scowled.

"Cretins in action," said Liz, not looking up.

"The CIA recruits the top—"

"The whole Cold War vision was a sick fantasy to start with," said their visitor of the day, "but these guys couldn't figure out it was all over even a week before it happened. That's not too centrally intelligent."

"Can you believe Bush going ahead with this SDI crap," Gwen said, "while one out of five kids in the country is hungry, can't read—"

"Sad dumb initiative," said Mary.

"Hey, Dad, isn't it amazing that these girls know better than the whole damn world what's good for us? The high and mighty leaders of the whole damn world aren't as clever as they are, how did that happen?"

"Don't make me throw up my Thanksgiving—"

"Mary," said her grandmother, "I don't think your father deserves to be talked to like that. You young people are too smart by half. Penny, everything is lovely," she added emphatically.

In her anxious, judgmental eyes he saw, imagined he saw, the woman's first favorable opinion of their guest change. From here on out her attitude toward this Liz would be set, you figured, and when the name of Mary's friend came up again, that evening, or next week on the phone to one of her daughters, or months from now on the eve, say, of Mary's graduation from college, she would let you know that something bothered her about that girl—just something about that girl that got under her skin. Not too pleased with her granddaughters just now either, her own sparkling flesh and blood. Watch your step with that daughter of yours, she had warned Gwen more than once over matters as trivial as . . . blue jeans, back talk, bubblegum. So you'd never breathe a word to the woman about alcohol, sex, teenage insomnia, never breathe a word to your own mother about something real, so by the time your kids were teenagers, the whole family was leading a secret life and these folks who cared about you more than anything in the world didn't have a clue about what was really going on and didn't want to know.

Most in her cozy world of acquaintances would accept her view of what was what, spun out of thin air. Meanwhile, someone like Clare was driven to the conclusion . . . as if it was only the likes of Patricia Wells who got to get old, sit back, tell what it was like, what happened, who was who, getting most of it wrong.

"Well, if reading a fat make-believe book will help Peter feel in touch with the major players," Penny was saying, "I guess that's no worse than any other form of brainwashing."

"Now there's going to be an argument here," Curly cautioned. "That's enough literary discussion for one day."

A welcome lull.

W ho's into the end of civilization? I noticed the book in the other room. Is that sweeping the campuses?"

"I thought we all were," said Gwen.

"That's Mom's," Mary answered. "All about the earth cooling, right? The imminent ice age. Drought, famine, fire, wind."

"Christ," said Peter, "don't get her started on that."

"The title happens to be the survival of . . . but maybe it should be called the end, Jack. The point, quite simply, is that the whole shebang will be over before we know it if mankind doesn't wake up. In this context everything else, everything happening in the world, is—"

"Oh, Penny, why do you waste your time?" her mother asked.

"It's Deborah's latest crusade," said Peter. "When you have money to burn, you need a cause to keep you busy." He stood and went around the table pouring wine. "Deborah's father was Tinker Toys or one of those—"

"Elaborate," said Liz, leaning forward with interest.

"Well, glaciation occurs every hundred thousand years or so. Roughly."

"Not right to the minute. Roughly."

"Shut up, Peter. Glaciation, glaciers, that's the earth's way of remineralizing its life-giving skin—the soil—"

"I like that—life-giving skin. How's that, Fletch? Is that poetry or what?"

" . . . which eventually becomes exhausted, unable to sustain the plant life necessary—that is, elements in the soil support the microorganisms that supply the protoplasm that feed the plant life. All that gets used up."

"I warned you."

"Carlton, would you pass these girls the stuffing and vegetables. Will you look at your grandfather sitting there with everything in front of him. Mary, you hardly put a thing on your plate for goodness'—"

"I'm full, Gram."

"Glaciation is the earth's way . . ." Gwen repeated.

"You don't want to hear it," Penny said.

Gwen, Liz, Fletcher wanted to hear.

"Carbon dioxide is the crux. Plant life absorbs the excess that goes into the atmosphere, like a by-product of growth and decay and so forth, and the planet keeps up with the whole process by producing more plant life, maintaining a carbon balance—"

"Key phrase—carbon balance. Everybody got that in their notebooks?"

"You bastard."

"Penny, honestly—"

"Really, Peter, you're too much. They asked me, so I'm just giving a brief . . . but you always—"

"Hey, Pen, I'm sorry, I've got my own problems with plants right now, all right? It's hard for me to take some of Deborah's stuff seriously. That book was published in 'eighty-one, wasn't it? We're talking ten-year-old science here."

"The thesis of the book is very timely," Penny told them.

"Ignore him, Penny. What about the carbon balance?" her sister asked. "I'm interested, what about it?"

"I think it's really very disturbing. In other words, once the soil becomes depleted and can no longer support the green world which absorbs the excess, then you have this tremendous buildup of atmospheric CO_2. Diseased, weakened forests, for instance, become vulnerable to fire, for example, caused by lightning, which creates even more carbon dioxide, et cetera."

"Has this kid done her homework?"

"You better be quiet," Gwen told him. "I thought fire was a good thing, necessary."

"Everything's more complicated now."

"Gwendolyn, please," her mother said, "what are we going to do with this food?"

"Enter the greenhouse effect," Mary said. "Right? So are we warming or cooling?"

"According to this version, the warmer air causes greater evaporation from the oceans which cools by the time it reaches the polar regions, forming cloud masses and snowfall so the glacial mass actually— Terrific, Bo, now get a paper towel and start cleaning it up. Peter, will you see if your son has eaten anything over there."

"He stuffed all his vegetables on my plate, Mom."

"So, I get it," said Liz, "the glacial mass actually—"

"In other words, the temperate zone, like us, warms temporarily until the colder air mass from the growing ice cap eventually creates cooler temperatures. So the onset of the whole process is characterized by hotter and dryer conditions in warm places and gradual cooling in temperate . . . and meantime the conflict between cold air meets warm causes violent worldwide weather systems featuring hurricanes, tornadoes, tidal waves, floods, the works." Her right arm turning the whole time, suggesting the churning force of rampant . . .

"Okay, Mother, don't get too carried away."

"Everybody got that?" asked Peter. "Sam, give Bo a hand before that milk rots the floorboards."

"Forget it," Penny said. "Fine."

"Hell of a story, Pen," said Fletcher, "but I thought I heard the ice cap was melting, oceans rising, places like the Cape going under in no time. If someone would just pass the brussels sprouts."

"Who said something about the Cape?"

"Don't worry, Gram."

"Well, I guess we know something about violent weather systems," Curly contributed. "First, we had Bob—that's an awful friendly name for a hurricane, isn't it?—then that terrible coastal storm in October, people never saw anything like it. You kids don't know what it was like, do they, Pat? Trees down everywhere, all those old trees along 6A, whole stands of locust, a terrible thing for the poor old Cape. The whole parking lot in Chatham toppled right into the ocean. Penny, that's the best turkey, it was fresh, wasn't it, not frozen."

"Yes, none of you has seen what a mess it is now," said Patricia Wells. "There's just heaps and piles of fallen trees and branches everywhere, I don't know how in the world they're going to clean it up. It used to be so beautiful."

"So let's say it's getting colder ultimately," Liz said encouragingly.

"So the point is we're approaching the end of this interglacial period, this ten thousand years. The cycle of events is under way. It doesn't take much imagination to observe that the weather is wacko. Have you noticed it's always unseasonably warm or unseasonably cold? It's never seasonably anything anymore," Penny pleaded. "The drought in Africa is a symptom of global cooling, for instance. Russia's growing season isn't long enough to feed the people anymore."

"Oh, we'll feed them," said Curly. "God, that kills me."

"For fifty years we've been fighting the wrong cold war," Gwen said. "Perfect. I love it."

Fletcher finished the brussels sprouts, greedily

wolfed brussels sprouts, willing to believe all members of the cabbage family to be cancer's enemies.

"Presumably, the tropics, like the equatorial region, will survive as the source of new life once the glacier . . . I guess it grinds the earth's crust to dust, which is carried over the surface by winds, remineralizing—"

"For the love of God, Penny," her mother said, "don't you have better things to worry about?"

"The non sequiturs are flying, aren't they?" Peter put in.

"So, what's the point, Mom, the ice age is coming and that's that? How about the hole in the ozone, we can't leave that out."

"Can we be excused?" Becky asked from the children's smaller table. The three, laughing, fled, Bo shouting, "Thanks, Mom," and Sam, "Everything was delish, Aunt Pen," the sound of a thumping tumble and roll the second they cleared the corner.

"The point is that everything we're doing, the exploitation of everything, is only making everything worse. The destruction of the Amazon . . . agricultural lands ruined with all these chemicals, our dependency on fossil fuels robbing the earth . . . I won't go through the whole thing again. Those fires in Kuwait, for example, Bush's fires, that's just what the doctor ordered."

Peter sat back and applauded. "Jesus Christ, you're fantastic. Pen should be running for office. Don't tell me the end is upon us? Come on."

Penny's expression was strained, a deep crease between her clear dark eyes. "If you lived in Ethiopia, you'd think so. Half of Africa, in fact, or Asia for that matter. Widespread famine is inevitable."

Kate recalled for them statistics from her paper on drought. "Millions will die," said Fletcher's daughter solemnly.

"Remember the Kingston Trio?" said Peter. He sang, "They're starving in Africa la la lalalalala. That was thirty-five years ago."

"That's awful, Dad. You didn't hear that, Liz."

"It was a song. Three guys in striped shirts, that was a friendlier world, I'll tell you. My question is how, given the host of goddamn problems, right, how can well-off American women pick out something like that? We've got the deficit, diseases you never heard of, the economy in a tailspin, these goddamn upstart nations all over the place, tribal warfare, dope gangs, farmers going down the tubes, garbage piling up, Japan and Germany taking over the world, right? And Pen and Deborah go out to lunch and get all worked up about glaciers. Something so beyond anyone's control—"

"I thought it was the survival of," Fletcher decided to say. "You haven't told us about that part yet." Clare would have enjoyed this, he imagined, informed us all, shed light from another point of view altogether. If she'd had the patience to remain at the table.

"The point is that it's not beyond our control yet, but it will be if governments don't get things straight, start seeing the earth as an organic whole, a global—"

"For heaven's sake, Penny," her mother said, "you're going to give yourself one of those headaches. That's enough."

"I know, it's a big joke. Laugh it up, Peter." Yet Pen, you figured, was one of them, one of us, more concerned with Becky's braces and Bo's breakfast than Africa, for example. Her life.

"I say bring on the ice age," Liz smiled, "before we mess things up so even glaciers can't fix it. Like you were saying, new life after the ice does its thing."

"I get such a kick out of you kids, I'm telling you."

Kate asked, "Why are you so quiet, Dad?"

"Just digesting."

Penny came to her feet, began gathering the dinner plates nearest her, scraping food from each plate into the bowl that had held the brussels sprouts. Enough garbage to feed another family, figure. Are you through, are you through . . . ?

Patricia Wells said, "Well, I don't live in Ethiopia, if you don't mind. It's Thanksgiving. We've heard enough about the world's problems today to last until . . . kingdom come."

"It almost looks like it could do something out there, doesn't it?" said Curly, turning to the window near him. "Has anyone heard the weather today?"

"Much darker," Mary forecast, "with a chance of famine in the afternoon."

Peter roared his laugh.

Patricia Wells stood, laying her folded napkin on the table, smoothing her skirt both front and rear. "This has been just lovely, Penny, everything was lovely. I feel so fortunate for this day, having us all together. I really do."

"Very fortunate," Curly seconded.

"I'm glad, Mother." Little gladness in her voice.

"Isn't it sad to think," Patricia Wells said thoughtfully, looking at her husband, "that we'll be gone in a few years?" She didn't mean the species, but themselves, Mr. and Mrs. Carlton. . . .

Howls of good-natured indignant protest assaulted the woman from every corner of the table.

W ith cheerful efficiency and constant chatter, six
women (including Kate) cleared the table for
dessert. Cheerfully constant, they inefficiently chattered
as they cleared their six minds for dessert. While the
master of the house, still game after a mealtime of master baiting, went for his snifters and Armagnac. His
shitkickers and knapsack.

Fletcher, too full, stepped out onto the north porch
of the ell and took several deep breaths, leaning over the
railing, holding his face out to the welcome breeze, the
sky today. Call me Ish. . . .

We've heard that before. The woman could still get
under his skin with a simple harmless phrase. Come on,
Jack.

On its post near the dogwood tree, the birdfeeder
was visited by a gray bird he couldn't identify for sure.
Peter had mounted his feeder on a cedar post that would
last a lifetime or fifty years, whichever came first, and
had advised Fletcher to do the same. That was two years
ago now, still hadn't put up the damn birdfeeder. Somewhere on the shelf in the back of the garage, sitting
there to give him a little prod each time he spotted it.
You raised the roof to fill it with seed, planes of glass
funneled birdseed into the feeding platform, squirrel-
proof presumably. He had stained his handiwork a
familiar colonial red. Fletcher saw: Peter, a busy, suc-
cessful man, at his exceptional workbench in his well-
lighted basement constructing his clever birdfeeder for
the Fletchers, cutting the pieces, carefully assembling,
painting. Or a wooden truck for Sam, a dollhouse
for Kate years ago. Many things. Fletcher had re-
marked upon the orderliness of his workroom; Peter
explained, When you have as little free time as I do,

you can't waste it looking for tools. Listening to fools. His *Popular Mechanics* mentality stood him in good stead with his fellow man. No, Peter was okay, decent enough, screw Jane Austen, his half-assed ideas about movies, the defense budget, cretins in action, what's good for you, or the planet. Get out the bird book, learn something about creatures while there still were such.

I get a kick out of you.

Lines like, So long as men can breathe or eyes can see, So long lives this and this gives life. . . . Ever mindful of Devouring Time, there was the consolation of the eternalizing power of poetry, popular Renaissance theme. Kiss it good-bye. We're talking the end of devouring time here, the end of forever. Stuck with our futureless future, as another sonneteer aptly . . . That made civilization anybody's ball game, truth and beauty up for grabs. You needed to go with the passing moment, get it while you can, don't look back, there's no tomorrow. That made it Peter's world. That meant you had to build police stations and grammar schools, if you were lucky, you had to hustle orthopedic surgeons about lame projects, make a silk purse of an old house into a sow's ear hospital for cats and dogs. Architect! The future, as it flew out ahead of itself, leaving a wake of endings, had the effect of compressing time and space. Shakespeare seemed like yesterday, an old friend, really did, in light of the advancing strangeness, the rapidly approaching unknown. Civilization more like a too brief episode bounded by prehistoric darkness at one end and pitch-darkness at the other. You don't say, Jack.

The lawn sloped gradually toward the row of venerable sugar maples by the road. Their days were numbered. Imagine New England without its sugar maples, if we may descend from our lofty peak and take one everyday example of the way we don't know what we're doing. Getting and spending at the expense of all. Like that wildly ugly modular metal building some dumb-ass high-tech outfit plunked down right in the middle of the largest sugar bush left in Fletcher's area, hundred-year-old roots hacked up to squeeze in an eyesore they'd be throwing out in ten years, asphalt packed right up around the mighty trunks so these well-groomed state-of-the-art hotshots wouldn't have to walk more than two steps to the front door under the doomed limbs of grand trees killed for nothing. Inside clucking over printouts, proud as hell of themselves at the cutting edge, the world by the tail, while woeful branches arched bewildered over the shitty little mint-green building. Might make a children's story.

The past was shrouded, as it receded, in a mist. One of Kate's more felicitous grade-school phoneticisms: mystery spelled like history. That was preserved in his end-bound notebook. As if the least moments of his life—a child learning to spell, a bird observed, a thought, a passing thought while standing apart on the porch—were matters of memorable importance. To Fletcher, such moments represented a way to seize the day. We live in our skins, the here and now, despite what is past, passing, or to come. The skin of the moment, that was one of Clare's lines.

I was awakened . . . pinned to the bed.

Precociously, Noah had taken his law degree by the time he was in his early twenties. Within a year he had also married and fathered a child, which makes me an awfully young grandmother for a white woman, Clare had written. With an older friend he had opened a free legal clinic in a three-story brownstone in a black St.

Louis neighborhood. The business was on the first floor and Noah lived upstairs with his wife and daughter. The live-in clinic had been a plan Fletcher had heard about for years. An unexpected letter began, There is nothing like rape to get your head together. Visiting from California in June, she had been babysitting for her granddaughter in St. Louis. A man climbed the fire escape and came through the window. I was awakened, pinned to the bed. . . . I didn't fight him; there was no way I could have. A stab of fright for his one-time lover fled downward from Fletcher's shoulder to his chest. What had he made of that sentence the first time he'd read it? She had been made to live that moment in her skin, and relive it and relive it. In parentheses she added, It seems I've come full circle from being accused of rape to being the victim of it. Fletcher assumed she was referring to her relationship with the Vietnam vet whose release from prison she had won many years before, but that was a murky part of Clare's story, which he hadn't sought to clarify. Otherwise, she went on, she was tending her garden—in California by then, not Missouri—and contemplating her next career move. She wanted to come and visit, maybe later in the fall. Please write! Let me know if I can come. I won't be a burden, she had written, and I won't stay more than a day or two. Right now I can't leave my garden. It's the only thing I've created all year and I can't bear the thought of it going to weed or seed. He and Gwen had called and talked to her about what had happened. The rape had left her feeling cut off, she said, that was probably the worst of it. Everyone—Noah and his wife, even some of Clare's friends—seemed afraid of it, afraid of her. She recalled coming down the stairs that night when Noah came in. I've been raped, she said, and she could see it in his face, a fear, a turning away. Later when Gwen tried to tell Penny about it, hoping Penny would rise to the occasion and seize upon Clare's crisis as an opportunity to heal the break between them, Penny didn't want to be involved. She expressed skepticism concerning the incident, in fact, insinuating that here was another example of Clare's instability. Over the years, that had become, for the rest of the family, the most common explanation for Clare's out-and-out rejection of them. She was disturbed, she needed help, Clare the loon. Each bit of news about her tended to confirm their baseless presupposition. He and Gwen had urged her to come out to see them. In October. I'll call you in a month, she'd said. But she didn't call in a month. Clare didn't come east in October, or any other time. Her occasional postcards stopped, and neither he nor Gwen took time to write to her. That was wrong. They might have flown to San Francisco, or he might have gone alone, spent time . . . She had felt cut off even from her son. What more had she needed to say?

Tanya, that was the granddaughter's name. Didn't that make him a granduncle? The thought was disturbing.

There was another interval of silence, punctuated by one or two uninformative Christmas cards. Gwen must have sent cards in return. Yes, he considered, two Christmases must have passed with no more than season's greetings going between them. When they heard from her again, it was the spring of '90, of that Fletcher was absolutely certain, a letter on blue paper. She was holed up in a friend's cabin north of San Francisco, working on a manuscript, which had suddenly come together for her in a blaze of glory, she wrote. For the first time in a while, she'd landed a new job she was excited about, teaching at a primarily Hispanic high school. I'm hungry for young blank faces. She wouldn't begin until fall, of course, so this summer she was going to take some time off and disappear herself in the Sierra Nevadas, she'd been away too long. Friends have been coming out of the woodwork, she wrote, i.e., my head. Another passage, which had meant little to him at the time, frankly, but which he had subsequently learned by heart: It is unbelievable to me that last year I was practically suicidal, life was over. The years of torment are over. I may come down again, but never again as bad as that. Noah was becoming a force with his clinic in St. Louis, she was obnoxiously proud of him, she confessed. She had enclosed a picture of Tanya, a gorgeous kid with curly white-blond hair. So, she went on, I really want to know about you guys, life is too damn short, we've been out of touch too long. I feel so good I assume everyone else does too, but, good or bad, write and let me know what's happening. She was more determined than ever to get back east, she'd let them know when she was coming. They were relieved to hear from her, relieved that she was apparently doing so well, grateful that she didn't hold their casual neglect against them. That summer they visited Monhegan Island. Clare haunted him the whole week. This was her kind of place! He and Gwen agreed that it would be wonderful to bring her there, possibly before September. They sent her a postcard made from an old black-and-white photograph of the small harbor—lobster boats, wood piers, shingled houses with gulls perched on steep roofs—proposing the plan. And they had a card from her that summer—snow-capped mountains—saying she was foraging for berries, sleeping under the stars, wearing pigtails, felt twenty-five again, but there was no mention of Monhegan. Their card, they figured, must have reached San Francisco just after she'd left.

Friends were coming out of the woodwork. . . .

The sugar maples there. Don't die out on us, he thought. They looked like the souls of trees. Heard that before? God love us, even our Mr. Foley has become a jogger, building his body while the souls of his flock withered and died. Anything that makes me feel that good can't be bad. A hot ticket, Mary's Liz, speaking up to the man of the house, centered-seeming, intelligent. Tools of seduction; she had known two.

From his forty-odd acres of woods across the road, Peter cut cords of hardwood each year for recreation. Roy, a giant teenage neighbor, helped. Fletcher could just make out the break in the trees that led into the woods. Now little more than a path just wide enough for a pickup, it had once been a public road connecting two towns. It was lined with stone walls on both sides. There were stone walls in various states of disrepair, mossy and adorned with lichens, all through the woods so that one was able to imagine former pasturelands and the monumental effort, the vision, that had brought them into being. To Peter they were monuments as significant in their way, he had once solemnly confided to Fletcher, as Stonehenge.

Maybe a third of a mile into the woods there was a small mowing, which a nearby farmer limed and fertilized and, twice each year, hayed. Before you reached the unexpected field, he remembered, you came upon a small rectangular graveyard enclosed by stone walls on four sides and containing the dead of two or three families, perhaps twenty antique gravestones. The historical society of the town looked after it. Bordering the back line of Peter's property, farther than you could go by truck, flowed a year-round stream. When Peter bought the house and fifty-plus acres, he hadn't known that the land across the road held these treasures: an open field, a graveyard, a stream. During one of their visits here, Peter, in Maine Hunting Shoes, led both families on a hike to see his discoveries. Mary was a little girl in black pigtails who protectively held Kate's hand. Penny, he thought, had been beautiful. Was his memory of her in a white sweater accurate? Peter seemed to have changed less than his wife over the years, although Fletcher could recall being startled by photographs from those days in which Peter looked rounder, boyish, less sure than he had ever seemed to Fletcher in life. Jack Fletcher had been someone else altogether, as it looked from here, while Gwen had only been younger, with big mothering breasts, and happier. Yes, Sam was already around then—the baby strapped to Fletcher's back that day like a knapsack. Clare wasn't present, Clare was never there.

I was awakened. . . . I won't be a burden.

Later he would take a walk, read names on the old stones, check out the stream. With his back to the house, focusing on the entrance to the once public road, he fantastically foresaw himself exploring Peter's private woods with Mary's friend, the vegetarian who was too smart for her own good. Seeking her innermost, hungry for young blank faces, the skin of the moment. You fool. Oh, fuck you, I'll talk about what I damn please.

The low sky almost looked like snow, although surely it was too mild for that. The holidays upon them again: season of recurrent themes. Handel's sing-along,

Corelli's concerto, Pachelbel's canon, for example, you
know the one. A decade of that to go along with the
brie, cross-country skis, mulled wine, drunk enough by
the end of the day to be moved mulling over life a year
later. A certain fruitcake, coveted by Fletcher, which
had come from the old country in Grama Wells's
head—containing cherries, currants, raisins.

His father-in-law placed a hand on Fletcher's shoulder. "Jesus, time flies. Damn near looks like it could
snow already, doesn't it, Jack?"

"You startled me. I didn't hear you come out."

"What's this I hear about a grammar school?" Curly
asked. "That sounds awfully interesting to me."

"We'll be out on the street if that doesn't come
through. We're working on it."

"You'll be all right," his father-in-law assured him.
"You're young, you ain't seen nothing yet."

Fletcher changed the subject to the Cape. "What a
shame, the trees down everywhere."

"It's one thing or another. We had another incident
with pilot whales, I don't know how many beached
themselves again at Wellfleet. They were all over the
papers for a week."

"Died, you mean?"

"It took a week to bury them. A mass grave right
where they landed. The leader was sick, someone said,
one of our experts, and turned toward land and they
all went right along. No one knows. Of course, Pat,
she wouldn't be interested in anything like that, but I
went and had a look. All sorts of people were running
around trying to do something for them. I'll never
understand it."

His children's T-shirts one year: a breaching sperm
whale superimposed upon a globe. Save them.

Curly shook his head grimly, pouting. "You'd think they'd know better, wouldn't you?" He clapped his hands together. "Say"—struck by a good idea—"give that marathon a go, why don't you? Quigley next door tells me his boy wouldn't miss it for the world."

"I'd like to give it a shot once. Time is the problem, training, you can't just pull on your shorts and—"

"Tell you what, you go ahead and give it a shot, and I'll be there at the finish line to cheer you in." He lightly socked him on the shoulder. "We'll have dinner somewhere in Copley Square, how's that for a deal?" With that thought, Curly left him.

Friends are coming out of the woodwork . . . I won't be a burden . . . please write . . . the years of torment are over.

He didn't turn away from the sky, the light, the trees until Becky burst onto the porch. "Uncle Jack, dessert! What are you doing out here, completing your navel? That's what my dad said." Laughing, she fled, the door left open for him, shouting behind, "Time for dessert."

*H*e would have a sliver of each—pumpkin, apple, mince—preferring a brief flirtation with different tastes to a solid wedge of sameness.

"Jesus wept," Peter blustered from his end, "now we have a vegetarian and an asshole who flirts with desserts."

"Don't shout, Peter," said Penny.

The phrase "Jesus wept" derived, you figured, from their colorful Irish friend, Cora.

"Mary, don't tell me you aren't going to have pie? What gets into you girls?"

"It's delicious, Gram," Kate volunteered. "What's the story, is this a Native American contribution or what?"

"They were definitely into pumpkins," said Mary. "I think pie was a little later."

"Very clever," said Kate.

"Ask your grandfather, he's part Indian, aren't you, Dad? What did you use to do, just boil them in water and eat them with a clam shell?" Half of Peter's piece, pumpkin, uplifted on his fork.

"Poor Injuns," Mary said.

"Thanksgiving wouldn't be complete without them," said Peter.

"No, it wouldn't," said Curly. "Their idea, wasn't it?"

"Imagine turning up to take on the unknown with your bare hands, no problem. Those Pilgrims must have been something."

"Now that you mention it," said Gwen, "you don't look much like a Wampanoag, Peter."

"He's got a desk full of scalps, though," Penny said. "Everyone who's ever crossed him."

Liz, Fletcher noticed, was frowning at her plate as if biting her tongue, troubled, then she looked toward Peter at the head of the table, addressing herself to him. "That whole mythmaking saga about our forefathers heroically clearing the intractable wilderness is mostly propaganda. Do people realize that?"

"Does everyone realize that?" Peter asked.

"The Indians here were agrarian. They'd cleared and cultivated all up the coast and along rivers, inland, for centuries. Apparently their land looked like a park. The English sailed into prime farmland, that's why they thought it looked like paradise."

Kate was impressed. "Did you know that, Dad? So what happened, they just said, here, take it?"

"That European export called the plague disappeared a lot of native people, entire tribes, followed by a smallpox epidemic later, equally devastating. Not pretty."

"And I thought Plymouth Plantation was so great in junior high," Kate said.

"They had every kind of bean," Sam called from the kid's table. "Squash, pumpkins, tobacco, strawberries, blueberries, grapes, nuts, mushrooms, tons of fish, ducks, turkeys, deer, rabbits, skunks, beavers, maple syrup, watermelons." Red in the face from his recitation. "We studied it in school," he declared. "Wild rice!" he shouted. "Popcorn!" Popping his arms into the air.

General laughter followed.

"Don't tell me they had grapenuts," Peter said.

"Jerusalem artichokes," said Fletcher, "right? Smoked salmon."

"American history," Mary said. "Great story."

"As though they sent these diseases over to wipe out the population and lay the groundwork for a general takeover," said Peter. "It just happened. Now we have AIDS. Next you'll tell me they were nonviolent, Deerfield massacre never happened—"

"As a matter of fact," Liz said, "they were very generous and hospitable initially. White man was definitely the problem."

Patricia Wells said, "I've never cared for wild rice."

"Mom," Peter said, "I bet Liz here would like your joke about—"

"Don't be an asshole, Peter," said Penny.

Gwen said, "After all these years, Mother, I still don't know how you get the crust to—"

"Everyone in our gourmet club is envious of your mother's pies," said Curly. "Jesse won't even talk to her anymore, will she, Pat?"

"Shed a little light on our dark history, Dad, you're the only Indian at the table."

"You're not going to get me involved in this one," said Curly, the cup raised to his lips, pouting as to kiss, blowing before he sipped.

"Here was this pristine place and these people living in complete harmony with it," Liz said. "The English thought it was theirs for the taking, God wanted them to have it."

"A few hundred years later it's all gone," Gwen said. "That's sad."

"When you're pushing fifty," Penny observed, "you begin to realize how recent all that was. Like yesterday."

"Is this Thanksgiving," asked Patricia Wells, "or is this the day of doom? What can we do about the poor Indians in 1991?"

"Okay, Gramp, tell us about the Indian part," Mary said. "What tribe?"

"The Golf-All-Day tribe," said his wife.

"My father's grandmother was a full-blooded New York State Indian," Curly said. "She stood about as tall as a broom, smoked a pipe every day of her life, and lived to over a hundred. I met her once. She just looked at me, never said a word. I guess she'd married a seaward Dutchman when she was just a slip of a girl."

Fletcher asked Liz, "What's got you so stirred up about Indians lately?"

"I read a book." She didn't look up. The tenor of this table talk, he gathered, had pissed her off.

"Speaking of paradise," said Peter, "let me tell you about Kamchatka. The easternmost peninsula of the Soviet Union. Is it still the Soviet Union?" He looked at his lovely watch. "It's between the Sea of Okhotsk and the Bering Sea, Fletch."

"For Christ's sake, Peter," said Penny. "Isn't he unbelievable? The Sea of Okhotsk!"

"Absolute untouched wildnerness, Fletch. Gorgeous. I think they did some lumbering in the Stalin era, one little corner. The peninsula is seven hundred and fifty miles long. It's got everything—pure rivers, virgin forest, mountains, geysers, hot springs, meadows of wildflowers, snow-covered peaks, waterfalls. You get the picture."

"Got it," said Fletcher. "What's the point?"

"There's every sort of game, beast and fowl, the rivers are full of blue trout and king salmon, so thick with salmon you can walk across their backs."

"Who lives there?" Mary asked. "It can't be uninhabited."

"I think there's a small population of reindeer herdsmen, nomadic Eskimo types, the sun rises and sets on the reindeer, which provides all life's necessities type-thing. Very few westerners have set foot on the Kamchatka peninsula since 1860 something. We're talking wilderness, Dad, one of the last places like it on earth."

"What's it called," Liz asked, "Come-whatsky?"

Fletcher asked, "How did you get involved in Come-whatsky, Peter?"

"The art deal, it's the same group, basically. Anyway, people have gone in there to check it out. Untouched wilderness, that's the word, a sportsman's paradise."

"What sportsman?" Penny asked indignantly.

"Fletch, are you paying attention, people from all over the world would give their eyeteeth to hunt and fish there. We've got enough people right in New England to make it worthwhile. They don't realize what they've got, see, the Russkies don't have a clue as to how to set it up. They don't know how to run a business."

Patricia Wells stood and began picking up the dishes near her.

"Relax, Mother, we're hardly finished."

"I'll relax in my grave."

"Don't be so sure," said Penny.

"I hope you're kidding," Mary said to her father. "The last unspoiled wilderness means nothing to you but a business opportunity."

"It would last longer as a sportsman's preserve than anything else you can think of."

"I wonder how the reindeer people will like the idea," Liz said. She and Mary were looking at each other, shaking their heads.

"It's fascinating," Peter went on. "We may get a group together by spring to go over."

"They can't feed themselves, Peter," Fletcher said, "the economy is a total disaster, and you're going to set up an international sportsman's paradise?" You had to laugh.

"You're what's fascinating," Penny said to her husband. "You should be preserved for future study."

"Listen to them, Dad," Peter said. "But we know who pays the bills, don't we?"

"Shit," said Mary, "don't start that."

Peter sipped his brandy and sat up straighter in his chair. He pointed a finger at his daughter. "Let me tell you something, my dear." He tapped his stout chest. "I'm not spending twenty thousand dollars a year plus to send you to that school so you can sit there and criticize me for the way I earn the money. I put a tremendous amount of time and creativity into what I do and I get pretty damn tired—"

"What are you sending me for?"

"Mary, drop it," her mother warned.

Curly's arm went up, his napkin a white flag. "Now . . . no arguments on Thanksgiving."

Peter raised his snifter. "Say a few words about Armagnac, Dad."

"Excellent. Just excellent."

Mary gave her chair an abrupt shove as she came to her feet, more vexed than the situation seemed to warrant. Her fair face was pink. She dropped her napkin on the table and glared at her father. "You embarrass me."

Fletcher stood and extended both arms toward his blushing niece. With corny bravado, addressing Peter, he recited, "This were to be new made when thou art old, and see thy blood warm when thou feelest it cold."

"Dad," Kate said, "don't be a jerk."

All the women were up from the table, lending a hand. While Mary's guest collected linen napkins— salmon, beige, pale gray, off-white—Fletcher extinguished ivory candles in the center of the table with his fingertips. She wouldn't look at him.

"Who does she remind you of?" Patricia Wells was saying to Penny at the sink as he reached around his sister-in-law, if he could just get a glass of . . . "I can't get over it," she said, disturbed. "When she was going on about the damned Indians, her expression, it was just uncanny, honestly, Penny, I thought I'd—"

"Skip it, Mother. Don't stand there, Jack, pick up a dish towel, if you want to hang out with us."

They settled like fatigued travelers in the low-ceilinged living room. The tall wide fireplace was based on Count Rumford's design, he knew. Let's see, that was Sir Benjamin Thompson, born here but loyal to George III, a spy in the Revolutionary War, a student of heat, among other things.

"Peter, it's not even cold outside," said Penny as he stood back from the blaze he'd just ignited.

"Got to have a fire, don't we, Dad?"

Curly gestured toward the open hearth. "My God, that throws the heat, though, doesn't it?"

Fletcher recalled a passage from *Walden* in which Thoreau considered boxing his fire tantamount to the lamentable loss of a companion. "For you can always see a face in the fire," he said.

"Count on Jack to remember what Thoreau said about his new stove," said Gwen.

"I'm glad we can count on him for something." Peter laughed.

Count von, yes, don't leave out the von, he thought. Count von Rumford. Count on Rumford to throw the heat, by God.

Reread, he thought. A book that reminded us of what we believe: we could be poor and have what we want. Thoreau it all away.

The Oriental rug on the floor was worth more today, you figured, far more, than the author of *Walden* had earned in a lifetime. A brief life. Serapi, that was the name. The small black tavern table they'd had for ten years, a museum piece, God knows what that was worth. A small vase of feathers sat on the old table's patined surface. Pheasant, turkey, hawk. The primitive American portrait by somebody or other was one of their treasures. Decoration. The woman in the painting, dressed in black, wore an extraordinarily detailed white lace cap, fanciful in contrast to her fairly grim, possibly toothless, expression. Those pinched eyes had looked upon Thoreau's world. Not with his vision, to be sure. Not likely. What were Peter and Penny doing with this stuff, if the truth be known? The dead and gone world. Penny's doing by and large. Peter wouldn't know the difference between a repro and the real thing. Last year they had acquired an oil painting by Metcalf: American Impressionism in Connecticut. What money could buy. A fussy rural scene. They didn't own a painting by a living artist, for example. Dry up, Jack, we like it.

Simplify.

Affluent gay men like Ted and John collected Shaker, for example, an austere setting for promiscuous weekend parties unimaginable to the weird celibate religious sect. Then AIDS suddenly complicating everything tragically, reassuring the straight world that gay men weren't having all the fun after all with nothing to worry about but their own skins, taking over islands and vacation spots, old houses and cities, the arts and other lucrative creative professions. Fuck you, I'll talk about what I damn well please. Oh, please.

You wouldn't find Thoreau's masterpiece in this house, would you? Fletcher glanced with interest at the handsome bookcase behind him. The *Encyclopaedia Britannica*, Time-Life Library of Art, of Gardening, children's books. Penny's smattering of novels, a former book club joiner, and her coffee-table-type English Style, French Style, wines from around the world, orchids, colonial furniture. Field guides to birds, wildflowers, insects, mushrooms. Years of *Antiques* magazine. A set of leatherbound something bought at auction. Pretty there, Penny. Ah, Peter's passion: a shelf of Trollope.

Your personal library, Peter?

Like running into an old friend in a strange city, he spotted the narrow spine of a familiar book, *Dubliners*. He'd given a copy to Gwen during his Joyce phase, insisting that she read one of the best stories ever written as far as Fletcher was concerned. What are you thinking, Gretta, I think I know, and she turns and says, that song, "The Lass of. . . ." Thinking of the young fellow who caught his death. I think he died for me. Curious, Penny owning a copy, too, for she'd never mentioned Joyce to him once, he was sure, never. One shelf below he noticed the black and white spine of another unlikely title, the collected poems of Rexroth. Impulsively he reached for the paperback book. Its pages had the feel of a book that had never been read. Anxiously, he opened the cover. There was an inscription in a cramped half-printed indecipherable hand, which to Fletcher was immediately recognizable and plainly readable. *For Mary, I wish I could build a fire in you that would never go out. May you flame into being. With love, Clare.* It was dated 1987. The girl's graduation from high school, he guessed. Greedily, he read it again, her living hand. Beautiful person! He looked up in alarm.

Mary and Liz along with Kate and Gwen, who might have been an older sister, had arranged themselves hip to hip on the velvet camelback sofa to delve into Penny's coat box of family snapshots, which his daughter, seated in the middle, held on her lap. He thought, Oh God. Gwen's father, arms folded and legs crossed, sat with the television set in a slant of light at the other end of the room, the monotonous drone of the game turned down to an unobtrusive background murmur. He idly rocked, already succumbing to that stuporous drugged state, feasting's aftermath, from which only the small children seemed exempt. Gwen's mother, seated in a tall crewel wing chair, knitted something blue—a Christmas present, he presumed—watching the work of her hands through heavy-lidded eyes. Apart from the rapid fuss of needles along the length of yarn, she appeared to be asleep. The yarn stretched from a shopping bag at her feet.

Fletcher brought the book to his face and breathed in the disappointing almost non-scent of its opened pages. He turned to the Rumford hearth. The uprush of flames occasioned by newspaper and kindling and pinecones had subsided, leaving a steady modest fire to gradually consume three cleanly split lengths of ash. You can always see a face. . . .

The Maine air had made her face ruddy, a cluster of thin veins faintly perceptible on her bright cheeks. All that funny flattery concerning his private-first-class phallus, she called it, the engorged glans soft as a rose petal, for example, impressive enough to reach someplace inside her that former lovers had rarely reached, she claimed, while also robustly round, made her seem more phallocentric than he was, if that was possible, bewitchingly teasing him with hands and mouth as if she was the entranced person here. Once she took him by surprise in the dory while he was still rowing, once he awoke to find himself getting hard in her mouth. Oh, Jack, elate, was one of their deep-throat jokes. I like you pink like this, the color of my nipples, almost exactly, rather than all those varieties of darker meat. Taking him in her female fist, she thoughtfully spread his prostate's translucent viscid fluid over the nub of his private rose with her narrow thumb. How strange penises are. One day she discovered that he'd developed a new vein like a thin skin-deep cord just below the flared glans, and decided that was all right, no harm done, probably a sign of maturing maleness. Exploited by her, used, now he knew, he said, how women felt. Lying in the sun on warm granite, she occasionally preferred to masturbate, you can watch, which just went to show they could more successfully manage the mutual orgasm thing at a distance, proving, she said, it's all in our heads. Our beautiful heads. She made him feel as if he had tapped in her a dormant source of erotic feeling, a healing force. More than once, in a loving mood, Clare had quoted to him the words he'd just found inscribed in Mary's book: I wish I could build a fire in you that would never go out. Maybe she had.

The banjo clock on the wall by the doorway struck the hour with a thin ping. It was three o'clock. This was the clock that had almost put him to sleep Thanksgivings ago when he'd first come here with Gwen. The thrill that ran through the tedium of such an afternoon, wanting her that day. Warm, full, girl-scented woman! Was that love? Now this hardly seemed the clock that had hypnotically counted the interminable minutes of his frustration as he sat waiting for Gwen Wells to rescue him from her family, to rescue them. Yet it was. He turned to the couch. His wife, he saw, had been looking at him. Now she looked away. Reaching behind, he returned the Rexroth volume to the bookcase.

It was only after they had visited Clare on the vineyard in Missouri and he'd realized that nothing would be possible between them again, that he confided to Gwen what had happened on the island at Weir Harbor. They had driven straight through Kansas and Colorado to reach Bryce Canyon in two days. They stood huddled together before the awesome view with Kate between them. Their first canyon, another first for them. There had been many. He was telling her about Clare, he said, because it had been important. He explained that Clare had ended the thing when the summer ended, refusing to further jeopardize her relationship with Gwen, for one thing. Gwen said, I wondered why you got so drunk the last night at the vineyard. Maybe the extraordinary vista of Bryce Canyon, setting all merely human dramas into perspective, at least temporarily, helped get them both through that potentially hazardous moment. The possibility had crossed my mind, Gwen said, I was afraid to ask. At that moment they didn't know—Gwen had not yet realized—that she was pregnant. She never questioned him about his affair with her sister. He figured she didn't want to know. Whether the disclosure changed her feeling toward Clare he wasn't sure. As for how she then felt about him . . . their life together continued to evolve, each adaptation adding another layer to something solid. Last fall, when he entered the living room to tell Gwen what he'd just learned from Noah's wife— Clare is dead—they clung to one another, sobbing. I loved her, too, he said, I really loved her. Gwen said, I know. That was the only other implicit reference either of them ever made to the Weir Harbor episode.

In grab-bag fashion they drew snapshots from the large lavender box, sifting at random through a jumbled cache of babyhoods, life changes, summer holidays. Kate and Mary greedily sought images of their mothers as young women. Today the presence of an outsider, Liz, rekindled their enthusiasm for family history.

"Let's not drag that out today."

"No one cares what you used to look like, Penny," said Gwen, who viewed old pictures of herself with enviable detachment and composure, Fletcher had observed over the years, as if they were photographs of an old dear friend.

"Gram, you're unbelievable," Kate said, holding up her grandmother's high-school graduation picture.

Young Patricia Wells—what was her maiden name, come to think of it?—had looked something like Ingrid Bergman of *Casablanca*. Unbelievably. Her full darkened mouth and commanding eyes. Fletcher knew the picture well. Everything ahead of her, smiling as though happiness was a cinch, everything possible. She had lived to see grandchildren reach the same point of beginning. May they flame into being. Who was that?

"I used to weigh ninety-eight pounds soaking wet. Your grandfather could put me over his shoulder with his right arm. Couldn't you, sweetheart?" she asked rhetorically.

They came upon one of Penny's prom pictures, some Larry, who that night had probably been allowed, you figured, to stuff his hand into the stiff bodice of her circa '61 dress and, an hour later, to tease with one venturesome finger her strange girl-damp pussy. Sweet. All that happened in no time, like falling on ice.

"Mother, is that you?" Kate asked. "Look at you."

"I was such a happy, positive person, I was so damned innocent I could cry."

"You're still innocent, Mom."

He reached behind him and took down the green Modern Library edition of *Dubliners*, an episode of youth. Something between them then. Fiction as foreplay, a fancy tool of seduction. His soul swooned slowly. . . . Never write a sentence like that today.

"That's my favorite in the whole world of Kate," said Gwen. "One of the first summers in Wellfleet."

He knew the one: a toddler in sunbonnet and pale cotton nightgown, a barefooted gnome on a bright vacant beach.

"I was so cute."

Fletcher thumbed the pages of the book just for the feel of it. Not a book he'd ever read again, he was sure. There was an inscription written on the endpaper. *I want you. Jack.*

Gwen's book: it was!

His face flushed with prickling heat. That Dylan song from long ago. You had to laugh. He didn't recall writing that inside. He knew the handwriting like the back of his . . .

"And that," said Gwen triumphantly, "is your father just after we returned from Italy. God, Jack, I could never stand you in this picture."

"The artist," said Penny.

All were acquainted with the mortifying black-and-white picture of Fletcher with shoulder-length hair and incoming beard looking straight into the camera as though peering into the very soul of something. Architecture had seemed like art in those days.

"Check it out, Liz, my dad just out of college or something. You look . . ." but words failed her.

"Pretty intense," their visitor said kindly.

"I was deep, drunk on my own depths. There was a lot of that going around in those days."

"Oh, Jack has mellowed," Penny told them. "I like you a lot more now than I did then. You were trying so hard to prove how different you were."

Fletcher, looking up, grinned to conceal the sting of Penny's offhand remark. Patricia Wells looked up from her rapid knitting. The four young women on the couch (Gwen included) looked up from their box of photographs. Peter—oh Jesus, come on—was focusing on him with his camera, aiming the goddamn camera at him. Looking away, he met Penny's clear intelligent eyes. Our exhibit this afternoon: mellow Jack. He was grinning, but it wasn't good. His face felt slapped. No, he had never thought for a moment, not in the last fifteen years, not seriously, that his sister-in-law had ever not liked him. On the contrary. . . . His mind raced as if struggling to absorb sudden shocking news.

"Can that be true?" he asked. "The old Pen, my own sister-in-law?"

"You've improved with age, my dear. Just a few more years and you'll be—"

"Go easy on that boy over there," Curly called from his corner of the room, unexpectedly alert to their conversation. "I'd say Jack has proved he's one of us by now. What do you say, Jack?"

Saving him a reply, Peter's camera flashed in his eyes.

"Beautiful," said the photographer. He turned to his wife, squatting, focusing—white light—then swung on his mother-in-law, her eyes at half-mast.

"Peter, please don't, really."

He went to his knees before the foursome on the

couch. "Hey, kids, get a little closer." The room snapping with the rapid succession of flashes.

"Come on, Dad, we need you in this. Fletch, pop over there between your delicious spouse and Mom. Where are the little guys, anyway?"

Fletch didn't pop. He turned and slipped the small book back into its place on the shelf. His gift. How did it get here?

"I guess she was different, wasn't she?" Mary was saying, apropos of another snapshot chanced-upon. "We hardly have any pictures of her."

"I don't know," Gwen answered, her voice changed. "She was something, I don't know what."

Glancing toward her mother, who was paying no attention to the review of old pictures, Penny said, "Let's put those away now, Mary, it's depressing."

"I'd like to get everyone in this, okay? Dad, how about it, you're a major player here. Fletch, damnit . . ."

As Peter attempted to herd them together for the picture of the day, Sam, their gymnast, cartwheeled into the room, his legs stiff as spokes. Little Becky, square and solid as her father, somersaulted behind him, a wobbly denim ball. She had changed her dress.

"Sam!" Gwen said sharply as Sam went into his excellent headstand.

"Okay, Becky, cool it," said Penny. Becky came to rest against her grandmother's legs.

Little Bo entered the room with an armload of plastic bowling pins dragged out from somewhere. He stumbled toward his hero, Uncle Jack, who can do anything. One plastic pin dropped, then another. Bo struggled on stout legs, bending from the waist to pick up the fallen pins, nearly spilling the lot. At last he stood before his uncle and held them up, holding his breath, the whole bunch held tight in his big beautiful hands. Six or seven bowling pins. Without a hint of doubt in his voice, the words bursting, he demanded, "Juggle these!"

H is face uplifted, he took deep breaths in the autumn air. The sky raced from north to south. Call me. . . . He might have thrown his running stuff in the trunk, get away for an hour. He couldn't have run now if his life depended on it. With his tongue he coaxed a piece of white meat from between two molars on his lower jaw. A puffed-up bluejay alighted on the bird-feeder. He knew a bluejay when he saw one. It takes guts and imagination to wake up, to face what's right in front of you, assess your part in it, and care about the outcome. That was Clare talking. You have to believe in yourself, Fletcher, and the people in your life.

My mother never taught me how to fight.

Call me . . . why didn't you call me?

Cozy in their cocoon of conventions, supported by the prevailing conformity, they succeeded this day in avoiding the absent person in their midst. Avoidance wasn't a basis for belief. This family. Between holidays there were often months of silence. If you don't call, then we won't call, and if we don't call, then . . . Everyone wanted the same thing, and withdrew, wounded by indifference. It never ended. Not even death broke through.

Don't get carried away, Jack.

Yet five, ten, fifteen years of holiday seasons had not yielded relationships with these people that helped, that offered . . . support. Fifteen years had not created

bonds, call it, of love. That was failure any way you cut
it. I need your faith.

"Hey, Dad, all the way." At the north end of the
front lawn, before a cluster of three leafless crab apple
trees, dense with red fruit, Sam waved his arms. With a
small hop and skip, a practiced gesture of old, Fletcher
approached the black-and-white soccer ball slowly rolling toward him and sent it sailing on the wind, a nice
clean boot.

It was the girls, Mary, Kate, Liz, and Becky, against
Sam, Bo, and Fletcher. They used pieces of cordwood
for goals. The disadvantage of their skirts was good for
laughs. Intermittently the wind made it difficult for
them to move at all. All their hair blowing around was
some kind of excitement. Red hair, blond hair, Mary's
wild dark hair. The children squealed, turning in circles
with arms spread, their voices blowing away, faces rosy.
This special fall wind as exhilarating as Maine surf. The
sky was patchily breaking up, shadows of clouds blowing across the lawn.

"And there was light," Liz shouted. "Like light."

Mary lifted her skirt to defend the oncoming Jack
and he scored a goal between her laced leather boots
from France.

"Dad, pass, will you, once in a while. You're hog-
ging the ball." Sam cartwheeled in anger.

Kate became fierce, as always in games against her
father. She had played soccer since six or so, mainly
with boys, and had only given it up in high school
because the team was dominated by pushy female jocks.
She wanted to be a poet, a traveler, an oceanographer,
a pianist, a dazzling human being. Now she gave a show
of her fancy footwork, leaving Fletcher flatfooted, going all the way. Everything ahead of her. May they be

taken with the true burning, he thought, suddenly re-
covering the line, yes, Roethke, learned all those years
ago on a Maine island. That was it. May they flame into
being. Just now that seemed plausible, rather than a line
of poetry, a lie.

May I flame into being, he prayed, catching his
breath.

With a laughing bark, Buster raced the ball from
player to player. Sam got tangled up in his big sister's
feet and they both went down. Ecstatically, swooning,
Bo collapsed on top of them as if this tumble and clutch
was what the game was all about.

Liz went after Fletcher, stamping away as if the field
were on fire. She'd had enough of this male superiority
bit. As he was breaking free, she grabbed his arm and
held on so that Kate was able to recover the ball.

"Go for it, Katie," she cheered, "you've got it,"
beads of spittle on her lips . . . coral more red . . . eyes
nothing like the sun . . . breasts bouncy . . . fuzzy chin
with tender blemish healing.

"Flame into being," he declared, his head back.
"Be inflamed."

Mary's friend glanced at him skeptically. "What?"

Fletcher raced to prevent the imminent goal and
was stopped by a pain behind his ribs about the size of
a fist. Like a hand had reached in there, grabbed,
squeezed. He bent, hands to his knees, a crimson leaf at
his feet. This pain passed.

In twenty minutes everyone had had enough. Both
sides claimed victory. The sun was just above the
wooded hillside. Purple lavender clouds. Fletcher
brought Sam to the ground in a bear hug, craving contact with the boy's sturdy body, and rolled with him in
his Thanksgiving clothes over sweet fading grass. Becky

and Bo piled on with shouts. Fletcher burrowed beneath their warm outdoor-scented bodies, holding them, then came to his feet, struggling upright, kids hanging off him, Buster excitedly circling, and shouted to the clouds blowing overhead, "This life, you guys, I love this goddamn life. I do." Ludicrously, tears, that surge of feeling, fleetingly surfaced.

"Don't mind my dad," said Kate, "he's going crazy."

A s chance would have it . . . a pheasant—the pheasant?—appeared at the edge of the woods as he and the three young women walked toward the front of the house. He knew a pheasant when he saw one. They froze. Too bad the children—they'd already dashed off—were missing this. The bird scuttled across the corner of the yard to the large fanned shrub near the road, forsythia, he seemed to recall. They drew near, stalking, and stopped within ten yards of it. There, in all its brilliant colors, erect, agitated, under the weeping bare branches of the tawny bush, as if submitting to their desire, permitting itself to be seen, its eyes twitching with fright.

"He's so beautiful," Mary whispered. "He looks exotic, doesn't he?"

"Oriental, in fact," said Fletcher.

"Imagine wanting to shoot it?" That was Kate. "How could you?"

Solemnly they observed the bird's especial beauty. When had he last seen a pheasant? When would he see suchlike again?

A red pickup came into view, tooling down Jongleur Road, and the pheasant, frightened from its cover, made its move to cross, darting in the wrong direction, just as the truck . . . Mary anxiously sucked air between her teeth. Kate grabbed her father's wrist.

"Oh shit," Liz said.

The truck never slowed—fucker!—they watched the bird go under it, right under—ouch!—then saw the critter gamely scuttle, still scuttling, stiff as a soldier, into the leafless undergrowth on the opposite side of the road. Christ, that was close, the three girls clapped, they cheered, Liz and Mary hugged breast to breast, relieved.

"Not a feather out of place," he said.

Mary, chilled from tending goal, and Kate, who was boiling and really thirsty all of a sudden, returned to the house. The other two walked down the lawn, looked both ways, and crossed into the woods hoping to have another gander at rarely glimpsed wildlife.

The old road into the woods was all russet leaves and pine needles with outcroppings of granite ledge. Here they were out of the wind, which gusted over-head in the treetops. A hemlock, its convergent twin trunks rubbing high up, sounded to Fletcher like a creaking door in a comic-book mystery.

Speaking of close calls, Liz had been run over in Vermont at six in the morning, no kidding, just this past summer. "All of a sudden I'm on the ground. He was about your age, in a suit, going to New York, all in-volved in his attaché case to make sure he had his shit together instead of watching the road. Monday morn-ing. Nothing was supposed to get in his way, right? What are you doing in the middle of the road? he asked me. Like it was my fault. You just ran me over, I said. He never even apologized. I was getting him off to a bad start, interfering with his day. What about my day? He had to get to New York to save the world—his ass, that is. God, how I hated those damned New York plates when I lived up there. I seemed to be okay, so he jumped in his nifty little car and took off. I never saw him again all summer. I couldn't move a muscle for three days. The moral is, watch out, there are some peculiar points of view going around."

Fletcher was only half listening, stirred, oddly disturbed, having entered silent woods, a place revisited.

"How did you run into Mary? You aren't twenty-one, are you?"

She laughed. "Let's see, twenty-one was five years ago, almost six, come to think of it."

"Did someone say you were in the Peace Corps?" Gwen, in fact, had told him that, following a conversation she'd had with her sister concerning the impending holiday. The detail had escaped him until just then, as he posed the question.

"Sri Lanka for two years. I was in Kalutara, south of Colombo, the wet lowlands, but I got around, I even made my pilgrimage to Adam's Peak."

"Never been," said Fletcher.

"Paradise, except now things are pretty fucked up there, too. Civil strife. I taught English, I loved it, I even married one of them."

"In Sri Lanka?" he asked. "In the Peace Corps?"

"I met him there. He was a medical student at Columbia. We got married in New York. That only lasted a year. So now I'm going to law school part-time. I was working at a gallery in SoHo. Mary kept coming in to look at the exhibit."

The graveyard intrigued her, the various decorative symbols—primitive winged skulls, vases, willows—cut into black slate.

"Samuel Phillips Potter," he read, "son of Ezekiel

and Mrs. Lucy Potter, died seven September 1771 in the fourth year of his age, his death occasioned by the cut of an ax upon his neck which severed the jugular vein. What does that mean?" he asked.

Liz stooped and traced the engraved lettering with thin fingers, evidently touched. He observed her hand lightly tracing over neck . . . jugular vein.

"Lucy."

"What?"

"Nothing. My mother's name." She touched the letters. "Lucy."

The woods opened before them, revealing a secluded upward-sloping mowing, still a vigorous green. Two crows, cawing raucously, rose from the field.

"Wow." She galavanted gaily, plunging into ankle-deep grass, arms spread as though someone directly ahead, invisible to Fletcher, waited to embrace her. "This is so great." Reminding him again of Clare, that eagerness, for example, that unqualified yes.

At the top of the field a towering sycamore with far-flung lateral branches stood out clearly—the whiteness of it!—against gray-black woods. A detail Fletcher had forgotten, if he had ever really noticed the tree before. They walked toward it through already dampening grass. The sky behind the woods was bittersweet, a corona of light above the dark hill.

"In the fall," she said, "sunsets look like sunrises."

"What a wonderful site," said Fletcher, "a contoured enclosure."

"That's right, you're the architect. It would be a shame to mess up this field with somebody's lousy house."

He agreed with her.

"Have you had any exciting projects lately?"

"I'm trying to make a living, that's all there is to it."

"You've been awfully quiet all day, but you don't necessarily seem the quiet type. Boxing in your fire, you know, like Thoreau's stove."

"Preoccupied, I guess. These holidays aren't exactly a hell of a lot of fun, are they?"

She asked, "What's fun?" A challenge in her voice, possibly, a definite ring: she knew what fun was.

He touched the beautiful smooth skin of the sycamore, the bared white of it where the gray outer bark had peeled away. Funny thing Sam said once, everyone talking about naming their new dog at dinner one night. Say, how about Moby Dick, whale of a name? Rather impatiently, in the knowing tone the boy sometimes adopted to inform the old man of things he evidently didn't know about, Sam said, Dad, Dick is a nickname for penis.

Her smile was generous, one front tooth capped, he saw, surely the result of a youthful mishap. "I like your kids," she said. "You seem to get along together pretty well, you're lucky." Looking up at him closely, half squinting.

Even cute stories concerning one's children could serve as tools of seduction, you figured, in the wrong hands. That hadn't occurred to him as he told the story.

"What are you preoccupied about," she asked, "work?"

"Someone absent. Gwen's older sister died a year ago. To the day. I woke up thinking about her and I can't shake it. Suddenly she's become omnipresent."

"Clare," she said, startling him with the name. "Mary's told me a little about her. The legendary aunt."

"Has she?" Mary was hardly a reliable source where Clare was concerned.

"It sounded like a sad story. I guess she was pretty messed up."

"There was nothing sad about her. You got the wrong story."

She raised her hands so her palms faced him. "I don't know a thing about it, Jack. I'm only repeating . . ."

The sound of his name on her lips, that also startled him.

"She was a marvelous person. Mary didn't know her. She only knows the official family version, while the real Clare and what actually happened gets buried under all the guilt and denial."

"I'll buy that." She smiled. "We should go back." She reached for his arm.

Black silhouettes of trees against a bittersweet sky. Black stone walls. Stillness as in 1771. This was 1991. What's fun?

Intercepting her hand, exerting a discreet pressure, which brought her face to face with him, Fletcher stepped forward to give Mary's older friend the benefit of the doubt, so to speak, at dusk in Peter's woods. She looked good, but that didn't have all that much to do with how he felt. They seemed to understand one another at the moment, that was probably most of it. The light just then, Fletcher's favorite time of day, undoubtedly contributed. . . . Yet this was reckless, not to be believed following their annual stuffing at Penny's, not one of us by a long shot. The best to be said in his favor, this was unpremeditated, an unexpected intensity as spontaneous as the brilliance on the horizon: a kiss in the middle of a secluded field, dark descending like curtains. She smelled, breathing her in, like the fragrant autumn afternoon, like one of the kids, with just a hint of something creamy, a lotion, behind it. Whether this was going to work was clear instantaneously. Hard to know what she had in mind, or meant, but her answer was wholehearted, giving. He felt her hands clasp at the small of his back as she relaxed into it. Liz, the vegetarian, didn't shy away from his body. She's been here before. He didn't want to make a fool of himself, although that wasn't going to be easy now. He refrained from blurting out, for example, I love you, yet for all intents and purposes this was love, as far as Fletcher was concerned at the moment, though surely just a lark from the lady's point of view, like a sperm-of-the-moment adventure on Thanksgiving with an older . . . He lambasted her nice face with a smattering of lip-smacks, not to put too fine a point . . . and they ended up eyeing each other curiously as if, having surfaced, they wondered where they were, who's here, what now. Or: as if there's no tomorrow. There wasn't.

She tugged his tie enticingly, and kissed Fletcher in return, the crazy Liz. That's all he wanted to do with her, really, but found both hands had gotten hold of her solid runner's behind in the wool skirt, as if the palms of his hands had plans of their own, and pressed warmly up her straight sturdy back to full breasts over here on the front of her under her bulky brightly colored extra-large sweater. Don't be a fool, he thought as his hands then came up under her skirt, warmly grasping her warm woman's . . . that thrill again, at once brand-new and wholly familiar, and led him, still spontaneously, most spontaneously, to pass over her warm bare back and gently explore with extended fingers the whole globe of her breast, aroused nipple just noticeably nudging the sensitive center of his hand, before venturing downward again over likewise smooth belly and, in all sincerity, his only defense, deftly plunging beneath silky underpants into her soft warm bush, let's see, where are you . . . ? She made a glancing pass at his nickname as if to establish the facts, then drew back, placing two fingers to his lips, blushing pilgrims under the sorghum stenches.

"Don't be a jerk, Dad."

Deadpan he said, "I love you."

"You crack me up," laughing with head back, smooth neck exposed. "Maybe we shouldn't be out in the woods after dark, you know, even though no one would believe this."

"Why did that just happen?" he asked.

"I felt like it."

He stopped when they reached the antique graveyard, returning. "What did Mary say about her legendary aunt?"

"I thought we'd dropped that."

"I want to know."

"I think Mary has adopted Clare—right?—as her family hero. She didn't know her, but I guess she remembers a few occasions when her aunt made an impression. The fact that someone in the family was an activist on the front lines means a lot to Mary. She's having a little trouble relating to her parents at the moment."

"What's the sad story?" he asked.

Her smile was condescending. "Suicide tends to seem like a sad end for someone like that. Mary thinks—"

"What does Mary think?" He was annoyed now.

"That the family thing, the conflict or whatever, was an important factor—"

"I thought Mary believed she was messed up, is that the phrase you used?"

"I said that, Mary didn't. Walking away from your family like that doesn't make sense to me. The whole sexual abuse thing sounded a little fishy. But what do I know? Frankly, I'm not that interested, believe it or not." She took his arm. "Can we walk and talk at the same time?"

"I'm surprised Mary knew anything about that subject."

"She and her mother have gone at it over Aunt Clare, I gather. Poor Penny must feel like she's losing her daughter to this phantom of her past."

"Poor hardly seems the adjective to describe our Penny."

"That ice age business, Jesus."

"What's fishy about the sexual abuse thing?" he asked.

"Wasn't that the so-called turning point, the mother couldn't handle Clare's belated accusations about her brother? Do I have that right?"

"Evidently Clare tried to talk about some trauma of childhood and her mother wouldn't listen. The uncle used to live with them in the fifties or something. He died young—in Korea maybe."

"So the mother says it never happened, Penny agrees with her, but Mary can't believe her wonderful aunt would invent such a story. That's about as much as I know. They were arguing about it last night, for crying out loud. I thought Peter was going to strangle both of them."

"What was the argument exactly?"

"You know, she didn't have actual concrete memories of her uncle . . . whatever he did. She extrapolated what must have happened from years of symptoms—dreams, I guess, and suddenly awakening with this scary sense of suffocation, with numb arms and legs. Mary has done her research. Children deny it so completely they have no memory, et cetera, but the grown-up knows something's wrong somewhere. Penny thinks it's all bullshit."

"And you think it sounds fishy?"

"It's none of my business. All families have their fishy stories, that's what I figure."

"We didn't know anything about any of that until after Clare's death. Maybe Penny knew. She finally told Gwen, but of course Penny presented it as evidence of Clare's instability, a neurotic's fantasy, with her death the final proof."

"What's Jack's theory?" she asked.

Fletcher didn't have a theory. "She wanted to be in control of her dying, that's what her daughter-in-law told me the night she called me. She'd been losing control of her life, so she wanted to take control of her death. Do you know what that means? I don't have the faintest idea what the hell she meant by that. She probably didn't either."

It had fallen to Noah's wife, Sarah, to notify Clare's family. He wouldn't communicate with anyone. They chose Fletcher, perhaps as the most marginal member of the family, to be the recipient of their grim news. Gwen actually answered the phone, and Sarah, whom neither of them had ever met, asked to speak to Jack. With a succinctness that sounded rehearsed, she brought him up to date on Clare's recent life, briefly sketching a context in which he might attempt to grasp the ungraspable fact of her death. Clare had been low the past few years, she'd had some difficulty finding work that satisfied her. She'd gone back to teaching, but that turned out to be disillusioning, and she had resigned a month before. Clare's neighbor had discovered her body a week before. We've been going through her address book, Sarah said, letting some people know. She would have preferred, he sensed, to end the conversation there.

He had asked, in the confusion of his own fear and panic, How is Noah? Clare's son, he realized later, probably had been right there, listening to his wife deal with his mother's friends—go over it again.

Pretty well, she answered. Noah felt he had done all he could. They believed it had been a considered decision on her part. Then, without offering any clear glimpse of the sort of day-to-day existence that had allowed such an exceptional person to go to the bottom and not want to come up, if that was what had happened, the young woman on the other end of the line explained, Clare wanted to be in control of her dying. She felt she'd been losing control of her life. He mentioned the last letter they'd received from her only months before, a happy letter. Clare had used the word *suicidal* but he had not, not for a moment, taken it literally. Clare was the last person in the world . . . In the letter she left for them, Sarah went on, Clare said she couldn't keep fighting. Her mother had never taught her how to fight. Apparently Noah just happened to call her soon after she'd taken the pills, Sarah volunteered further, because there was another note that said, You must have sensed I was drugged. I'm glad you're the last person I talked to. For the first time there was a ripple of emotion in her controlled voice, a quavering. She had been determined to get through the phone call unruffled. He heard her draw in her breath.

Fletcher attempted to press through the opening in her composure. How did this happen? He didn't understand. Sarah's silence iced his advance. When she spoke again, it was to ask that Fletcher notify Clare's family. When he asked her what the funeral arrangements were, presuming that was the next order of business, she informed him that Clare's body had been cremated days before, there had been a memorial service in San Francisco. That's impossible, Fletcher blurted, losing control for the first time. Clare's parents, the rest of her family, they were entitled to be informed. Noah had no right. . . . Sarah cut him off. Clare had left specific instructions concerning her death. Noah had carried them out. This phone call had been her own idea; Noah hadn't intended to do even that much. Now in her clipped speech he heard the toughness, the wherewithal, that the young woman who had thrown in her life with the likes of Clare's son and his free legal clinic in St. Louis surely possessed. At the time he felt that further probings on his part would have been impertinent. He asked her to convey his sympathy to Noah, he thanked her for calling. Hanging up the phone was like closing a book against his will—just as he was beginning to get it, just as the questions were beginning to present themselves. Numerous questions. Eventually he wrote a long letter, ostensibly to Noah, in which he attempted to express how much Clare had meant to him. He didn't know where to send it.

Even as he pleaded his sense of loss and frustration concerning Clare, he was keenly aware of the person beside him, more taken up with the immediate moment, the pressure of her body against his arm, for example, than with the woman who, just a year ago, had died. That didn't sit right, as if this was merely another good story, a grotesque seducer's heavy tool. Holding his arm tight against her side as he talked, Liz frowned at the dark leaves they shuffled through, putting at Fletcher's disposal her most attentive listening self, it would seem. What did he expect Clare's story to mean to the day's blond guest, a complete stranger?

"Do you think you could have done something? Intervened?"

"No." Her discouraging question confirmed his misgivings.

"Maybe you could have." She gave his arm a jerk, jostling against him. "You know, maybe . . ."

"Anyone involved in her life probably feels they could have made a difference, given the chance, especially her son. Clare had drifted out of reach, she hadn't given him or anyone else an opportunity to intervene."

She let go of his arm. "I don't believe that. Every relationship is an opportunity. If you'd been in touch . . ."

The last word he'd heard from Clare had been good news, he reminded her. "That's not an excuse, it's a fact. You don't know what's actually going on in other people's lives. I just didn't know. It seemed ridiculous, it's still very hard to believe. I think about her, I can't believe it. It happened."

"You weren't there."

"Right. I wasn't invited."

"Here was this terrific person, this wonderful person—"

"This is getting too damn depressing," Fletcher said. "Let's drop it."

"It's like this family in their nice house. What do they know? One of them is going to the bottom, as you put it, and no one knows a thing about it, and after it's too late no one feels they could have done anything about it. She was alone, you said, maybe she couldn't go it alone anymore. Well"—she socked his shoulder, a stiff shove with the heel of her hand, sudden real anger deepening her voice—"where was everybody?"

"Hey, come on," his hand reflexively going to the spot.

"Goddamn it, where was everybody? You're right, how did this happen? These fucking useless people."

"All right, Liz, it's probably not that simple. I don't need this, all right? Can we drop it?"

She stooped and took a stick from the ground, brandishing it before her. "You don't know what you need." She whacked a tree—hundred-year-old sugar maple just happened to be standing there—and the end of the stick zinged into the woods. "You people are too much."

"I'm sorry I brought it up. You were right before, it's really not your business. Where are you coming from all of a sudden?" He stepped past her and proceeded down the old road, dusk deeper.

"You'll never know, Jack," she shouted, almost shouted, after him. "Where does my business begin and your business end. You can feel me up, but I can't talk back. You're just like that asshole who ran me over in his damn car. What are you guys afraid of?"

Win some, lose some. Winsome law student named Liz becomes loose wheel on the flip side, a volatile store of stuff you couldn't see piled up in her attractive skull. One kiss, the human touch, and suddenly you've plunged into the unknown person. See you later. He heard her come hurrying up behind him, running, it sounded like, and resisted the impulse to turn around. Seconds later he was jumped from behind, his assailant wrapped her arms around his neck, locking her legs around his hips, startling the daylights . . . Fletcher reaching behind, bending forward, stumbling, to keep from going down. What the . . . ?

"Listen, wait." She had his head in a stranglehold, breathing heavily. "Wait a minute."

Only a moment before, it had become crystal clear (come to think of it—brook imagery—he'd forgotten the stream that bordered Peter's land just beyond the field) to him that this Liz, whoever she was, wasn't Fletcher's cup of poison, but here he was holding her again just to clear the air, let bygones be . . . just holding, but tight for some reason like they both needed this.

"I'm sorry about Clare." Rubbing her face against his shoulder as if her nose itched. "I really am."

Holding her face with both hands, he smoothed the delicate skin of her temples, crow's feet invisible in this light, with his large thumbs. "So am I."

By the time they resumed their walk, they were friends again.

"Does Mary know you're bad news, packing dynamite to blow away our traditional Thanksgiving before the day's over?"

"I love Mary. She's a friend."

"What was that about just now? You weren't kidding, you went off the handle."

"Nothing." She grabbed the front of his jacket with both hands and hoisted herself up to Fletcher's face. "Still love me?"

"No, that's over." Deadpan he said, "I could have loved you."

"Hold on." She pulled up her bulky sweater and unbuttoned a small breast pocket on her dark dress, fingering down into it, fishing. "I just happen to have a little something right here that I've been saving for an emergency. I don't think I can handle the evening straight."

They walked back along the narrow road through rapidly darkening woods, shuffled through redolent fall leaves, hand-in-hand no less, smoking an expertly rolled joint. Apart from his children, Fletcher couldn't recall the last time he'd held hands with anyone. Loved the sight, he explained, of little kids and old fuzzy white-haired gentlefolk doing it. Seemed innocent compared to everything else, didn't it, holding hands like so, hitting it off so nicely with no one you knew for a stolen minute or two, yet how horrifying to all the folks back at the holiday. Nice getting stoned with all these old stone walls around, monuments to the old world, which never thought it would come to this. Wonder who hit the little kid, Samuel what's-his-name, with the ax, Christ, that must have been a bad day. Figure he'd dwell on their little walk for days, turning it every which way to the light, getting everything said straight, recalling her this and her that, drumming up variations of what happened, things not to come. He would have said the likes of Liz was behind him, or beyond him. She was, actually, wasn't she?

Really, said Liz often, as in, You said it. She took deep long hits with her head up, knew what fun was.

Penny's stately home, all its cozy lights on, brought everyone inside back to mind. Hungrily, before they crossed the road, they kissed again, knowing their minutes were numbered, and this time when he thrust his hands into her thin underpants, the visitor of the day permitted him, catching her breath a little, to get a feeling for what Liz might really be like.

"Jack . . . stop!"

On the side porch by the large mock orange bush, still stubbornly clinging to some of its leaves, reckless Fletcher gave Liz a last kiss quickly—lastly gave Liz a quickie—which seemed, like everything else now, kinda funny.

"Shh, I think we're home, Uncle Jack."

Fool, Fletcher, he thought. Just stupid, really.

Sperm of the moment: a phrase lately popular among Kate's friends. Sorghum stenches: from a phonetic version of Little Red Riding Hood (Ladle Rat Rotten Hut) with which he had once delighted his children. Mural: yonder nor sorghum stenches dun stopper torque wet strainers.

They entered the warm illuminated kitchen too boldly grinning, he was afraid. Kate turned from the sink with a glass of water in her hand.

"Did you see it again? I walked over, but I didn't see it."

They had walked all the way back to the field, past the graveyard. "No more pheasants," said Fletcher. "Just maple trees and pleasantries."

His daughter glanced at him uncertainly.

"Boy, it's pretty back there," said Liz. She went up to Kate and brushed a strand of hair away from the girl's face. "Isn't she gorgeous?" Kate shy to the touch. Their guest, he saw in incandescent light, looked better to him than she had yet.

"What can you see in the dark?" Penny asked. She was picking the bones of the turkey at the counter by the sink. Penny's soapstone sink.

"I know." Liz smiled, unruffled. "The sunset was

great, but then—kaboom—night falls before you know it."

Fletcher, wiping his washed hands on a dish towel, asked, "Where are those delicious small rolls this year, Pen? Not the dinner rolls. The ones that are yellowish and come in great numbers." He wanted to make bite-size turkey and cranberry sauce sandwiches.

"Dad, you can't be hungry already."

He was.

"If you want to know the stupid truth, Jack, I was too depressed all week to make them."

"You're kidding?"

Liz and Kate went arm in arm to find Mary. Excuse us.

"Am I?" said Penny. She finished stripping the turkey, fingers reddened, greasy. The meat filled a large white bowl. The bones went into a stainless-steel pan already simmering on the stove. She busily covered the bowl with tinfoil and put it in the refrigerator. With rapid circular sweeps, she wiped her kitchen counter, running the checkered cloth along edges, into corners. She was on the wrong track, he thought, stoned, lucid in the laid-back glow of Liz's marijuana. Penny snapped open the cupboard beneath the sink— garbage—then snapped it shut. The large Canton platter that had held the turkey was wiped dry and put away. Her movements were merely efficient. Efficient, impatient, without pleasure. Everything—living —was a chore.

A pair of Canada geese in synchronized flight, southward presumably, attractively adorned the bib of her muslin apron. A block print in the left-hand corner. A lovely idea! Lovely of her, lovelier than Fletcher had hitherto realized. She had made three such aprons the

year before, gifts for her mother, her sister, herself.
From Penny.

When she turned from the sink, emboldened
Fletcher, who had stepped up behind her, embraced
her closely, half a lark, half love. "Penny, Penny, Penny,
easy does it. Where's the fire?"

Her eyes darted, shoulders tensed, then momentarily she rested her forehead against his shoulder, an
unexpected response. Her arms hung at her sides. The
day had worn off her makeup. Her handsome face was
pale with reddened patches on her cheeks. Twin vertical creases, more pronounced than he seemed to recall, between her large eyes. A handsome woman's
aging face. Fletcher smiled affectionately. Suddenly: her
full lower lip telltale of tears, childlike.

"What is it?"

Penny pressed her face against his shoulder. Fletcher
breathed in turkey and perfume. Pen, he thought.
Aware of her dish towel over his tail as in touch football. With rigid arms, she held tighter.

"I don't know. Everything, I guess."

She didn't cry. Fletcher squeezed back, letting her
know he was up to it. She was taller and broader,
altogether more substantial, than the younger woman
he had last held. As if transmitted by her touch, her
sadness began to well up in him—What's the matter
with us?—but that passed. Relax into it. Hugs good for
your health, six hugs a day, he seemed to recall, pro-
moted longevity in somebody's book. He felt the dish
towel, dangling behind him, drop silently from her hand
to the floor.

Superb Peter entered the room, crushing an aluminum beer can in the palm of his hand. "What's cooking
out here?" he crowed. "Break it up, you two." Did he

think the unlikely and unlooked-for moment transpiring in his kitchen—years and years might pass before anything like this occurred again—was commonplace, the ordinary glow of an everyday evening rather than the liquid fire of a thrilling sunset?

Penny let go. Her serious eyes were darker, more beautiful to Fletcher just now, than her daughter's.

"I'm all right." She smiled.

What does Fletcher know? Nothing.

"You smell funny, Jack, like a pile of burning— Peter, please! Let go, you're hurting . . ."

T he heat of the living room was now tropical. Gwen's dad out cold in the chair of yellow damask. The heat of living, thought Fletcher. In his camel pants, his pale yellow V-neck sweater, Curly blended in with the walls here, the decor, as he did in his own home, his wife's tastes prevailing. In colors and the general appearance of things, Penny's taste, while more expensive, was much the same as her mother's, no getting away from it. Gwen had escaped that, too, he considered, the pastel palette.

" . . . difficulty urinating was the first thing. Everyone we know has had that benign enlargement business, for goodness' sake, but then everyone can't be lucky. So now, the poor fellow, even if they get it all, I don't think he's ready for that . . ."

Patricia Wells discussing some poor fellow's prostate, he gathered, a good sport from their bridge club, you assumed. Every week, it seemed, another recent friend, who had also retired to the Cape from the old life, fell mortally ill with one cancer or another, heart disease, emphysema, Alzheimer's, diseases of the day.

The Wellses had been lucky so far, well as their name, Jesus, Jack, not funny.

Gwen's view was that things could always be worse. With surgery and radiation therapy, if necessary, the prognosis was excellent, it really was. "All anyone can do is wait and see, and hope for the best, I guess."

"One day at a time," said Patricia Wells. "I can't tell you how often you hear people say that today. Everyone you know is living one day at a time, for goodness' sake. We never had expressions like that."

"It's hard," Gwen agreed.

"Thank goodness you've still got your job," her mother said, switching subjects. "God knows, the building industry has collapsed in a heap. Are you managing?"

"Things are tight, Mother, but we're all right. Jack has been working very hard on the grammar-school project, and there are a number of other possibilities. I think we'll be fine."

Loyal life mate!

"I hope so, Gwendolyn, for your sake. That architecture business is so . . ."

We've heard that before.

"Jack is very enterprising, Mother. Don't worry about us."

He thought he might quietly slip away here, his eavesdropping unnoticed, but Gwen had already seen him.

"I was just telling Mother how great you are, Jack. Isn't that peculiar? I don't know what came over me."

"I just want this recession to come to an end before we're all living out of shopping carts," said Patricia

Wells. "Our tax-free mutual fund barely pays six percent anymore."

"I've thought of designing a new shopping cart,"
said Fletcher, "better suited to today's needs."

"That's not a bit funny."

"Do me a favor while I've got you right here, Jack,"
said his mother-in-law. She took the back side of a blue
sweater from the silver bag at her feet. Lord & Taylor.
It was composed of thick braided cables. "Turn around
like a good fellow and let me see if this is going to fit."

She stretched the sweater section across the top of
his back and pinned it to his shoulders with her fingertips. Fletcher the dummy.

"Now, what do you think, Gwen, Peter is just that
much broader, so it should be perfect, shouldn't it?"

"It's lovely, Mother. I can't believe you did all that
since Monday, I really can't. He'll love it."

"Thank you, Jack."

"My pleasure," said stoned Fletcher pleasantly.
"You're some knitter, though, aren't you? I've always
known it, but honestly, who knits sweaters like this?
Can I see it?" They had sweaters by Patricia Wells
going back to Kate's infancy. Tirelessly knitting from
cradle to grave.

"I try."

He handled her handiwork admiringly. "Patricia
Wells must be one of the great living knitters of New
England. Do you think so?" he asked her. "No, I mean
it. This is remarkably beautiful, isn't it, Gwen?"

Patricia Wells was flattered, appeared to be flattered.
A smile, an authentic grin, blossomed on her day's-end
face, the upper lip lifted above the gums, revealing
bony semitransparent teeth, her sallow soft skin mottled

by shadows in the lamplight, eyes raised to him with relaxed candor, tired, not unfriendly. A real face looking out from its hiding place, real person here all along. A flattering bit of acknowledgment, he considered, a scrap of goodwill, had brought her to the fore. It was an innocent face.

"A Rembrandt," he said, "among knitters. Gwen, this kind of work deserves recognition. Can't you have a knitting exhibit at the museum? You've got quilts, right, how about—"

"Now, that's enough of that." She took back the completed section of her sweater. "I'm glad you like it, I really am."

Gwen's glance was suspicious. "You've cheered up, Jack. What did you do, get a blood transfusion?"

M y mother never taught me how to fight.
November, one year ago, the news was Bush's military buildup in the Persian Gulf, shameless jingoism sweeping the nation, flags and yellow ribbons to beat the band, mindless war imminent, a half million troops in place, fifty thousand body bags shipped from Washington. One year ago that universal madness reigned, the whole world conspiring, even National Public Radio caught up in the fervor, so the likes of Fletcher, anyone opposed, had to feel a stranger in a strange land. Iran-Contra, Panama, Persian Gulf. A decade of Reagan-Bush could make you feel that it wasn't your world. "Decade of Destruction" had been televised on PBS that fall, according to Fletcher's notebook, the desperate decimation of the Amazon. "Race to Save the Planet" was another timely preview of disaster. Skimming those year-old months in his notebook the

night before, he had also noticed Helms reelected in North Carolina, Bush vetoes Civil Rights Act, a spell-binding thriller entitled "Motherlove." And "The Civil War" had been a major television event they'd watched for a week, a documentary that managed to celebrate heroes and maintain myths of glory despite the depiction of rampant death-dealing absurdity. Clare's period of study. As sheer entertainment it didn't hold a candle to the actual Bush war once that was under way. She hadn't stuck around to watch. My mother never taught me how to fight.

You mean you decided it was no longer your ball game, your show? Leave it to the assholes who waltzed around without a thought in their heads? Suicide meant you could be alive, it meant someone wasn't there—maybe anyone. What were you thinking? Your old record albums, your treasure chest of tapes and stacks of books, your garden, your San Francisco, your Sierra Nevadas, your Noah and Sarah, friends coming out of the woodwork and friends in need, blank young faces, your glass of Scotch at the end of the day, the sunset, a cup of coffee the way you liked it, a chance encounter, the chance of someone new turning up, the survival of civilization, or for that matter its prevailing decline, the long shot of resolving long-troubled relationships, the life of the ever-present moment, the ongoing here and now. A list of reasons to live as eloquent as any. Wasn't it?

Where was everyone?

I'm glad you're the last one I talked to.

Seated in an armchair of bird's-eye maple by the Rumford hearth, he suddenly saw Clare, or rather was seized by the idea of her, alone in a room—how long had she been there alone? What had she done that day?

Had she come in from somewhere? Had she been with other people?—alone with her death, the idea of her death, alone with her decision to die suddenly present in the room with her. She wrote a letter containing the sentences, I can't keep fighting. My mother never taught me how to fight. Or, if the letter had already been written, wouldn't she have read it again? Focused on the flames as they fled above and between the split wood they consumed, Fletcher seemed to see her, for the first time, alone in her room the night she took her life. November 28, 1990. Gwen had informed him that it was the day after her birthday. She had been forty-nine or fifty, he wasn't sure. Alone in her room. Where was everybody? He imagined her looking in the mirror, applying moisturizing lotion to her face with thin fingers. Lying back on the bed in the red flannel nightshirt from L. L. Bean, she extended her arm, smiling. . . . I'm glad you're the last one. . . . The room he momentarily pictured her in, he realized, was the small wallpapered room in the steeply pitched dwelling on Weir Harbor. Pierce's place. There had been a mirror above an old pine dresser which stood between two multipaned windows. Pills, her daughter-in-law had said. She knew the number of pills that would assure her death, no mistake. Of course, Weir Harbor was a far cry from where Clare had died. The actual room was airy, off-white, austere. Tall windows looked out to the sparkling city, the dark bay, and darker hills beyond. What were you thinking? You'll never know. Then, extraordinarily, or expectedly, the phone rang. Would you hesitate to answer? he wondered, looking into Peter's fire. While she was alive, she couldn't ignore the phone going off in a room. Who did she imagine it was? What did she imagine she might say? She had already swallowed her fatal

dose. What in fact had she said to her son at that moment—an entirely ordinary conversation pertaining to
everyday life, simple questions and replies? Yet she
wanted to believe that Noah somehow knew. You must
have sensed I was drugged, she wrote. I'm glad you're
the last one I spoke to. I can't keep fighting. My mother
never taught me how to fight.

Abruptly he looked up. With her eyes closed, and
her narrow mouth slightly, unconsciously open, Patricia Wells nodded in her chair, the knitting needles momentarily stalled in her hands.

Over the years, though less often as the years went
by, he had imagined Clare visiting the Fletchers. She
would have enjoyed sitting at their kitchen table discussing the enormous changes occurring then in the
world, the weather, other people's lives, a collection of
poems or essays, the movies that came and went, the
way to live, the way we lived, the food. She would
have gotten a kick, he liked to think, out of Kate and
Sam as they came into their own.

There was plenty in Fletcher's corner of the world
that was right up her alley. The organic gardeners with
their common market in the center of town Saturday
mornings, the artists and artisans out in the woods trying to live as they pleased, the bumper stickers on small
efficient cars. There were halfway houses, Cambodian
refugees and Russian dissidents from years before, good
bookstores, an excellent bakery, a congenial little world
of cafés, coffee shops, health-food stores, used-clothing
shops, trading posts. The women's movement had not
been forgotten. There was a free bus to take you around
town. There were talks and concerts, readings and con-
tredanses every night of the week. There were healers
for whatever ailed you. You could take a balloon ride

over the valley, hike into the hills, ski out your back door, linger in the park with your Sunday *Times*, waiting for a fiddle contest to begin, stand shoulder to shoulder in the weekly vigil for the day's most pressing global cause. You could visit the Buddhist Peace Pagoda and share a hopeful vision with blissed-out strangers. In May you could ride the Ferris wheel that came to town. You could join groups to practice yoga, meditate, play the recorder, read books, comfort the sick, rub each other's backs, to relax.

Come east!

San Francisco had its list of attributes, but if the city by the bay wasn't working for you . . . It sounded a little too simple, yet in the look and feel of the life around him, Fletcher received constant reminders that Clare would have fit, maybe thrived. I know, Gwen said. She'd had the same thought, watching a woman with a knapsack boarding a bus, for example. On another occasion, a sunset with hamburgers, his wife became impatient. What does that mean, Clare would have . . . ? So what, Jack?

She had missed Fletcher's backyard, Gwen's herb garden, mussels at Andiamo's on a festive Friday night in February. For example. She had missed Bush's stupid war, and its disastrous aftermath, she had missed the end of the so-called Cold War, the end of the Soviet Union, the end of the world as we knew it. Oh, Clare, he thought, seated by the Rumford hearth. How she would have thrilled to all that unraveling, the new unknown.

Come east!

I'm glad you're the last one I talked to. My mother never taught me . . .

They liked to have candles at either end of the bed,

enhancing everything between the flames. Twice, he recalled, they pulled the dresser with its attached mirror up to the side of the double bed to observe themselves from new stimulating angles. The flannel nightshirt contributed its splash of color. Still in his twenties, he had been up to hey-jack-elating twice of an evening and yet again at dawn. Those days were gone. He had been about the age Liz was now, it occurred to him, as he was now about the age Clare had been back then. The young guest of the day seemed a fleeting windfall. Was that how the older woman had viewed eager Fletcher? I could have loved you.

C urly stood, stretching, "I've tried on sweaters till I'm blue in the face," and trudged stiffly to the front door, needing air. Just what Fletcher needed.

On the porch he greeted his father-in-law with a handshake, always enjoyed a good handshake, struck again by the meaty width of the man's grip—the size of Sam's baseball mitt.

"Is that all you can muster? You're getting worn out on us."

Without apparent exertion, Curly put the screws on, an effortless crushing of Fletcher's knuckles, his architect's grip hardly up to strength. Curly, a modest man, smiled good-naturedly and let go.

"The toolmaker's hand," said Fletcher.

Curly looked out at the evening sky. Clouds blowing past the moon, pinpricks of stars. Fletcher recognized his father-in-law's meditative mood by the set of his jaw. Still a handsome man in kind light. Skin like his mother's, Grama Wells. The hairline no more receded than a boy's. That was in the genes, you figured, good for the children of Fletcher. The older man frowned: about to speak.

Patricia Wells complained that he had nothing to say to her from one day to the next—might as well be living alone, she'd been telling Gwen over the phone for years, since Curly had somewhat prematurely retired. She'd be less lonely living alone, she said. Sure she would. Probably go right on telling him, do this, don't do that, all day long even if he wasn't there. All the while, of course, Curly, sitting there silent as a Trappist, loved talk, hungered for the opportunity of one-on-one, longed, Fletcher knew, for a listener. Something his wife of more than fifty years was not.

"You realize," he said, nodding in anticipation of his own words, "our galaxy contains maybe one, two hundred billion stars, something like that."

"Give or take a few, huh?"

"Our sun takes some two hundred billion years to make one trip around it. That's how big it is." Curly held out both arms to embrace this idea of size.

Takes, he thought. Like it takes two hours to get to Boston.

"And that's just our galaxy," he went on. "There are maybe billions of galaxies in the universe. I was watching a show on the tube. I bought a book on it, the whole bit." He held his left hand at chest level and firmly took his sizable little finger between the thumb and index finger of the other hand. "You've got moons and whatnot going around our planets . . ."

Our planets, thought Fletcher, pleased.

"You've got the planets orbiting the sun," he said, taking his next thick finger. "You've got the whole damn solar system some billions of miles across, streaming through the galaxy of billions of stars, and on top of that, you've got the galaxy itself winging through space with billions of other galaxies. The whole thing revolving out there, Jack, like a bat outta hell." He paused, shook his head, bemused, his lips compressed. "It's really something." He extended one arm over the porch railing, gesturing presumably to the universe, thrilled with the colossal idea, the enormity of it. "Have you seen that show? Excellent."

Fletcher stood before him with arms crossed, grinning from ear to ear. Curly was a show.

"What's the sun, maybe ninety-three million miles away? We get one billionth of its light and heat. And in some places that's too much for us, isn't it? Can you imagine the distance of those stars right there? My God, there must be every kind of thing imaginable out there that we don't have the faintest idea about. It's anybody's ball game."

We, thought Fletcher. Earthlings.

"Tell on," he urged. "Tell on, Copernicus. You think there's life out there? Other life?"

"Absolutely." Curly dismissed the question with a wave of his hand. "All these movies and books over the years about people making contact . . . We used to think there was nothing out there, we were the only brains in the universe, for heaven's sake."

It took just a second here for Fletcher to grasp the implication of Curly's unfinished sentence. "You mean Spielberg's an alien? Hollywood hotshots in blue jeans have been preparing us for the real thing? It's not just some clever bastards making a killing?"

"I don't know about that, Jack. At this point my guess is that anything's possible. Did you know—the other night they had it on—a factory somewhere, I don't even remember what they were making, not a man working in it. Nothing but robots. My God, I felt silly just watching it. How about this virtual reality thing I've been hearing about? You can put on a pair of goggles and feel like you're walking through a house. Now, where that's going to lead . . . that'll be our next vacation, Jack, a pair of goggles."

"Does the wife know you're sitting there at the table with this stuff on your mind?"

"Pat? Oh, I don't think Pat . . ."

Fletcher laid his arm over his father-in-law's stout shoulder. "Curly, you're all right." He enjoyed speaking the man's friendly, fitting name.

"What puzzles me, Jack, is how we could win the war, then manage to set things up so that Germany and Japan come out on top forty-five years later. That doesn't make a bit of sense, does it? How did the most powerful nation on earth let that happen, can you explain it?"

The subject of space had evidently roused his pride in Planet Earth—Earth's most powerful nation.

"I'd say the most powerful nation on earth has fucked up," said Fletcher amiably. "We've been on the wrong track."

"Now that crackpot Saddam there," Curly went on as though he and Fletcher were in agreement, "why is he still alive? Some backasswards little place you never heard of causing all that damn fuss. But now I see we're going to get some of the hostages released anyway. I guess that's something, the poor devils." He scratched his jaw, frowning. "You don't know what to think. The deficit, Jack, trillions at this point, that's beyond me."

Fletcher sat on the porch railing, facing now the lighted windows of the house. The three older girls had returned to the living room. Kate fanned her face with her hand, and whatever she said—their wit—caused Liz to laugh, tilting her head back. High: their secret. So that's what she looks like, he saw through Penny's sheer curtains. Hi yourself.

Hostage crisis.

Anything's possible, Curly would say, except you couldn't take the young woman by the hand, for instance, and guide her upstairs to the master . . . We can have outer-space cadets in the movie business, madmen ruling nations, yet the mind couldn't accommodate the likes of down-to-earth Fletcher making it in the midst of Thanksgiving. A universe awhirl with billions upon billions, worlds within worlds, didn't make a little thing like fucking on earth easier to forgive. He turned to his father-in-law, wishing to express the big irony of it all, stretch the man's imagination a tad further here. . . .

"Life today," said Curly, announcing his favorite topic with customary gravity. "I'll tell you, Jack, you don't know what to think." Curly had often told him that before. Tonight it was like hearing an old song you hadn't heard for a while. "Gimme, gimme, gimme, that's all you hear today. God love us, this S and L fiasco Peter was talking about, what did one fellow call it, the mother of all government mistakes. That's going to cost us hundreds and hundreds of billions before we're done with it."

"Just part of the Reagan legacy," Fletcher suggested, "along with the recession, the homeless, environmental—"

"They could have saved a couple of hundred billion if they'd faced it in 'eighty-eight, shut down the sick banks before it was out of control, but that was an election year, wasn't it?"

"And look who we elected?" Fletcher laughed. "Wonderful."

"We didn't have much," Curly went on, "but what did we know? Look at people today. Let me tell you something . . ." He leaned toward Fletcher and touched his son-in-law's arm. "People used to be happy."

"Did they?"

"People don't realize that today. Take me, Jack, I used to love going to work," the word *love* underlined. "I couldn't wait for Monday morning, couldn't wait to get there, now that's the truth. Up at five-thirty, you'd stop at Lazote's for breakfast, look at the paper. You walk into the mill and Bobbie Skully has people laughing already at six-thirty in the morning. The girls in the office, you know, wave and smile behind the glass, you've got a cup of coffee at your elbow five minutes later. You made a tool. They needed something for this or that, so you made it. If it did the job, you might make a line of tools for a machine as big as this house. That's when I was starting out, I loved that."

How often, Fletcher reflected, he and Gwen had driven past American Brass and Manufacturing, a foul sprawling blight dominating a dying cityscape—fuming cylindrical chimneys, grinding noise, stench, a haze of pollution hanging over acres of corrugated roofing— and shook their heads, appalled at the ghastly sight of Curly's daily lot. As you drove overhead on the inter- state, the place presented itself as a cartoonist's vision of industrial hard times, a life of brutish imprisonment. Her father had spent his life there, working his way up from the bottom to plant manager in the course of forty years. Who could blame him, Gwen asked, for the way he was?

Curly was smiling, hands in pockets, looking at the moon.

Couldn't wait to get there, Gwen, as though, all those years, he had lived a secret life of strange pleasures unknown and unknowable to his family. One of Gwen's memories—he knew her childhood memories well—was the sound of her father leaving the house hours before anyone else was up, before dawn, not to return until supper, and often not even then. She remembered men's voices on the phone asking for "Curly," calling him to work in the middle of the night because something had gone wrong. For decades he never worked less than six days a week. During the fifties he often worked Sundays as well.

Gwen, he loved it!

She remembered her father hanging up the phone in the kitchen and turning to her mother, who always seemed to know what had happened before he told her: Bobbie Skully died, Frankie Shay died. Faceless names from work. Accidents, cancers, heart attacks. Gwen's father spent a lot of time visiting people in the hospital. There was always a wake or a funeral to attend. His dark suit, Fletcher remembered, was one of Gwen's childhood memories—how different he looked in it. The white starched shirts in his mahogany dresser, where he also kept a beautiful old pocket watch that didn't work, a large gold ring with a diamond set in its black stone, silvery tinfoil packets depicting soldiers of Troy and not to be touched. He had a bowling night, a poker night with loud laughing voices downstairs, parties with the wives, too, an annual clambake, three weeks' vacation at the lake, or on the Cape.

The sisters were not to use their father's facecloth or towel because, Gwen grew up believing, their father came home contaminated by some sort of mysterious factory filth. To this day, Curly's personal towel hung on a special hook behind the bathroom door. Their mother had taught them that their father worked like a slave in a dangerous dirty place in order to give them everything they wanted—that was why they had to behave, or go to bed without a fuss, get good grades, be careful of the company they kept (at the first opportunity Clare changed all that)—and Curly, who never brought work home, had never suggested anything to the contrary. You just got up and out of there by five-thirty every morning—out into your world. The wife raised the children, the wife took the paycheck and called the shots. Well, what do you know, Gwen, the family slave couldn't wait for Monday morning.

Just now she was sitting on the small footstool with her hands in her lap, her head back-tilted, allowing Becky to brush her hair.

Fletcher turned to his father-in-law. "I'm delighted to hear that," he said. "I mean it. Gwen always told me you hated that goddamn place, like it was misery."

"The times we used to have," said Curly. "Freddy and his sax, have I ever told you . . . ? Frederick Douglass Washington. Nicest guy you'd ever want to meet. Black as the road. Fantastic worker. Freddy did the work of three men in that rod mill. His first love was his saxophone. You never heard anything like it, Jack. He played Thursday nights at a club in the east end, so Thursdays he brought it to work and kept it in his locker. Everyone was sitting around during the afternoon break and here comes the scrap truck pulling out of the mill. A huge truck full of scrap metal on its way back to casting. I was the youngest on the floor, so I was elected. I pointed to the truck and yelled, Hey,

Freddy." Gwen's father pointed toward the moon and called out, reliving the moment for Fletcher's sake, "Hey, Freddy, is that your sax on the scrap truck? Sitting right up there shining—he kept an awful shine on it—poking out of the heap of scrap brass is Freddy's sax, headed for the fire." Remembering, he laughed. "We had it all planned, of course. Freddy, is that your sax on that damn truck? His eyes opened up like silver dollars. He took after that truck hollering, Oh, Jesus, oh, Jesus, like he'd seen a ghost." Curly clapped his hands together. His pleasant face crinkled with mirth. "Oh, Jesus, he's hollering. For years you'd hear people telling that story."

"Fantastic," said Fletcher, grinning. Yet one could easily imagine—couldn't one?—a black man called Freddy running after his instrument, his first love, thrown onto a heap of scrap brass, running through a white man's mill with real fear.

"After twenty years on the same job, a cable broke." Curly snapped his fingers. "He was gone before we ever got to him, crushed to death. A horse of a man with a barrel chest."

"He wanted to play his music, the fucking job killed him. Perfect."

"We lost quite a few over the years. You'd have to go see the family, someone's wife or mother. It had to be done. Somebody was always having a problem with money or women or booze, sickness in the family, missing work. There was always one thing or another and you'd have to call them in and try to straighten it out. To me it was always the people, that was my interest. You wouldn't believe the stories, Jack. Everything in the world happened in that place."

Becky, it seemed, was braiding Gwen's hair. And

there was curious activity on the camelback couch. His daughter and the other two young women sat Indian style, their legs folded under them, all facing in the same direction as in a canoe, each with her straight back to the girl behind her. Kate was braiding Liz's hair while Liz braided Mary's hair. A vision through the curtain: damsels dressing their hair. Dazmels. Dear world of beauty. . . .

"They could call me in the middle of the night— Billy Sherman on the third shift—and I'd be off like a shot. We didn't think a thing of working seven days a week in those days. Leisure was a word they hadn't invented yet. We didn't make any money back then either—not like now. It was only the last years that everything went to pot with the unions and then the new blood. Hey, what the hell, they didn't know you . . . what we'd been through. They didn't want to know anything but the almighty dollar, so what could you expect. Overnight, it wasn't the same. Today it's like nobody needs anybody, isn't it? Well, that was years ago now. Ancient history."

The world had changed, the story went, and American Brass, trying to change with it, years ago had retired all personnel over fifty-eight or so. Curly, who had given his life to the place, hadn't believed it would happen to him, but it did. They yanked the life right out from under him, Gwen's mother had often explained to her. She had seen the change. He was never the same after that.

Fletcher draped an arm over his father-in-law's shoulder as he had before. "Those bastards. What did they know?"

"They saw the writing on the wall, Jack, the way we couldn't. It's all different now." The last he'd heard, the plant had been sold to an electronics outfit. "No one could have believed it wasn't going to last forever, any more than you could think the moon there . . . " He didn't finish his thought.

Through the sheer white curtains, Gwen's mother, knitting with rapid precision in the blue crewel chair, seemed rapt, entranced. Liz's fingers ran down Mary's dark hair like mice, leaving thin dark tails hanging from her skull. Cornrows, that's what you called them. With pouting concentration, Kate endeavored to braid their visitor's blond hair. Sam and Bo maneuvered matchbox cars along the edge of the brick hearth. Becky played with Gwen's hair, attempting to copy what she saw the older girls doing. Peter and Penny were not present.

Clare, he thought—again, with alarm, as though remembering too late something he'd meant to do—is not present.

"You know what my mistake was?" Curly had turned and was now facing the house as well.

"What?"

"Do you know what my mistake was?"

Fletcher turned to him. "That's what I thought you said. What mistake?"

Curly pinched his lower lip. Something to say.

"I lived for work. That was my downfall. Hey, Jack, that's all I ever did, go to work." He held up his open hands. "I didn't know anything else."

Fletcher, nodding, didn't press him. Downfall! In five, ten, fifteen years his father-in-law had never expressed to him the sort of sentiments he was airing on Penny's north porch. Never. His own affable and receptive mood owed something to Liz's surprise number, face it, but Curly was only himself. Had he always been so . . . available? It was you, Jack, was it, who withheld, gave off a caution to people, an uptight stench, to keep their distance? To what end?

Scrutinizing his father-in-law's face with affection, he was struck, startled, by a deep diagonal crease in the man's pendulous earlobe. The same crease pictured in the thick, hopeful (to Fletcher, foreboding) volume entitled *Life Extension: A Practical Scientific Approach*, through which he frequently browsed, bathroom reading, seeking reassurance maybe, hints to help survive today's hostile environment, his own bad habits. There was a correlation, researchers at a famous clinic had found, between this particular crease and heart disease, risk of sudden . . . He'd often noted the black-and-white photograph of the outrageously ugly ear, and occasionally checked out the lobules of his own ears in the mirror. This evening it was disturbing to find Curly wearing the telltale mark, though he'd already survived a heart attack years back. A lifetime of the prosperous American's rich diet. Start taking fistfuls of C and E, plenty of onions and garlic at every meal, chinook salmon like the once-upon-a-time Eskimos, old cod liver oil routine, quit meat, all these lovely desserts, stuff you love. But look at him, Curly was still a bull. Fletcher looked away.

"What are we coming to?" he went on, set off on yet another tack. "We're becoming a nation of morons and cripples and half-wits, aren't we?"

"I won't argue with you there," Fletcher answered cheerfully.

"Take women today. Women used to be different, you know. Do you know there are more infants born with something wrong with them than ever before in history? Think about it, Jack. What will become of the human race? You're laughing, but there are way too many idiots and deformed and God-knows-what today. Men have always been the same way. Can't help themselves, I guess. But women used to be different. Kept the home properly, took care of their kids. You counted on them to be better. That's the truth," said Curly. "Now they want to be like men. It's a damn shame."

"All that breast cancer going around," said Fletcher, "all that poverty, you think there'd be a law against it." He drummed his father-in-law's broad back. "Curly, you're a riot."

"No, I'm serious. You can't have everyone getting VD and AIDS and going around hyped up on crack and cocaine and one thing and another all day. These gangs of kids shooting each other every day of the week. They don't think a thing of somebody's life. That's something new, isn't it? I don't know how many people can't read today. That's not right."

Through the curtains, as through radiant fog, Fletcher dwelt upon the warm domestic scene in Penny's living room. Peaceful, safe, at home. Their heads were wild. Now Liz was doing Kate's hair, the two of them pleasantly chatting. She brushed his daughter's hair with long smooth strokes. Flattery made Kate shy. Through the curtains: like a ship in a bottle. He recalled Gwen—years before—in her new bedroom putting out the light near the window in an old-fashioned sheer nightgown, which he'd brought home for the fun of it. Her body like a ship in a bottle.

Don't be a jerk, Dad.

Do you come easily? he considered. A question he might have been bold to ask. Give her something to think about in an idle moment. When you come, is it conclusive? Do you come to your own conclusions? What are the chances of coming to see you? Of seeing you again? Of seeing you come? Sweet sight for sore eyes. There was nothing lackluster about Mary's friend Liz. A—like—lyrical quality. Really. Desire, the longing for desire, never ended. A longing human in his prime, a lonely creature. Aren't we all?

To himself, but aloud, unintentionally, he said, "Goddamnit, Clare."

Curly's body responded, he was sure, the man's shoulders shifted, and when Fletcher looked up, his father-in-law averted his glance, darting for cover. Fletcher felt there was no turning back.

"I've never quite known what all that was about," he said, "I'm sure it's complicated. I just thought she was a wonderful person. I miss her, Curly, even though we saw so little of her."

"Well . . . "

Curly, he realized, was not prepared to respond. Clare was a part of himself, or a subject maybe, an idea, a past, that he had walled off, or walled in, or walled out somehow. You didn't know. He had never discussed his eldest daughter with his youngest daughter's husband. Fletcher, emboldened for the moment, but also feeling unexpectedly close to the older man, decided to push against the wall, call it.

"We spent those weeks together in Maine," he said, "building that cabin in Weir Harbor all those years ago. She'd be up and have the boat loaded before I was out of bed. If you were setting sail for the New World, you'd want Clare in the boat, that's how I felt. She taught me a lot." When Curly remained silent, he continued, in a deliberately lighter vein, to describe the time they had raising the roof rafters, both of them damn near breaking their necks that day. . . .

Turning toward him, and roughly clasping him in an uncomfortable bear hug of sorts, Curly hoarsely said, "Don't. I loved that girl so much, Jack, I can't tell you."

At a loss, disturbed, Fletcher said, "I'm sorry."

Almost a whisper, as if imparting a secret in utmost confidence, Curly added, "I always thought she cared for me, I really did." He let go. "I don't know."

What could you say? Nothing.

Liz had finished Kate's cornrows. Becky was doubled up in laughter over the kooky job she'd done on her patient Aunt Gwen. To Fletcher the room seemed imbued with an even warmer golden glow.

His father-in-law had turned back to the sky, stargazing with his stout arms folded above his solid belly. "Do you know how it's going to end?" he asked, his genial informative tone restored. "Do you know what's going to happen?"

"Tell me about it. Let's hear it."

"They figure the sun is maybe five billion years old, and it's going to go on for another five billion years. It's a middle-aged star, let's put it that way," said Curly. "But by then reactions at the core—helium and hydrogen, right—are going to make the sun expand in size. The surface will be cooler, okay, but it will be radiating a lot more heat because of the size. Okay, Mercury and Venus are baked out of existence. Cremated. Kiss them good-bye."

"I hear you."

"Then, I don't know, a billion years, say, the earth will be boiling away, a cloud of steam. Poof! That's it for us, Jack. After pouring out this energy for so long, the old sun begins to shrink and die. It dies for billions of years. It gets smaller than the earth used to be, and cools to a white dwarf star. Finally it's a piece of coal in space, a cold black chunk of coal like we used to heat the house with." Curly was shaking his head, tipped up to the heavens. "That's too much, isn't it?"

Fletcher, crazy about Curly out here on the porch, could give him a kiss on his silver cheek, but doesn't.

"You know how they know all this?"

"No."

"They know it because they've seen it. Watched it happening out there with their telescopes. It's the life cycle of all stars."

"I like it," said Fletcher.

"Now, you know what I don't understand. I don't want to start a big discussion, Jack," he said kindly, "but I don't understand how you can look out there like we're doing now, and think about it, you know, all that, and not believe in . . . whatever you want to call it, Jack. God."

Surprised, Fletcher asked, "God?" Curly's cosmos, it seemed to him, argued the very opposite. He kept his mouth shut.

"Now, that's all I want to say on that subject," said Curly. To their grandparents' dismay, Fletcher's children had not been baptized. This was as close as Curly had come to expressing his disappointment. He briskly rubbed together the coarse large palms of his hands. "Jack, Jack, Jack, it's getting doggone chilly out here. They're going to think we fell through the ice." He waved his hand toward the yard dismissively, the darkness beyond the porch. "You know what?"

"What?"

"I don't think it's going to rain after all. I think it's changed its mind."

*T*ake him out and shoot him, Mort, that's how I feel. What does he think he's doing, anybody know? Two months ago it was a terrific property, great location, good solid middle-class tenants with pride . . . now they tell us it's only seventy percent occupied, nothing but Puerto Ricans with knives, dogs prowling the hallways, half the first floor looks like a halfway house for crazies from the state hospital. Do I have to go down there myself to find out who's living in it? I'm the troublemaker, Mort, because I'm not going to let it go down the goddamn tubes without taking a good shot at saving it. Meanwhile, everyone's sitting on their thumbs like I should be in a straitjacket, drool running down my chin. Sunderman's got to be removed for openers. You read his letter, the stuff about God bless you, the man is out of his mind . . . Alzheimer's . . . exactly, so we get his ass out of there and find someone who wants to save the property. I know the money isn't there, we'll have to raise it. I'm not going to let someone waltz in and pick it up for two point eight at foreclosure, boot out the Spanish and the pit bulls, turn around and sell it two years later for six fucking million, meanwhile my people have lost their money and come gunning for me, meanwhile Sunderman is out on his fucking boat smoking cigars like he had nothing to do with it. You're absolutely right, he has no goddamn character . . . take him out and shoot him, love to, but we don't shoot people anymore, Morton, we get them removed as general partner. Fishy? That's an understatement, my friend. Sunderman's buddy Anglin is probably sitting backstage waiting to pick it up for two point eight, exactly. They're down there on somebody's boat half the winter, they're waltzing around the

Plaza like they own the place, meanwhile my people are asking me, how did it happen, Peter, how did it happen. First thing tomorrow we get on it and straighten it out, that's the spirit, Mort. Jesus, don't bring that up, will you? Have I got enough to think about without thinking about those fucking orchids? Schneider is a major grower in Hawaii, anybody have any idea why he'd let himself in for this? He's going to jail, no question, directly to jail. The plants weren't there, Mort, as simple as that, it all hit the fan last week. You were smart not to be involved, all right. I never wanted to get into that can of worms in the first place. It sounded perfectly reasonable, you get seedlings from South America, grow them in Hawaii, sell the plants in California, simple. Ten million plants, that was the number. They were never there, okay? No orchids, Mort. Freeman and Reagan were actually distributing dividends purportedly on sales, right, but in fact they're paying it out of money raised from new investors. They were spending money like it was going out of style, they were into windmills, ranches in Montana . . . You got it, Mort, there was no money from actual sales because there were never ten million actual fucking plants in the first place, there were no plants, just suckers. Please don't laugh, Morton, it's not funny. Ten million plants from South America sounded great, just what the world needs, how could you lose. The dentist, the endodontist, he's got three units, he's sick about it, tells me he can't choke down his turkey today, you follow me? Three units, you're talking a lot of rotten teeth, Mort. Yes, I put the poor bastard in that, too, back when we thought there would be a market for gas. Exactly, if Penny's glacier would get a goddamn move on, we might be in business again. Meanwhile, everyone starts taking fluoride, right, and there are no teeth to fix, then what? That's another thing I wish you wouldn't bring up. It's Thanksgiving, for Christ's sake, I can't think about Andy's goddamn movie right now. I can't get through to him anymore, the son of a bitch won't take my phone calls. Tomorrow let's get the damn pit bulls out of the building, okay? That's right, take one fuck-up at a time like those clowns in the White House. Here we are trying to hold it together, Mort, keep the dream alive, and I've got people around here who want to give it back to the Indians. Hey, you, too, Kimosabe, happy Thanksgiving.

He hung up the phone, reaching for the freezer with his free hand. "Don't tell me to relax, Fletch, I'll strangle you."

"What the hell was that all about?"

"Don't ask, okay? Hand me that bottle of Scotch right behind you, will you, sport? It's pretty fucking difficult to be discussing this stuff with you standing there with that shit-eating grin all over your—"

"Sorry, Peter, I'm not laughing at you—it's the drool running down the chin, the dentist choking down the turkey, shoot the bastard, the pit bulls, the orchids. Sounds like you're having a hell of a time."

"Time of my life, just the time of my life."

"What, there were people selling ten million plants that didn't exist, or what?"

"You didn't hear that, Fletch, follow me? That's not public knowledge."

"Fishy. You said fishy. Then the guy's name—Anglin. Did you realize that? You didn't catch that, did you? Fishy. Anglin. The boys out on the boat. Then you get the can of worms in there. Catch that one? The poetry of everyday language. You're full of poetry, Peter."

"Turkey."

You said the magic . . .

Y ou don't think life with your father has been a bed
of roses, do you? Half the time I might as well not
exist. I'm not ready for this, Penelope, to be perfectly
frank. I try to make the most of things. I've learned to
hold my tongue."

"I bet you have, Mother."

Fletcher, enthroned in the john, imagined his
mother-in-law holding her tongue with her fingers.

"Your father's never been a demonstrative man.
He's so much like your grandfather . . . of course,
Grama Wells, I don't know what she was made of.
They don't make them like her anymore. Maybe it's
not my business, I just—"

"I know what's on your mind, Mother. You don't
need to say anything."

"I don't want to see you do something you'll regret
for the rest of your life."

They were setting out food and dishes for supper—
buffet style. Fletcher imagined Curly lying in a bed of
roses, for example. That wasn't pretty.

"Peter is a go-getter," said Patricia Wells, "you can
be thankful for that. He works hard and he's done very
well for himself. And he's wonderful with those children. No one can fault him on that score."

"Mother, please, I'm a middle-aged woman. I'm
not in the mood for a lecture."

I'm a middle-aged not-in-the-mood woman.

"I'm not lecturing, I'm just suggesting. Count your
blessings, Penelope."

Like counting sheep: stay asleep.

"Are you through?"

"God knows, I've got enough to worry about without worrying about you, too. I never thought I'd have to start worrying about you at this stage."

"Do us both a favor, Mother, don't worry."

"It just seems a terrible shame . . . "

Not a Bloomsday shit by a long shot, Fletcher. Into the mirror he muttered, "You miserable wretch." He opened the medicine cabinet just to see . . . several copper-colored plastic bottles with white childproof caps on the top shelf behind tinfoil packets of Alka-Seltzer, white jars of moisturizer, Mylanta, shampoo samples, small tin of Bag Balm. Each prescription label read, *Penelope West for Pain*. For pain, for pain, for pain. He unscrewed a cap: little pills.

"Ask Mary how wonderful Peter is," Penny said. "He's going to alienate her completely, if he doesn't wise up."

"All children go through that. God knows—"

"I know, you're an expert, Mother. I don't think I want Mary to follow in Clare's footsteps, thank you."

"Penelope, how can you say that to me?" Her alarmed voice broke in the middle of the sentence.

"Mother, honestly, I didn't mean that." Penny's voice suddenly scrambling. "Here, don't, please." Hurried shuffling, a chair, sounded like, dumped over. "That was a stupid thing to say, I'm sorry, I'm simply so strung out lately. Come on, please, Mother, you've done so well all day. "

For the first time in years he couldn't get out of the bathroom without fussing with the door. As he stepped into the kitchen, he said, "That was fun, Pen, the rush of panic associated with being locked in . . . "

His sister-in-law had both arms around her shorter,

rounder mother, her cheek pressed against the woman's thinning hair. Patricia Wells stifled sobs, her shoulders heaved with the effort, a cloth napkin raised to her face. Yes, the black Windsor lay on its fanned back.

"Never make the mistake of letting Peter fix that door," said Fletcher.

His mother-in-law released herself from her daughter, and with practiced self-control promptly composed her pained face. "I couldn't imagine who was in there," she said to no one in particular. She didn't look at him. "I didn't see anyone go into the bathroom, did you?"

D ear world of . . .
    Stoned goatish Fletcher, washing down cheese and chutney with Peter's very good single malt Scotch—Glenfuckit, Fletch—chose a nice spot near Penny's shiny-leafed gardenia to observe the life around him. He didn't mind the heat. The heat of living. He liked the amazing evergreen plant. Mary sat on the floor between the stereo speakers. Peter's super-duper sound system with tape deck, equalizer, disc player—the man never listened to music—was tucked away in a paneled cabinet, not to cause discord in the antique room. Kate and Becky sort of danced together. Liz stood across the room by the bookcase, swaying to the music in her swaying skirt, in pretty stocking feet. Gwen rocked rhythmically in the funny old rocker, watching Becky and Kate with a pleased smile. A mother's pleasure. The effect of Gwen's hairdo, a tangle of wispy braids going in all directions, sprouting rather than hanging from her head, wasn't flattering. It was funny. Her largish ears stuck out comically, her neck was skinny. A good sport. Fletcher liked her, his sporting wife.

Kate's coloring, pink and gold, gave her a glow just now like the sun going down at the end of the day. She'd never worn makeup, which had been making a comeback with kids since Madonna maybe, the so-called natural look rather fallen out of favor with the many.

Dear World of Beauty. . . . A letter she wrote, age twelve, to a cosmetics company that kept sending trays of makeup in fifty inhuman colors. She had been so bold as to send off a coupon for the first free kit, not realizing she was subscribing to a club. Fletcher had come across the rough draft of his daughter's letter while rummaging around her desk for something. Dear World of Beauty, I would like to resign my membership.

Kate! He loved her name. Right for her, a sturdy person.

The other four adults had been temporarily driven from the room. Supper's on the counter, help yourself.

The tape being played belonged to Kate, a random mix of favorite songs from three decades, featuring at the moment the former king of reggae. They'd left the house forgetting the shoe box of tape cassettes and he'd been annoyed to return for it. Now he was glad they had. "No Woman, No Cry," for instance, a tune that held up well from ten years before, more. I hear you, mahn. Poor bastard, dead at thirty something, doing Fletcher good from beyond. . . . The song pulled you somehow, really did. Don't cry no tear.

The three girls in their cornrow braids were exotic. Three primitive deities to grace their Thanksgiving. Liz was digging the music like she didn't care who was around, feeling her way, eyes closed, with hips and shoulders and the soles of her feet, swaying like a grace-ful long-stalked downy-stemmed plant in the corner of the room. Thin braids dancing and jangling. You wouldn't mind grabbing this juicy no woman, no cry, you miserable wretch. Everyone wants the same thing.

Our bodies are our gardens, where there's a will . . .

How comfortable the room was: tasteful, cozy, friendly. The base of the lamp near the door was a large glass jug filled with shells collected on vacations over the years. The vase of feathers there on the candle-stand—pheasant, turkey, hawk—found in Connecticut woods and fields. The chair holding Fletcher was up-holstered with a flamestitch fabric of brilliant, warm autumnal colors. Autumnal, Jack, you don't say? Bit-tersweet, yes. Penny's house was expensive, but its suc-cess was more than a matter of money. It was individual, thoughtful, imagined. A home. No mean accomplish-ment, Pen. You did it. Must tell her, remind her, before the day was done. You made a place to live, a life. Wasn't that enough?

For pain.

Count your blessings. Clare had lived in a trailer at the edge of the woods for years. Her brilliant son had decided to live in a goddamn ghetto. She should be here right now dancing with Liz, no woman, no cry, but her mother never taught her. . . .

Penny had once been like the young women in the room: poised for happiness. That was what informed their youth: the idea of possibility. Patricia Wells, Clare, Penny had once been like them. A narrowing, a hard-ening set in. Present and future diminished as the hope-ful, unsuspecting traveler drew near his long-anticipated destination. Meanwhile, the past became too long and hard to think about, too changed. We all set out plan-ning to come into our own someday, to arrive at what we meant, what we want, bound eventually to real-

ize. . . . We loved an old face that seemed happy. Grama
Wells, for instance, bravely smiling in the face of no
possibility. Her aged twinkling countenance cheered
everyone up. She exhibited the wisdom of living in
the dying moment. A child's vision, living without a
plan. If you were Peter, you had to laugh, refusing to
believe it could be that simple—living in your skin.
The skin of the moment. The likes of Curly laced up
in his wife's fears, trusting conventions to keep everyone safe. The woman's prevailing mood of closed-
mouth anxiety wasn't helpful in a life of narrowing
possibilities, fraught with disappointing pitfalls, the
body unveiling new discouragements from top to bottom, the skin in the mirror. You needed to skip,
dance, keep your chin up, don't look down. Go for
it. Flame into being.

What unhappiness had blinded Clare to the possibility looking out from every passing moment? He
knew she would have loved being here right now. She
would have loved the feel, the flow, the young people,
the music. She would have loved the drive through the
countryside, the sky today, the geese, the light over the
horizon of bare trees, the view from the north porch,
even Curly's views, the braiding of hair, the table talk,
the sugar maples. A chance pheasant passing. Above all
a brief flirtation with family life, a day in the bosom of
generations. She would have loved the whole thing, if
everything had been different. Everything is possible,
that had been her faith. How had she lost sight of it?
You'll never know.

Dear World of Beauty, I would like to resign my
membership.

Don't do it. You're making a mistake. Come east.

A tune sweet to Fletcher came next, a sound

handed down from father to daughter in a manner of speaking—a woman loved by the many for her getup and guts, one of Clare's standbys, come to think of it, going back to Maine. Take another piece of my . . . Mary came to her feet, she danced, a hopping step, toward Liz, turning and crowding up to her backasswards. Liz, taller, wrapped herself around her friend's shoulders like a shawl. Laughing, they sang along with the song, mouthing the words. Like friends saying hello or good-bye, they kissed, and his niece danced out of her guest's arms, leaving Liz to tear open her chest with pronged fingers, as it were, a pantomime of passion, as she wailed silently toward Fletcher with empty outstretched hands: Take another piece of my heart. . . .

Hot shit.

Becky trying to copy Kate's hotshot moves was a spastic doll. Kate going to town in her athletic body, give 'em hell, apple of my eye. Be you. He still owed five hundred for braces, which had come off six months ago. In truth, he liked less her perfected teeth, the old inimitable smile somewhat altered by a simple-minded orthodontist who didn't know any better. Too old for little kids, too young yet for the likes of Mary, Kate faced the giddy hardship of inventing herself day in and day out, smoldering years of it. Leaving the room, Gwen tossed a ball of paper on the live bed of glowing coals, she ran her hand over her strange hair self-consciously. Never keen on Janis. Her back said, I saw that, you bastard, I know you through and through. A red wedge of flame, a dancing lick of fire, flashed against the back of the blackened hearth.

He touched the shiny deep-green leaf of the four-foot plant beside him. A living thing. Gardenia. The plant, almost Becky's age, he figured, was part of their lives. Listen, another old song important to Fletcher, this rending voice about a town in north Ontario. . . . He nodded, remembering. This was an album Gwen had played constantly for months years ago, vaguely involved with that puffed-up artist-in-residence who moped around the museum in his paint-soiled shoes, a fraud for art. He made the mistake of meeting their guest's eyes. She shuffled toward him in the corner of the room by the remarkable plant, grinning too broadly. Be careful. She knew the words, soundlessly moving her lips. She said, leaning over him, "Aren't we savage, Dad, in our Meduzoid hairdos?" She shook her dozen snakey braids at him. Secretly out of her mind. Corny. Cornrows. She ruffled his hair with her hand, let her leg lean against his arm for seconds.

"Does this feel good," she asked, "or what?"

"Yes."

She strolled off, sashaying her skirt, arms raised.

Patricia Wells entered, moving to the music, her round bumble bee–like figure in the soft, creamy cashmere sweater. Yes, you needed to get on your feet, be moved. Fletcher saluted her, thumbs up, although she didn't notice. Kate engulfed her. Gram, you're so cute. They embraced in the center of the room, then, holding hands, they danced after a fashion, the older woman taking her cue from her granddaughter.

Fletcher snorted kindly muffled laughter. Our humble Thanksgiving celebration, our show of happiness, the best we can do. He closed his eyes, listening, a line about birds across the sky . . . and opened them to find that everyone had gotten together on this one, all arm in arm, all the women of the house, that is, Gwen and

Penny in from the kitchen, all slowly swaying back and forth in a wobbly circle. The words: Helpless helpless helpless.

Curly stood in the doorway, filled the doorway, with a glass in his hand, his evening martini, his pink face bathed in delight. All that marvelous stuff about the heavens in his head. For the nonce.

Fletcher placed two fingers on the underside of his upturned wrist—an impulse—and counted as sixty seconds ticked off on his digital watch: fifty-nine.

U pstairs in the master bedroom—let's see—Peter was stretched out on the queen-size bed with Sam and Bo watching television. A nature documentary. No, a close-to-nature documentary about a primitive tribe deep in the rain forest. Our fellowman. Naked painted bodies leaping.

"Dad, this is awesome, an undiscovered tribe."

"Awesome," Peter seconded.

"Dad," Sam asked without taking his eyes off the screen, "did you know that we have these microscopic things on our eyelids that look like miniature hippopotamuses? They were just on."

Peter rolled toward the night table, snatching up the phone before it rang twice. "Jesus, I was just thinking about you. I'm lying here with Bo and his awesome cousin Sam, watching this damn loving tribe with bones in the ears, poor bastards bound to lose everything now that they're movie stars. The phone rings—I thought, Jesus, that's Joy saying he's going to drop in on us."

Fletcher descended the stairs thinking about layers of reality. Many layers.

A lone in Penny's kitchen for the first time today, he observed his face reflected in the window above the sink with kind detachment. A face in the dark.

Friends are coming out of the woodwork.

The hands that reached before him for a glass of water belonged to Liz. "Excuse me."

She ate cold stuffing with her fingers. He placed his veined hand on her breast, a lovely wholesome something.

"This is the best stuffing. I hope your hand isn't greasy. I mean, this is my best dress at the moment."

"Do you come easily, readily, or is it a lot of trouble or . . . ?"

"Depends on where I'm coming from."

"I suppose we don't get to see you again."

"No, come on, you can't . . . " She buttoned the button he had undone. "You can't do that in here. I doubt it. I mean, we probably don't get to see us . . . "

"Don't get to doubt us, shout about us. Take this mince pie. Like"—he ate—"a layer of reality."

"What?"

Slipping his hand almost unconsciously, seemed like, over her backside, tailbone there. "I'd rather munch you than mince words."

"Shh . . . " Grabbing his hand away, straightening her dress. "Ever heard of sexual harassment, Jack?"

"Real is a many-layered thing. You know that song?"

"It's good grass, but it's not that good."

"Love is many splendors in the grass—or spenders. Did you see the movie?"

"Are you for real or what?"

"Real splendor is many-layered lovers laid in grass.

Okay, enough of that silliness. A friend of mine used to work in the emergency room. Now she's into mid-wifery, but she used to like the emergency room. One night a man came in with a potato stuck in his ass. Imagine."

She laughed. "What?"

"Respectable, upstanding, middle-aged man with a potato . . . how's that for real splendor?"

"The poor man, that must have been a bad night."

"The same night, all right, the very same night, a woman, a wife-and-mother-type woman, stuffed her hand into a food processor in a fit of despair. Probably making supper, thinking, I'm never going to make an-other goddamn meal as long as I live. It didn't work, she only mangled her poor hand."

"Yuck. I'm going back to the living room."

"The same night, you see what I mean? Poor lonely souls walking into the same emergency room. If they only could have, you know, gotten together. They just had it mixed up. Put the potato in the food processor, put her hand up his behind, everything would have been fine. They would have been happy that night, no emergency."

"Hmm, this mince pie is good. Listen"—licking fingertips—"I love this song." Spinning away on her toes somehow three hundred and sixty . . . skipping out of the room, happy.

"Used to be my theme song," he called after her.

The Stones: "Gimme Shelter."

He sat down next to Gwen on the velvet couch and placed a small green volume, *Dubliners*, on the soft wool of her lap.

"What's that for?" She didn't touch it.

"It was here in the bookcase. Do you recognize it?"

"No."

He opened the cover to his inscription. "Can you believe that?" He smiled.

She read the line. Meeting his eyes, she shook her funny head. The braids, which she'd taken out, had left her hair out of control.

"What's it doing here?" he asked.

"I want to leave pretty soon. I've had it."

*H*e remembered thinking as they pulled into the drive: the Fletchers are here. The young woman framed by the doorway turned out to be Liz. Peter wore his red suspenders, he expressed opinions on the Steal and Lie scandal, Cretins In Action, Clare the loon, waltzing assholes, buildings taken over by pit bulls, tropical plants that didn't exist. His toy intended to solve the world's problems had been restored. A thought about money: it grew like mold. During their literary discussion, he dismissed the innermost thoughts of a twenty-year-old girl. At the island in the kitchen they enjoyed the gossip concerning the adulteries of strangers. An update on the legendary Joys. Ripeness was all with brie. Glenfuckit was the single malt of the day. Penny said, I never used to like you. Her almost tears. Geese flew overhead. A gray bird alighted in the dogwood. Three beautiful girls stood by the window. Come quick: an iridescent pheasant, which led to a walk in the darkening woods, the stolen thrill of an off-the-cuff kiss. Don't be a jerk, Dad. A shared joint was a blood transfusion. With humor by and large, and briefly, the world's ills were addressed: Penny's ice age, recession, the Cold War era ended, widespread famine imminent, their dear world of beauty endangered. Like whales beaching themselves at Wellfleet, doomed. Think they'd know better. Diseases mentioned: cancer, heart disease, AIDS. The counting of blessings was advised. Their discussion of the arts revealed that one opinion was as good as another. All put in two cents concerning best-liked books, movies. . . . All a matter of dollars and cents; dolor and no sense. Bittersweet branched . . . remember? Marvelous plants the size of children numbered among the Thanksgiving company: Rosemary, Gardenia. Three joggers were present. Your father-in-law would be there when you came in. The coat box of photographs was laid across laps. . . . You've mellowed intensely, you've boxed in your fire. May you flame into being. An old book discovered: an old tool of seduction. His first love. Under the low winterish sky they had their game of soccer. Hooray. Hastening light-shot clouds. The wind was excitement. Shadows of clouds blew over the field. The day ended with the unexpected glow of a bittersweet sky. Jokes told: Curly's good one about a girl's handwriting in the snow. Two Dogs Screwing: an Indian name. Native Americans, they learned, had been farmers, they cleared the land. There was still a paradise remaining, Peter advised: Kamchatka! Gardens, past and present, played a part. Carbon dioxide was the crux. Of late, Sam's preferred mode of movement was the cartwheel. Clare was never far off—not for a moment. My mother never taught me how to fight. Call me . . . come east. A Maine adventure recalled, a shelter built. I could have loved you. In the bosom of her family Gwen was like a stranger this day. I'll talk about what I damn please. For Penny's pain there

were pills. Stone walls of romance stood around setting the mood. The sunset and silence talked to them
about the old dead past. Dick was a nickname. In a
twinkling they were bungling with one another,
strangers, their orchids blooming. Ten million tropical
plants represented a lot of rotten teeth. There was a
relationship between the destruction of the Amazon
and Penny's ice age. The food today, must mention
the food, you turkey. You said the magic . . . Curly.
The lowdown on our middle-aged star. His mind
awhirl with the heavens' millions and billions. Back to
earth, he found lamentable a world filling up with
cripples and morons. Literally. They enjoyed their
close encounter on the porch while, inside, young
women braided their hair. I thought she loved me. A
day of close encounters, as it were. Near misses.
Curly's wisdom: people used to be happy. Freddy's
sax shone like the moon, like scrap brass. Minute by
minute their braided heads, dancing, changed the look
of things. Do you know how it's going to end?

In his chair by the luxuriant gardenia he recalled the
day, endeavoring to remember what he was afraid he'd
forget. Like Kate's glow right now. This Liz swaying this
way. His wife, his first love. The geese on Penny's apron.
Flying south presumably. The mark she showed them
behind Peter's ear. Take him out and shoot him. The sky
today. Not to mention space. Time. Fifty billion years,
was it? Know how it's going to end? I'm glad you're the
last one I talked to. How did Curly put it—the life cycle
of all stars. Dear world of . . . there were layers and layers
of reality, layers too numerous. . . .

Stevie: juggle these!

In the back of his mind, Fletcher, the architect, felt
a tremendous poem unfurling, a bittersweet master-

piece. This life, happening right now, the skinny moment. That's it: The Skin of the Moment.

*H*e found that Peter had entered the room with a boy giant. Taller and broader than the master of the house, as blond as Liz, their day's guest. The boy's hands were dead weights at his sides. Oafish, handsome, agog. The music had the kids on their feet again. Madonna. Kate and her older cousin were dancing after a fashion while Becky tried hard to follow Liz's free-style laid-back body language. The music was probably louder than they realized. The boy didn't know what was going on here. His host had him firmly around the shoulder. Peter's flame face damn near the color of his suspenders, his smile was excellent. He pointed to individuals in the room and stretched up to speak into the young man's ear as if to give him a kiss. Liz smiled prettily, openly, and waved. Truth or dare? The boy looked away. Kate waved, too, and winked, the wiseguy, laughing with Liz. Fletcher remembered that their wild hair was hardly what one would expect. Savage. The hair, along with the music and the dancing and the heat of the room would easily account for their young visitor's baffled expression. Peter pointed toward Fletcher. Awkwardly, the boy made his way across the room and extended his large ruddy hand. Bending from the waist to make himself barely heard, he said he wanted to be an architect someday. Fletcher shook hands warmly without getting up, looking directly into the boy's heart and soul for a second, smiling.

As Peter ushered the fellow from the room, Fletcher thought, Roy, that's who. Peter's hand was on the small of his back. Penny had told Gwen that Peter thought the world of Roy, obvious that he'd give him the shirt off his back, and then some. Rather go out and chop wood with Roy at this stage of the game, basically, than stay home and fiddle with Penny's lonesome pussy of a Sunday afternoon, say. Minutes later Roy appeared in the doorway again, a Red Sox baseball cap on his head, and nodded farewell to the room in general. Fletcher waved, but Roy was all eyes for enticing Liz, the likes of which he'd surely seldom seen in his corner of rural Connecticut.

While Fletcher had thoroughly enjoyed it, he didn't know what Roy's appearance here at the tail end of their Thanksgiving meant. What did it have to do with all that had gone before?

S am stumbled through the doorway with an arrow through his head. His eyes were wide open, surprised. He clutched his throat. He staggered past Kate, lunged against the crewel wing chair, slowly turned in dizzying circles around Liz, the arrow crazily pointing north east south west. Fletcher watched with wonder as this genius, his son, struggled toward him across the room. Sam keeled over at his father's feet, rolled onto his back with outflung arms, his eyes closed. There was no letup here in the life of the moment. Everything kept happening. Fletcher threw himself onto the boy's body, gathered Sam into his arms. The flawless face was deadpan, eyes fast shut, the arrow sticking out both sides.

"That must hurt," Fletcher whispered. He slipped a finger into the right place under Sam's armpit and watched his son's face light up. They rolled, broadcasting laughter, in each other's arms.

Remember this! Remember this!

M aybe just a bit of white meat and stuffing with cranberry relish and one wee sliver more of pumpkin plus a sip of Penny's robust French roast would be just the thing before taking our leave. Day is done.

Or was it?

He came upon the kitchen in an uproar, as if a whole carload of revelers had just arrived with drinks in their hands. Peter was roaring away, one arm around his mother-in-law, the other encircling another woman's waist. Over by the back door, Curly was pumping some man's hand, old Curly running for office here at the end of the day. Penny dragged Gwen forward to meet . . . All talking in that boisterous I'm-so-glad-to-finally-meet-you sort of way.

"Jesus wept, Peter, are you positively daft to be filling your mother-in-law's poor head with such rubbish?"

Fletcher thought: Cora.

The woman wore a lightweight white wool coat with bright paisley scarf. Her hair was a soft, unreal strawberry-blond, shortish. Her face was soft, powdered pale, a pink blush on the cheeks, and vivid red lips. Along with the cool night air she had brought in a scent, a floral perfume, which momentarily masked the lingering cooking smells of Penny's kitchen.

Peter was going on about one of the finest Irish voices this side of the Atlantic. He was off to get the family guitar. "You must give us a song, Cora. We can't let you get away without a song."

"Heaven help us, Penny, Peter must be half mad with the jar. Now, Paul, I said, we simply can't go flying by, it wouldn't be right at all. We'll stop just for one minute. Penny would be just as happy if we kept going, says he. I won't hear of it, says I." She turned to Gwen's mother. "I'm so delighted, I've been amazed for years by the work of your hands, Mrs. Wells. You're an absolute cottage industry all to yourself, aren't you? That peach sweater you made Mary last year, how lovely it was. I'm nothing but ten thumbs myself, going in every direction." She laughed at herself. "You've a marvelous gift, Mrs. Wells."

"I enjoy it," said Patricia Wells, quite at a loss, paling, withdrawing in the face of such admiring enthusiasm.

"You'd have to be a marvelous woman yourself to have a daughter like Penny." She turned, smiling prettily, and took Gwen's hand. "This is Gwendolyn. It's such a treat for me to finally meet you. Penny thinks the world of you." She touched Gwen's face, incredibly. "You remind me of my own younger sister."

"You must be excited about your new house," said Gwen by way of seeming human.

"The new house," cried Cora. "Not a bloody stick of furniture in it. We haven't even a faucet on the bleeding kitchen sink. Penny, you must come and tell me what to do with the place. Penny has created one of the loveliest homes in Connecticut. You have. New England, in fact." She looked about. "Now, I must meet Kate and Sam. It's Kate and Sam, isn't it? I know all about awesome Sam from his adoring cousin Bo."

"They're here somewhere," said Penny.

"At long last," said Fletcher, intruding, "the legendary Cora Joy."

Fletcher was introduced by his sister-in-law.

"But of course," said Cora Joy, "the remarkable brother-in-law." She beamed, the eyes positively twinkling. "The whole family is extraordinary, isn't it?"

"Jack the remarkable." That was Gwen.

"Now, you said we'd only stop for a minute, love, no more." The man was a tad drunk, Fletcher was pleased to observe.

"Have you met my beloved husband?" She introduced Paul Joy to each person present. "Have you ever clapped an eye on a handsomer family?"

"Paul Joy," said Paul Joy soberly, taking Fletcher's hand. "She's a marvelous one for the chat, you know, if you let her get a foot in the door." He was an American, clearly, yet the Irish lilt of his wife's speech had evidently proved infectious.

Curly, Fletcher noticed, was already crazy about these two. He stood by, wearing a smile, as if he was responsible for having found them outside and brought them into the house for an unexpected treat.

"Now, love, I must see the children, then we're off." She flew to the living room.

"Wow," said Gwen.

Peter had the guitar by the neck, held before him like a trophy, a fresh kill.

"The Joys are already late, Peter. Not tonight."

Cora returned, bestowing smiles, bustling. "My name is Sam Fletcher," she mimicked in a serious boy's voice, then laughed. "He's a positive charmer," she told Gwen. "And the girls are stunning—the young women, I should say. Kate is absolutely lovely. The three of them with the hair, they're a dream." She looked about. "All right, Paul, if we must."

Mary had followed her back to the kitchen. Becky, Kate, and Liz looked in from the doorway.

Peter held out the guitar. "You can't go, Cora, without—"

"Peter, for goodness' sake, don't be a nuisance." Penny talking.

Mary said, "Please, Cora, one song."

"What possible good are we if we can't take a minute for a song?" Cora stated decisively.

Paul Joy glanced toward the ceiling, the eyes rolling back. . . .

"Honestly, Cora, it's not compulsory," Penny said.

"Oh, not at all." Cora Joy busily discarded her overcoat and scarf. Her dress was bright red, which matched her shoes and lipstick, while her stockings were white, and there was white lace on the cuffs and collar. "We won't guarantee a thing," she said, hastily plucking the strings to tune the guitar.

"Jaysus wept," muttered Paul Joy. Peter handed him a glass of whiskey. "I never thought you'd ask, Peter. There's a good lad."

All moved back a step as Cora made herself comfortable on the Windsor chair, hitching the guitar up under her arm. There was an instant—he noticed Gwen's eyes seek out her sister's—of enormous awkwardness, all tensed to witness a live performance, but I'll be damned, he thought, following the first slightly rusty note, the woman was altogether convincing, her voice ringing in the crowded kitchen, a song Irish, merry, and quick. The human voice, thought Fletcher. A woman's singing voice.

All politely applauded, while Peter brayed bravo.

She was back into her coat, held out by her husband. She buttoned up. "Now we're off." She looked from face to face. "I'm so glad we stopped. Now, Paul, the next time the Fletchers or the Wellses are in Connecticut, we must have them over. Penny will tell me when they're coming. Isn't it ridiculous, not to have met you before this?" She turned to Gwen. "Can we plan on it?" Taking Penny's face between her hands, she kissed her good-bye, then Peter, then Gwen as well, impulsively, and the four girls, Liz included, a hasty rush of good-bye kissings. Handshakes for Fletcher and Mr. and Mrs. Wells. "God bless." They're off.

Kate said, "I loved her."

Gwen was smiling. "She's almost a little much, isn't she?"

"The dress," said Patricia Wells. "I can't get over that dress."

"She's real," Penny assured them. "That's Cora for you, believe it or not."

Fletcher believed. He followed Peter outside. Paul Joy's car shone blackly, a block long. Peter leaned into the window for a good night kiss, a last handshake.

"Thank you so much, Peter, I adored meeting everyone. It was short but sweet. God bless, love."

Fletcher bungled up behind Peter, leaning toward the car window. "Loved every minute of it, Cora Joy. You were perfect. Perfect."

Paul Joy raised the drink he'd taken with him to the car. With affection he said to Peter, "Good night, asshole."

N ow everyone crowded into the front hall to bid the Fletchers good night.

Penny urged upon him a package of leftover meat and pie. Their kiss was awkward, unsatisfactory, Fletcher aiming for her lips while Pen turned her cheek, no more than a formality.

"Thanks for everything, Pen." He touched her arm above the elbow. "It was fun."

"I hope so."

He indicated the new antique chest near him and confided, "I like the recent acquisition."

"Jack, tell me one thing," said Curly. "What happened to our game of cribbage? Last time I needed one miserable point to go out," he told Peter, "but our friend here had first count. I'll be doggoned if he didn't do it with eleven points right on the nose." He warmly took his son-in-law's hand. "You devil."

Fletcher had no memory of their last game of cribbage.

Gwen turned to her father. They hugged each other. "Good luck, Dad, I'll be in touch." She kissed him.

"All I ask is that you drive carefully," said Patricia Wells. "God knows, what we don't need is an accident." Mother and daughter kissed. "Take care of everyone."

Fletcher picked up Becky and Bo for wholehearted hugs. The small boy clung.

Mary said, "Remember, you've been challenged. Next time we won't have skirts on." Her kiss was quick, his cheek pecked.

Behind Gwen's family, in the light from the kitchen at the end of the front hall, was Liz's braided head, a halo effect. Then her arm in its dark sleeve.

"Oh, Liz," Kate called, and she rushed back to hug good-bye.

"Yes, we're forgetting our guest of the day," said Fletcher. He raised his arm.

A chorus of good nights ushered them onto the porch. Parting, like the instant of greeting eight hours earlier, proved one of the sweet moments of the day. These faces.

Bo began to cry, a bravely muffled sobbing. His mother picked him up. "He's tired. Aren't you, you wonderful boy? You're the best boy."

"I'll be out your way with the Jag one of these days, Fletch," Peter promised, "and we'll make a day of it. No families, just the two of us. Safe home." A phrase borrowed from their Irish friend Cora. His dark eyes were houndishly sincere.

"I'll look forward to that, Peter. In the meantime, I'll send you my tax bill." Sincerely he added, "Thanks for everything."

As if they'd waited until the last possible moment, the two sisters hugged, Bo between them, and coolly exchanged kisses.

"I'll be in touch about Christmas," said Gwen.

"I'll talk to you next week," Penny told her.

"Come on," Peter hooted, "I hope we'll see you before Christmas, for Christ's sake." He lifted his sister-in-law off her feet in a hard hug. "I love you completely, remember that."

"Christmas is in less than a month, Peter," Penny reminded him. "I'm sure we won't see them before that."

Peter stood with Gwen's father by the lighted lamp-post at the edge of the drive while Fletcher turned the Saab around. As he pulled away, he tooted the horn twice and watched for two arms to go up. They did.

*T*wo broad paths of light, white and red, curved into space. Our Thanksgiving. Worn-out earthlings sped silently home through the dark, bearing back the pains and laughs of endless relationships. In all the on-coming traffic not a soul in sight—just this flow of light composed of identical light beams in ordered succes-sion. A wonder really. The family of Fletcher in the flow: another anonymous set of headlights. And yet closed up in your car you felt powerfully, visibly present, your life, the lives of loved ones, in your hands, absorbed with the special task of bearing your precious world home at the numb melancholy end of the day.

Kate and Sam slept, or seemed to, reclining at op-posite corners of the backseat.

Gwen, with her eyes closed and arms folded across her narrow chest, hadn't spoken a word since they'd left Penny's. That, thought Fletcher, was too damn bad.

"Are you asleep?"

No answer.

He turned on the radio and tuned in, as chance would have it, to a familiar pop tune, solid gold from years ago. Gwen's hand darted forward to snap it off. A slap in the face.

"I was listening to that."

As quickly as he turned it back on, she clicked it off again. "I'm not in the mood."

"Is this how the day is going to end?"

A moment later she said, "I'm all talked out, that's all. I'm finally just bummed out, I guess."

Bummed out: Sam's influence.

"I thought everyone seemed in pretty good form. I actually enjoyed myself in the end. Even your mother. She didn't put on her expression of martyrdom until late in the day."

Gwen shifted in her seat and kicked with her stock-inged foot, hard, striking his thigh with three rapid blows. "Leave my mother alone." She struck his shoulder with the side of her fist, then the underside of his upraised arm. "Just leave her alone."

"I'm driving," Fletcher protested. "You want an accident?" The mother's martyrdom was an old story between them; she knew what he meant. "What the hell was that about?"

His wife sat stiffly erect, her arms folded tight, turned away. Obnoxious to Fletcher.

"Under the circumstances, I thought she was fine all day. You don't know when to stop, Jack. Don't you have any feelings for her at all?"

"Clare, you mean? That's perfect, now that it's too late for anyone——"

Gwen faced him. "Not Clare. I don't mean Clare." She changed her tone. "No one said anything to you?"

His pulse quickened.

"Where have you been, Jack?"

"I've been at your sister's for Thanksgiving, Gwen, Let's hear it."

"You're remarkable, all right." Her father, she'd learned today, had cancer of the prostate. They'd received the results of a biopsy the day before yesterday. "Can you believe it?"

He struck the steering wheel with the heel of his hand. "For crying out loud."

Gwen summarized Curly's condition: confusing lower-back pain, some minor urinary symptoms, which had evidently been going on for a while and had finally forced him to the doctor, who had insisted on a biopsy immediately. He was scheduled to go into the hospital Wednesday for more extensive surgery. They'd know more then. His doctor was also talking about radiation therapy. "Mother said he hasn't been up to par since September. Don't you think he looked tired today?"

"No."

"You know, kill yourself for forty years, retire, then when you're beginning to get on top of things, get cancer. Or something else. Christ." Tears in her voice. "I feel sorry for him. I mean, goddamnit . . . "

People used to be happy.

"That's very treatable today, Gwen. Chances are they've caught it early. They're removing prostate glands all day long today." He reached out a friendly hand to squeeze her sturdy shoulder. "Don't torture yourself until we know what he's up against. Come on, Curly's a bull."

"They're trying to act like it's practically nothing—he didn't even mention it to me himself—but I know my mother is scared to pieces."

Statistics showed the cancer was more common in married men than single men. Because, Fletcher surmised, married men were less sexually active. Keep it to yourself, he thought. "Today he practically broke my hand. I went to shake hands, he broke it. The man is a bull."

"On top of that we had Penny's stunt. Perfect timing. Everyone's stuck in their own rut and can't get out of it, no matter what's happening to someone else."

"What stunt was that, Gwen?"

"Where the hell have you been? Jesus, Jack."

He took both hands off the wheel. "What do you want from me? I'm talking to people, no one's telling me anything."

"My super-reliable sister took off for five days, leaving everything in Peter's lap. The trouble was she didn't let anyone know . . . no one knew what had happened to her. So Peter was going absolutely nuts for five days thinking she'd driven off a cliff or something. That's not Penny at all, to up and leave like that. Peter couldn't believe she'd do that to him and the kids. He called Mother, naturally, thinking that's where she was, so Mother got to go crazy for a few days just when this whole thing with Dad was happening. They called the state police all over New England practically. Penny was at the Woodstock Inn, as it turned out, deciding what to do with the rest of her life, I suppose. Evidently she didn't come up with anything, so she came back. What kills me is she already knew they were waiting for the results of the biopsy. That stinks.''

"Why?" In the dark of the car, he smiled despite himself, shaking his head. The absurdity of it. "Don't tell me Penny's involved with someone? Has Peter been fucking around?"

"Of course not. She decided she's wasting her life or something cute like that. We didn't really get a chance to talk about it much. Mother was the one who mentioned it to me first.''

"Why now? I mean, just before the holidays?"

"I don't know what specifically triggered it. Nothing, probably. I thought that's what the holidays were all about now. Isn't that when everyone gets to go berserk?''

"It's not really surprising, is it?''

"Not really, no.''

"They'll be together to the bitter end. What did you say to her about it?"

"I told her hardly a week passes that I don't think about doing the same thing. Splitting. She should have done it ten years ago.''

"You must have been very comforting.''

"What else is there to think about? I'm sure your

concerns are loftier than ours, Jack, yours and Peter's,
you've got more important things to think about."

Didn't deserve an answer.

She had seen Penny and Fletcher in the kitchen
together before supper. "I thought that's what you were
talking about. Her flight."

"I didn't know what we were talking about."

Traffic thinned only slightly as they traveled north-
northwest through dark hills toward their heart of the
valley. Fletcher's spine, knotted now with tension, sent
fleeting spasms up the base of his skull. Relax. Remain
alert.

Replay the day. Things said and unsaid, the mood
and feel of the occasion, all were somewhat altered.
He had been present and not present, in a manner of
speaking, so that now Thanksgiving at Penny's consisted of the day and the day he had missed. Like recalling the puzzling backdrop of childhood now that
you knew what life was about: what, among the
grown-ups, must have been going on. He felt child-
ish, cheated. Curly and Penny must have assumed,
like Gwen, that he had heard their news somehow
from one or the other of those present, and simply
had nothing to say. Not his business. After five, ten,
fifteen years. What in truth might he have said? Everything's going to be all right? You'll be together to
the bitter end? Everyone had seemed in pretty good
form. Rerun. Reread.

"Why didn't anyone get in touch with us? That's
ridiculous, Gwen. It's your father. Your sister."

"Who knows?" As if his question was a hill she was
too exhausted to climb. "I guess they thought telling
me today was soon enough. Mother probably didn't
want to ruin my week sooner than necessary. When she

has a problem, she talks to Penny, not me. Boy oh boy."

Among Curly's memorable remarks: people used to be happy. Not like now.

"My family," said Gwen, discouraged. "Mother goes on and on about the family, we're all we've got, the only people you can really count on when the chips are down. We just don't do each other much good."

Clare, he thought. He said, "Come on, Gwen, your family is no different than every other family."

"My mother and I can talk about matters of life and death all day long, but it's not real talk at some level. It doesn't help somehow. The same with Penny. We don't get anywhere. What is that?" She stared blankly at the tolerable glare of oncoming traffic, her hands in her lap. "But, boy, we can hurt each other like blazes." She added, "I just want him to be all right. Give the guy a break."

To Curly's space people, say, with their special intergalactic lenses, the flow of light would appear a single organism, a singleminded entity. Family-of-man-type thing. All alike as ants, whales, wildebeests. Each car, you figured, was a turkey stuffed, roasted, carved up, picked clean, soup tomorrow. Each car was a feast, you figured, with its jogger, its joker, its genius, with its go–getter, its gossip, its good person, with its knitter and baker and book-reader, its jock, its juggler, its jerk, with its pretty young thing, its merry old soul, its sick and tired, its stick-in-the-mud, its dearly departed, with its failure, its oddball, its doomed. Each car was a nest of loved ones, a mixed bag.

We just don't do each other much good. Like my mother never taught me how to fight. Fight what? You mean, she never taught you how to go with it, the flow.

Relax, remain alert, don't let the assholes get ahead.

"The more I think about it, Gwen, I can't believe someone didn't say something to me all day. Christ, Peter is an asshole. Five, ten, fifteen years I'm sitting there one goddamn Thanksgiving after another, the invisible man, as far as anyone's concerned. Everything's going to hell and I'm not even informed. These are the people in my life, some of them anyway."

"How do you think I feel?" She faced him. "That's them, all right, that's the way they are, but you aren't any better. The first thing you did once we got there was disappear. After dinner you went outside to play, Jack, and then took off for a walk or something until dark. What do you expect?"

"It's not hard to understand where Clare was coming from, is it? She just said I can't deal with them, the hell with it."

"Don't identify with Clare, Jack. Clare was lost."

"Since when have you come to that conclusion?"

"I can't forgive her for what she did to my parents. Her flesh and blood, for crying out loud. Can you imagine Kate doing that to us someday? She was their daughter, they loved her."

"You just said you don't do each other any good. You're starting to sound like your brother-in-law."

"My mother can drive me up the wall, Jack, she's a frustrating, limited person, but she's not a monster. She didn't deserve the heartbreak Clare handed her. The whole thing is nuts," she said, defeated.

"The final falling-out was over the uncle, wasn't it? What if Kate came to you with something like that and you refused to listen? Your mother hides from everything, Gwen, she wouldn't face the truth about her brother. Was Clare supposed to forgive her for that?"

"Clare came to her with that desperate theory when she was already forty, for God's sake. Who knows what that was all about? I was maybe two when he died, but Penny remembers him. She thought he was terrific."

"What's that got to do with it?"

"No one knows what happened, or if anything happened, including Clare apparently. It doesn't make sense. I think she was more"—she waited for the right word to come to her—"disturbed than we realized, frankly. Maybe she wasn't all there, Jack."

On thin ice here, Fletcher wasn't inclined to venture too far out. Instinctively, so to speak, or intuitively, he accepted the discovery Clare had made, or believed she had made, about her blurred distant past, the out-of-bounds childhood trauma that began to trouble her sleep and haunt her days much later in life. At first, as he speculated on what may have taken place, he'd resented Penny's sad postmortem revelation, and yet nothing could soil his pure, loving, and carnal memories of Clare. His basis for believing what the others wished to dismiss, his special insight into the truth of the matter, wasn't to be shared with anyone, including Gwen. Not tonight, driving home from Penny's Thanksgiving, from the long day and the day he had missed.

As if to set the unresolvable matter aside with a wise piece of advice, he said, "She was a wonderful person, Gwen. Remember the good stuff. Don't let her go."

Gwen couldn't resist having the last word. "I was just her sister, Jack. I didn't know her as intimately as you did. I can't let myself think about that."

"Don't let her go," he repeated. "She was important, she is important."

"Be quiet, Jack, I don't want to talk about it."

Each car, you figured, had its toolmaker, its man in

the market, its monk, its mother-in-law, its not-in-the-mood wife, its would-be poet, princess, prince of peace, its could-be rock star, superstar, Rising Star, its pedant, pedophile, prisoner of sex, its has-been, might-have-been, its uptight, played-out, fed-up, its laid-back, tip-top, right-as-rain, its awesome, its excellent, its gross.

Take it, take another little piece of my heart now. . . . Liz tearing her chest open like . . . an offering. Her hand going up at the end of the hall, her blond head. If you were Fletcher, you couldn't pass it up, realizing this was it, very likely your last waltz in the woods at twilight with the likes of Liz, the sort of windfall moment that fell at your feet once in a blue moon. You would have been a fool to pass it up and you were a fool not to.

A thought, remember: not a soul in sight in the racing glare of night traffic. A homogeneous mass humming along, not a whit of difference, from a certain distance, between this one or that, God love us, and yet you in your car with your precious thoughts, your eyes, your hands, your pains and laughs, your loved ones, you are it, the world is on your back, the world is in your hands.

Its dreams, schemes, recurrent themes. . . .

As in that documentary on famine: hot barren acres of wasting human beings—a people of exceptional beauty, one could discern in the less ravaged face focused upon at random by the panning news camera—not a soul in sight in the glare of mass catastrophe, and yet you in your paper-thin parched skin, in your starved body with your unimaginable thoughts, your large eyes, your helpless hands, your loved ones. . . .

Clare was lost. She could not be reached.

Her son had called, unwittingly, after she had taken

enough pills to kill herself, but before she had died. He had intruded upon his mother's most private act. That is, Clare heard the phone ring for the last time in her life. The phone rang. And she answered it! And managed a conversation, some few words, about nothing of importance probably. Good night. Then scrawled her haunting postscript: You must have sensed I was drugged. I'm glad you were the last one I talked to. A last glimpse of her state of mind, her presence of mind, Clare's exceptional mind.

One year ago today.

Where was everybody?

Had Noah, in fact, sensed she was drugged? Or even if he'd sensed fatigue, a vagueness, would he have deduced from that . . . ? Clare's words intimated that he knew, as if nothing could have been more obvious, as if by assigning him knowledge she secured his implicit consent, his understanding. That was something she wanted, needed, even then, especially then.

We're all we've got. . . .

"Now what?" Suddenly they were stopped in westbound traffic. It extended bumper to bumper in both lanes the length of a long curving uphill slope, and beyond. Traffic piled up behind them in Fletcher's rearview mirror.

"Oh, brother."

A happy face popped up in the back window of the station wagon ahead of them, then ducked out of sight. Then two happy faces, two nearly toothless grins. Peek-a-boo. Fletcher stuck his thumbs in his ears and wagged his hands. Gwen waved, not to disappoint them. But the children, he realized then, couldn't see them in the dark behind their headlights.

Next to the station wagon was a red Honda with a young family packed inside. The woman's head of dark hair rested against the window. There was another couple in the car to Fletcher's left with two elderly white-haired ladies in the backseat. Not to be forgotten this day. The second time he looked, he saw that the woman was nursing an infant, judging from her arms like that, her bent head, the collar of her blouse opened. He couldn't see the baby. Sweet.

The traffic proceeded fitfully. The new mother pulled two car lengths ahead. An older couple pulled up beside Fletcher, the woman's neck in a fat white brace, I'D RATHER BE SAILING on the bumper, then a woman in a white Subaru, blondish, sitting up real straight, eyes fixed straight ahead, anxious, alone at the end of the day. Her bumper stickers: I LOVERMONT. ARMS ARE MEANT FOR HUGGING.

Kate asked, "Where are we?"

Blue light in the rearview mirror caused him to step harder on the brake. Sensation, like a current beneath the skin, ran through his shoulders. A state cruiser fled past in the breakdown lane at zealous speed, casting harsh thrilling light as it went. Receding before them, the flashing light scored the broad arc of highway, grew distant, and disappeared. Shooting star.

Come on, Curly, fight back.

A blue Volvo station wagon then pulled alongside, fortyish academic type, one boy, one girl in the backseat, the short-haired woman talking away at him, some well-taken point, the pinkie of her right hand inserted well up in her right nostril. A large pale dog, damn bandana around its neck, stared out the rear window, which displayed a rainbow decal plus a college parking sticker—cozy little house on leafy campus, witty colleagues in for cocktails, off to meetings all over the place, new pocketful of coeds like Mary each year, sabbatical coming up, oh, to England with jaunts to Rome, Paris, Istanbul, not a bad life if you could stomach it.

A siren. Turn and look: AMBULANCE. Whirling red light swept past, ascended the hill, and was gone.

"It must have just happened."

Up ahead a pickup pulled into the emergency lane, and the car behind Fletcher, the back end of it up in the air like a baboon, the girl curled up like a squirrel in the fellow's lap, followed suit. Assholes! Need to get ahead.

Kate asked, "How long are we going to be stuck in this? Turn on the radio."

"Forget the radio, Kate." She didn't realize. Someone's hardship, someone's loved one, it happened so suddenly.

Another state police car sped past, bleeping its weird Klaxon intermittently. A dazzling white tow truck, its cab decked out with dozens of blinking yellow lights, followed.

Sam, awake now, thought the tow truck was excellent.

I lovermont, the straitlaced damsel in the white Subaru, had lit a cigarette, which struck Fletcher as out of keeping. Alongside the young mother again, there was the infant up over the shoulder. Brand-new looking. Fuzzy soft skull. You had to support its wobbly head, little face all surprised, mouth slack. A bubble. There, let's have a big burp. What a good boy! The woman noticed him watching and smiled. Her happi-

ness. Fletcher winked back. Walking and talking before
you know it, preschool, kindergarten, off to college
before you know what hit you.

"It's so cute," said Kate. "Mom, I want one."

"I wish you'd told me you were going for a walk,"
Gwen said. "I would have enjoyed that." She'd decided
to be friendly now.

"We were following a pheasant after our game of
soccer." We smooched, made glancing farfetched passes
at private parts, argued, and made up. Nothing to do
with you, really.

"I can't remember the last time I was back in those
woods," she said. "The laurel and the ferns and the lichens on the stone walls. They have it rough, don't
they?"

"Do you think lichens and ferns would make you
happy?"

"Maybe it doesn't make any difference what you
have, but when you think of how much Peter and Penny
have, it's hard to feel sorry for them. When you can scoot
up to Vermont in your new Wagoneer and stay in a
classy country inn for a week because you're fed up, it's
hard to see that as suffering. Who can afford to do that?"

"That's the trap she's in."

"I guess Peter's having his problems these days, too.
Penny said something about a lawsuit pending."

"I have a feeling that Peter will land on his feet one
way or the other." A moment later he laughed.

"What?"

"Just thought of something." The bookmark in
Pen's survival of civilization book: her Thanksgiving list
on Woodstock Inn stationery. She took off, scaring the
daylights out of Peter, only to sit up there planning the

holiday. Wasn't that the truth? Locked into our lives while the glacier slouched toward us.

Their lane edged forward. Oops, a little trouble in the Honda, Mom reaching into the backseat to wildly swat I'm-not-going-to-tell-you-again at her nest of boys, who threw up arms in self-defense. Wasn't *my* fault, *I* didn't do it, don't hit *me*. . . .

"Those kids are in trouble."

Sam laughed, "Holy cow," identifying with the culprits.

On the bumper of an old Chevy: TOOT IF YOU BELIEVE IN JESUS. Good one!

"But I'm sure she really is unhappy, that's the thing."

"What's wrong with Penny?" Kate asked.

"Nothing."

"She's unhappy," her father told her. "Maybe a few days shopping in New York will cheer her up."

"I wish we could go somewhere. Mary's going to Europe next summer, for instance."

"I thought you were going to April in Paris," he said. Her high school's foreign exchange program was something Kate had hoped to participate in.

"Can I? Really?"

"If we get lucky." If the grammar school comes through, if the orthopedic surgeon decides to go ahead with his addition, if IIF survives the inevitably lean new year.

He recalled Peter's proposed present to Gwen's parents. A Bermuda holiday. That was Peter's promise to Curly that everything would be all right. Peter was a decent shit, loyal, hopeful, hardworking, he was, despite his nonsense.

"Peter's all right," he said. "Penny could do a lot worse."

"I love Peter. He's just so . . . blind."

They stopped again. The oncoming traffic, the glaring flow of light in the eastbound lanes, continued without pause, as if this had nothing to do with them. Only glad they weren't caught in it.

"I miss having a baby around the house. Look at that little guy."

"Then you have one, Jack, okay?"

I'd rather be sailing. I lovermont. Toot if you believe. . . .

"Kate, how did you like Mary's friend Liz? The three of you seemed to be having a good time."

"She's fun. I might visit them in New York."

"Her father lives in Switzerland, right, and her mother lives in California?"

"No, her stepmother lives in California. Her real mother died when Liz was like twelve or thirteen or something." She hesitated. "Mary said not to say anything, all right, so don't mention it to Penny. I mean it, Mom, I told her I wouldn't tell you. She committed suicide. In Europe somewhere. Like Greece, I think, or Spain."

"Really? Why should that be a secret?" Gwen asked.

"Mary said she found her or something horrible like that."

"How awful."

Fletcher sought his daughter's face in the rearview mirror, then turned to the backseat. "Spain? They were living in Spain?"

"I don't know."

"Liz was twelve? Did Mary say what happened, I mean why . . . ?"

"I don't know, Dad."

"Jack, we're moving."

"Her mother must have been a young woman. Did Mary say what they were doing in Spain or—?"

"No."

"Liz found her? What did Mary say about that?"

"She only mentioned it, Dad, she didn't go into it. That's all I know. It was after soccer when we were going back to the house. Why are you so hyper about it?"

"Where was her father? Were the parents together then?"

"Kate doesn't know," Gwen said sharply. "For heaven's sake, Jack, you sound like it happened yesterday. Why are you so interested in Liz's mother, who's been dead for . . . how long? Leave her alone."

"Yeah, Dad."

"Thirteen years old in a foreign country, you walk in and find your mother one day . . . what a nightmare."

Where was everybody?

"I guess she gets pretty depressed sometimes."

"I'd say Liz is fine. I'm sure Liz takes very good care of herself. She certainly wasn't depressed today."

"You know who you sound like? Exactly? You sound exactly like your mother. That's just the sort of remark—"

"Okay, Jack."

The name on the gravestone: what was the woman's name on the gravestone?

Another ambulance, the size and shape of a bread

truck, streamed down the breakdown lane of the eastbound highway with its lights going.

"I wonder if that's us or something else?"

Sam had to pee, forgot to go before they left, and
really had to pee, Dad.

"Well, you're really going to have to hold it, handsome."

Below them the scene of the accident, an anoma-
lous pulsing dazzle of multicolored lights in the passing
lane, loomed on the highway. Like the carnival on the
green at the top of Fletcher's town in May. Irresistible
as a barn burning in its field at night. A diagonal line of
flares sparkled pink-red, the traffic merged gradually
into one lane, Fletcher behind I'd rather be sailing.
Families filed past as if this was why they'd come. It
happened to someone else, not them, not us. Matter of
percentages, as if a decree had gone out, so many shall
perish in cars this day. A tall mustachioed state trooper,
stately in hat and boots, kept the traffic moving with a
lazy twist of his wrist, his back to the confusion. He'd
seen it all before.

Several cars had pulled off the highway, involved as
witnesses, you figured, or one of them could be Red
Cross certified, or just nosy. Then you saw a U-Haul
truck, its cab somehow askew from the body, which
had been whacked broadside. The alarming glare of
emergency vehicles screened the mustard-yellow car
until they passed directly in front of it. The hood of the
automobile had been smashed back toward the windshield, which had shattered, the driver's side totally . . .
totaled was the word they used. The car pointed east in
the westbound lane. There was activity around the
other side. Look away.

"Doesn't look good," he said.

Two men in the road with brooms swept glass. Another man shoveled sand onto the asphalt from an orange pickup. Two other cars somewhat banged up there, it looked like, snatched from the orderly flow, although nothing compared to . . .

Gwen turned in her seat. "Sam, come here. Don't look," she whispered as Sam nimbly climbed onto her lap from the backseat, all eyes for the action outside.

On the grass bank, silhouette-like, shadowy in the play of light, were two or three clusters of people, just standing, arms folded. Happened so suddenly, and suddenly—bang—a different ball game. There were two, three people sitting down, huddled, hugging updrawn knees. Long night ahead. Then, a bit farther along the bank, what the . . . ?

Fletcher pointed. "Are those cows? Gwen, look, there are two cows standing there." Yes, contentedly grazing with heads down, a man with them, holding a rope in one hand and a long stick in the other. Herefords, not dairy cows.

"For goodness' sake," she said.

Sam wanted to know how they got there.

"Could they have been in the U-Haul?" Fletcher asked.

You drove past, and it was behind you.

"How the hell did that happen?" He held his hand straight out before him. "I'm shaking. Are you?"

"That's an end to the day for you," Gwen said, "the poor people."

Going directly to the heart of the matter, Sam wanted to know if anyone had been killed.

"Maybe everybody got lucky tonight," Fletcher suggested. "Let's hope so."

The clear night opened before them, two wide un-cluttered lanes, and soon, sooner than you'd think, the holiday traffic resumed normal speed. They rounded a broad curve in the highway and the distracting com-motion in Fletcher's mirror, the momentary fuss of flashing lights, was gone.

Kate sat at the edge of her seat, leaning into the space between the front seats, but remained silent, looking out the windshield. Her experience, he thought, her accident coming home from Connecti-cut. It would go down in her journal, along with other matters of the day, as it would go down in his journal—the accident they'd passed, along with other matters, whatever seemed noteworthy, including his daughter's silence, Sam in his mother's lap, I'd rather be sailing. . . .

"Now, damnit, Jack, will you put on that seat belt now. Something like that and you sit there like . . . I mean it, it's so dumb."

He reached with his right hand, drew the wide black strap across his chest, but how the devil do you get the metal part into the . . . Kate took it from his hand impatiently and snapped it into place.

Traffic thinned as they proceeded west, the road beyond his headlights curving along the broken white line into rural darkness, dark New England hills rising familiar, their dormant winter forests, the dim smatter-ing of distant lights, our dwelling places, like a cry in the wilderness, Curly's moon there, the galactic night. How did one space traveler put it, the planet seen from a distance, suspended in space: fragile, alone, a lovely creature. From a distance.

"Mother is scared to death, saying things like I don't know what I'd do without him. She was in tears before dinner, did you notice? It's frightening, getting old, losing your best friend."

"It's all unknown, Gwen. Like that back there. Your parents could outlive all of us for all anyone knows."

Moments later she said, "I didn't mean that about Clare being lost. I've been thinking about her all day—since you mentioned it this morning. It must be terrible for Noah."

He could feel her sitting alertly beside him staring out at the night beyond the headlights, wide awake with vague imaginings. They have known little so far of what people suffer. She placed a hand on the back of his neck and gently squeezed, an unexpected touch. "Jack." His name, spoken that way, meant, I understand, we have each other. Then, as suddenly, she took her hand back.

"I hope our Camperdown makes it. I love the way it looks in the garden. I scratched one of the branches with my fingernail, you know, a couple of days ago, and it was green underneath. Very green."

"It will."

"The business about Dad, I thought that's what the two of you were discussing on the side porch. I saw you with your hand on his shoulder. I couldn't imagine what you were doing out there. He never says a word to me."

No, they'd been discussing all manner of far-reaching subjects. "The old days, life today, the universe. The sun"—he smiled—"I learned all about the sun. The life cycle of all stars."

S till awake? Shouldn't you be sweet dreaming by now?"

"Hi, Uncle Jack. Me and Gram and Bo are playing Scrabble. Even though Bo can't spell. He just spelled bird *b r d*. Dad," she hollered, the phone striking the wall. "It's Uncle Jack."

"I couldn't imagine who the hell would be calling at ten of eleven Thanksgiving night. Shouldn't alarm people like that, Fletch. You got home all right?"

"Half hour ago."

"That wasn't too bad, was it?"

"There was quite an accident just past Sturbridge. A U-Haul, I don't know how many cars. That slowed us down a little."

"Never fails, does it? So what's up?"

"I just wanted to call and thank you for the day, Peter. Great day. I loved the sky, that low winter-ish—"

"I really can't take credit for the sky, Fletch."

"I hadn't been back in your woods for years. That's a splendid tree back there in the mowing, that syc-amore. The little graveyard . . . I remember when you first walked us back there, Peter, in your L. L. Bean boots. I had Sam on my back. Mary and Kate hand in hand. It's hard to believe, isn't it? Where's the time gone, you know? I just wanted to call . . . lovely day. Everyone was in pretty good form, weren't they? The food, as usual, was out of sight. That Scotch, where did you get that? Wonderful Scotch."

"It was a nice day, wasn't it? Our pleasure, Fletch. I felt the same . . . "

"You've got a nice spot there, Peter. I love that Rumford hearth, wonderful heat . . . While I've got you . . . you know the birdfeeder you gave us a couple of years ago, what do you do, just take a bolt and drill a hole . . . ?"

"Birdfeeder?"

"The birdfeeder you made us like the one out by your dogwood, I want to put it up out there in Gwen's garden. What do I need, a cedar post, a bolt . . . ? I'll tell you what, why don't you give me a hand with it when you come out?"

"Jesus, Fletch, God knows when I'll find time. This is it, you know, from now until the new year, we're straight out. It gets worse every year."

"Screw that. Just take the day, Peter, get in the goddamn car, we'll put up the birdfeeder. You think I'm busy? Everybody's busy."

He laughed. "Love to, Fletch, can't think of a thing I'd rather do, honest to God. I'll tell you, next week I'm in Florida again, then Pennsylvania. I've got to get to California at some point. If I don't get to California before Christmas, I'll be up shit's creek, my friend. And then New York, we've got the whole family in New York the week after next."

"I'm counting on it, Peter. Fuck Florida. Bring the family out, we'll cook pasta, have a hell of a time."

"Listen, I've got a couple of calls to make before—"

"I thought you were done on the phone for one holiday. I loved that, the Itzak Perlman of the telephone."

"California, Fletch—eight o'clock out there. I'm just up to my eyeballs—"

"I'm counting on it, Peter. Fuck California. Is Penny there? Let me speak to her for a minute, will you?"

"Hold on, weirdo. Hey, Pen," he called, "some weirdo wants to talk to you."

"Yes?"

"Hi, listen, I was just saying to Peter I just wanted to call and thank you for such a . . . The food, as usual, Pen, was probably the best food I've ever eaten. And the setting, your house on its hill with the trees, those maples, and the sky, it's—"

"Did you call up to be sarcastic?"

"No, absolutely not. I was thinking, remember that old watercolor Gwen did when she was a pollywog practically? The one in our kitchen, the white farmhouse with the woods and the clouds—has it ever occurred to you that it looks a lot like your place? On a day like today."

"I don't remember, I'd have to look at it, Jack."

"Take a look at it next time you're out here. It occurred to me that you've sort of created or achieved that vision your sister had back then, you know, Gwen's idea of a place to live. That's interesting, don't you think?"

"Fascinating, Jack. Listen, I'm glad you enjoyed—"

"Your home, Pen, what you've done there, it's no small accomplishment, it's wonderful really. The whole thing, I kept thinking today, is very imaginative, interesting, pleasing. The vase of feathers, the shells, the bittersweet, those plants of yours."

"Just between you and me, Jack, I'm sick to death of it. I'm mortified when I think of the time I've invested . . . but let's not get into that."

"Forget sick to death. Don't give me that, Pen. Here you've created this terrific place, you have a wonderful family. Your kids are fantastic, the three of them. That's a lot. You've done well, Pen. Everything's going berserk, and you manage to maintain this safe, sane—"

"What's gotten into you tonight, Jack?"

"I loved you in your apron, incidentally, the geese in flight. I have a question, are they flying north or south? Did you ask yourself that as you did the design? I like to think they're going south because geese mean more to me in the fall."

"As a matter of fact, they are, Jack. I knew you'd ask, so I made a point—"

"So here we are driving home and Gwen tells me you took off for the hills or something. I had no idea, Penny. When we were in the kitchen, I didn't realize there was a subtext, so to speak, but I wanted you to know—"

"Is that why you called?" A laugh. "I wanted some time to myself. I'm not going off the deep end, Jack."

"I know, we all need time to ourselves. It's a little different, though, when you don't let people know, when you let people go nuts for a week wondering whether you're dead or alive, right? I'm sympathetic, Pen, honestly, but what I mean is, here we are one Thanksgiving to the next, and no one ever knows what's going on, so you end up alone in some inn with nowhere to go, reading about the end of civilization, I mean the survival, and making up your Thanksgiving list—"

"Is this going to cost me anything, Jack, or do you do this for nothing?"

"This is free. I'm just saying—"

"What are you saying?"

"It doesn't make much sense, does it? Five, ten, fifteen years later, and what happens? Any one of us could get in the car tomorrow and never come back. It's not right."

"It's getting pretty late, Jack. I've got to get these

kids to bed. Can we postpone this discussion until Christmas?"

"That's what I love about you, Pen, that reserve, that composure. I was thinking today, once in twenty years or whatever it's been I gave you a kiss. Remember that? Against your refrigerator."

"You're in a funny mood, aren't you? Are you drunk?"

"One kiss in a lifetime, eventually we die, get cremated, flame into extinction. I was thinking we probably would have done each other more good if we'd gotten together once a year to get in the sack, to sin, instead—"

"I'm really too tired to listen to this, Jack. It's eleven o'clock. Try me some morning after I've seen the kids off to school and had a cup of coffee."

"I saw those little bottles in the bathroom for pain, it bothered me. What's that about? What pain?"

"What bottles? Oh, those, they're nothing. My problem right now is I can't keep my eyes open."

"I'll let you go. Oh, send me copies of those school pictures, will you? I forgot them, damnit."

"You don't want those."

"Yes, I want them—autographed. I love those kids, and I love you, Penny, I mean it. Listen, thanks again."

"Oh, don't be silly. I'm glad—"

"Is your guest, Liz, around?"

"Liz?"

"Put her on, will you?"

"I think they've gone to bed already."

"Go see, okay? Something I meant to ask her . . . about her mother . . . "

"What are you up to, Jack?"

223

"See if she's up, will you?"

"Just a minute."

He stretched for the refrigerator, tethered by the spiraled phone cord, and managed to get his hand on a beer. Waiting, he placed two fingers on the underside of his wrist, the phone wedged between chin and collarbone, and counted against the passing moment displayed on his digital watch. Ninety-five.

"Hello? This is Liz."

"God, that was a long minute. She's not going to come to the phone, I'm thinking, but you did. How nice of you."

"Oh shit. Becky said phone for Liz, I couldn't imagine who . . . I thought you were my father or . . . " Off the phone she said, "It's Uncle Jack."

"You weren't sleeping?"

"I just got ready for bed."

"Sounds good to me. What do you wear to bed—anything?" There was the sound, a faint click, of a phone being disconnected. "Was that someone hanging up another phone? Where are you?"

"Mary's room. It must have been. I'm wearing a nightgown, in fact, this one is flannel with little flowers, I think. It's Mary's. I don't think this is too smart."

"Is Mary there?"

"She just went to take a shower."

"By the way, didn't someone say your father was an architect, he restores castles in Scotland or something?"

"I don't want to talk about my father."

"I hardly had a chance to speak to you once we returned to the house. Never said good-bye and good luck, you know, which began to bother me about half-way home."

"Don't sweat it."

224

"Chances are I'll never lay eyes on you again, it occurred to me, and the more I thought about it . . . It's not every day you go to Penny's for Thanksgiving and grab hold of—"

"That was pretty strange, I guess. Grab hold of what?"

"The skin of the moment. The skinny moment."

"What?"

"Listen, you were a great addition to the holiday. All that stuff about the Indians was wild. I loved the soccer game, the pheasant, our walk. You were important."

"Boy, that's big of you."

"You gave me a lift—like the other day I turned onto a dirt road and there was a deer right there. I was thrilled. The guy I was with, Ingari, acted like it was nothing. We were looking at the proposed site for the grammar school, a beautiful pasture that used to belong to a dairy farm that went under last year. We're dying to get the contract for the grammar school and destroy this beautiful piece of land, we need the money. Ingari probably thought it was a Great Dane."

"Listen—"

"I didn't tell you my deer story, did I, come to think of it? I was running about six in the morning. Last fall. Part of my route I pop over the fence surrounding the college athletic field—it's locked but there's a low spot where you can get over—and dash around the track a couple of times. I was dashing along and I saw what looked like a blanket maybe at the other end of the field. I couldn't tell until I was practically on top of it. A deer had impaled itself on the wrought-iron fence, those pointy bars."

225

"Ouch. Where do you get these stories? Potatoes and . . . Was it dead?"

"Of course. I thought, shit, you'd think it would know what it could handle—fence-wise. Like Curly's whales at Wellfleet, you think they'd know better. Maybe dogs had been chasing it, I decided, it must have panicked."

"What did you do?"

"Kept running. I called the maintenance department when I got home. That haunted me for months. Clare, who we were talking about, Mary's aunt, that happened about the same time. Last year."

"Well . . . Look, Mary is going to be out of the bathroom in a few minutes. I'm sure this must seem pretty strange to whoever . . . What do you think they're going to think?"

"Why am I pestering you? I regretted the way we left it, I just wanted to call and say I had a great time on our walk—loved the stone walls, the marvelous light on the horizon. You gave me a lift like to the lark at break of day—do you know that one?"

"This has been a real neat chat, Jack, I really appreciate it."

"By the way, one more thing, the woman's name on the gravestone—remember? Your mother's name, you said. What was it?"

"Lucy."

"That's it. I couldn't remember."

"Why? What about it?"

"Kate said she might visit Mary in the big city. Is it safe down there?"

"Don't worry, we'll take good care of her."

"By the time I got back here, I just had this strange

feeling. You said where was everybody, you know. Like today. Everybody was right there, we're all right there, but . . . where was everybody?"

"Really, I've got to go. I hear Mary coming."

"I'm crazy about Mary, she's a terrific kid."

"I think so, too."

"Do me a favor, tell Curly I'd like to speak to him."

"Curly?"

"Mary's grandfather. He's quite a guy. Ask him about the sun tomorrow."

"What? His son?"

"The sun in the sky, the center of the solar system, ask him to tell you about it. You'll love it."

"Look, I think everyone's in bed."

"I'd like to speak to Curly if you don't mind. He's probably downstairs watching the news."

"All right, I'll go see."

"Listen, I loved the cornrows, the dancing, holding hands, the whole thing. You were outstanding. Take care."

Off the phone she said, "Your fucking uncle . . . wow . . . "

"Hi, Jack, what are you doing, harassing my friend Liz?"

"Every time I looked at you today I said, My God, Mary is a beautiful young woman. Sight for sore eyes. Liz was a wonderful addition to the day, I'm glad you brought her home with you. I like her."

"I know, she's great. Tell Kate we really expect her to visit us in New York. She's really grown up a lot in the last year, Jack. A lot."

"Do me a favor, don't be so hard on the old man, will you? Your father has a lot on his mind. I don't like

227

to see him get pushed around. You don't know what it's like having a Mop who becomes a Mary overnight."

"I don't think I have to worry about my father."

"He loves you more than anything in the world, you know that, don't you?"

"Jack? Hello?"

"Bye, bye, Jack."

"Hello? Jack?"

"What are you doing, watching the news? So what happened in the world today?"

"Not a damn thing. What can I do for you?" Off the phone he said, "Yes, it's Jack . . . I don't know, I just picked up the phone." He cleared his throat. "You got home all right? Everyone's all right, Gwen and the kids?"

"All snug in their beds."

"Peter said you saw a humdinger of an accident. Near Sturbridge?"

"It wasn't pretty. Maybe everybody got lucky, I don't know."

"Years ago we saw an accident, Pat and I, on our way to Canada, I'll never forget it. Gosh, it must be thirty years now. One of those VW Beetles you never see anymore. One fellow was decapitated, I'll never know how."

"It's scary."

"It is, that's a good word for it, Jack. Well, you're home anyway, that's the important thing."

"So what's the weather? Have you heard a weather report?"

"I was just waiting to hear what they said, Jack. They don't know."

"Say, how about that food today, not bad, was it?"

"The food? Out of this world. Absolutely."

"I really enjoyed our talk this evening. Your talk, I should say."

"She had that bird fresh, you know. Penny got it right down the road here. You can taste the difference, can't you?"

"The turkey? Yeah, the turkey was terrific. But when we were outside . . . you take things for granted, you know what I mean, and then ten, fifteen years later you realize it never happened again, a one-time deal. That knocks me out."

"Oh, there are more where that one came from."

"It was a good day, wasn't it? A full day."

"Yes, it was."

"That must make you feel good—two wonderful daughters like Gwen and Penny, all those gorgeous grandchildren."

"Yes, I guess . . . "

"I was thinking about something you said, your mistake was work, all you ever did was work. I don't think it should be viewed that way. You were happy, you enjoyed it. That was your life, right?"

"Well . . . "

"You've done well."

"Oh, I suppose we could have done worse."

"A lot worse."

"Jesus, Jack, I've got people turning out the lights on me down here. I think I'm going to have to say good night."

"In most cases it doesn't matter what you do anyway, does it? You live until you die, you know what I mean?"

"Well . . . "

"I don't want to keep you up. Listen, Gwen tells

me you're going into the hospital for some damn thing
next week. The damn prostate gland, right?"

"I don't worry about things like that, Jack."

"I didn't realize it, or I would have said something.
I'm sorry you have to go through that, Curly, goddamnit, but I'm sure you'll be fine. They're removing
prostates all day long today, they're pretty good at it.
What are they going to have you in for, a few days?"

"That's all."

"You don't seem too alarmed about the whole
thing."

"It would take a lot more than that to alarm me."

"Well, I just wanted to say good luck. Take care.
We'll be talking to you."

"You bet. Thanks for calling, Jack."

"By the way, that story about Freddy and his sax—
was Freddy, wasn't it? I want to hear some more of
those stories next time I see you."

"Well . . . oops . . . God love us, here's someone
else to say good night. He's got every stuffed thing he
owns with him. Hold on now . . . just a second . . . here
we are."

"Good night, Uncle Jack."

"Good night, Bo."

Fletcher, scared shitless thrill-seeker, tried flying
once. You had to run, leap out into the air, although it was a beginner's steep slope rather than a
sheer cliff, adrenaline glands pouring open, and in the
instant of your brief glide, a suspended falling, your
great Day-Glo wings stretched above you, you entered
a big silence, full of the uprush of your strange being,
which had suddenly acquired a humbling fragility. You

momentarily departed the ground, your former place of all importance, and falling, your life, its trappings and certainties, fell away. The silence following his phone call was like that, a precipitous solitude, his sense of the room, his place here, all the stuff that added up to a life, and even the people upstairs, falling away from him. . . . Then you were dealing with the upcoming ground, the hard dirt—this is it—and you were stumbling, jolted, bounced, dragged, just trying to get your feet under you, hold it together.

I needed that.

You entered the San Francisco apartment at the first-floor level, but when you continued into the living room you were in midair, far above the white buildings of the steep city, whose flat rooftops descended like massed steps to the distant bay with its mounded treeless hills beyond. Buena Vista Terrace, in fact, was the name of her street. You were aware, Fletcher was aware, of entering a single woman's austere life, a private place. The person who lived here lived alone. There seemed a permanence in the selection and relationship of furnishings, as if these possessions were the outcome of patient accumulation and, once acquired, had settled the whole question of things. A flat woven rug on the wood floor—a kilim, he decided when he attempted mentally to re-create the place he'd visited only briefly years before—an oval Queen Anne table and chairs, a Victorian love seat, two antique, Spanish-looking tapestried armchairs, a wall of books. Another table in a sort of alcove was piled with papers, an electronic typewriter, the wall above papered with postcards, photographs, printed messages. A gathering of tall plants stood near one of the three wall-length windows. The kitchen was standing room only, the food cupboards mostly bare. She insisted that they stay with her the two nights of their visit. Kate and Sam slept together on a futon in the guest room, Gwen and Jack took the bedroom, while Clare managed with a pad and her sleeping bag on the living-room floor. Clare's bedroom was Spartan: bed, side table, chest of drawers, a vase of cut flowers. To Fletcher the spareness and simplicity of the place felt right: he could have lived like this. On the mantel above the fireplace in the living room she had arranged, like sacred relics, various mementos from important journeys and significant periods of her life: shells, coral, fragments of wood and bark, shards of rock, and distinctive stones. The largest of these—and instantly recognizable to Fletcher—was a perfectly smooth and symmetrical black stone from the island at Weir Harbor, Maine.

The July weekend in San Francisco was so cold and windy they had to borrow sweaters and jackets from Clare to walk down the panhandle into the park. That night Gwen and the children went to bed by ten, bushed from the long day outdoors. He and Clare finished the large bottle of California red wine they'd started at dinner. The glittering dazzle of city lights in Clare's broad windows shimmered and blinked and intermittently disappeared behind dense billows of blowing fog. She suggested a brief walk around the neighborhood before they crashed for the night. They strolled down the sidewalk opposite the small park that rose steeply from the street, black and forbidding as a forest. The cold fog gusted before them, cascading off the shoulder of the wooded hill, shredded by the dark towering pines there. Clare took his arm and held it

snugly against her side. Doesn't this feel good? Yes. I
love the fog, she said, then added—exactly what
Fletcher was thinking—It always reminds me of Maine.
Tugging his arm close with both hands as they walked,
and laughing, she said, Weren't we bad? emphasizing
the last word with pleasure. She said, I was in heat, I
was an animal. She said, Fucking astonished me, as if I'd
discovered my true self. He placed his hands on her
shoulders. The ten or so years since he'd last, and first,
kissed her seemed like no time at all when he kissed her
again. I needed that, she said, smiling, then steered him
back toward her building. He hadn't asked her what she
meant.

On the slant top desk in their living room, along
with Sam's inimitable carving of a robin and Kate's
ceramic multicolored duck, Gwen had placed a framed
photograph of Clare and beside it one of the smooth
oval stones, polished by immemorial tides, which
Fletcher had brought home with him from Maine more
than a decade before. They turned up in drawers and
baskets throughout the house, valued for their feel, their
reality, their stoneness. Gwen had set out the two ob-
jects soon after Clare's death and they had stayed put,
this stone, out of all the possibilities, steadily acquiring
worth for Fletcher in its now established proximity to
the picture. Kate had been the photographer, spontaneously shooting from the cab window with his zoom
lens at the last possible moment, just as the Fletchers
were leaving for the airport. Clare, wearing a green
sweater and Levi's, stood in the arched doorway of her
Buena Vista apartment building, by a large terra-cotta
pot of rosemary, looking directly at the camera. Her left
hand was in her jeans pocket, while the open palm of
her right hand was raised to eye level, a subdued wave:

good-bye. Her short wavy blond hair, her smile. Beautiful person! The stone, flatter on one side and as convex as a mirror on the other, fit the palm of his hand perfectly. It was dense and felt surprisingly heavy. Basalt, he thought. Thanks to Kate's headlong infatuation with her awesome aunt, they'd ended up with a photograph of that now astounding moment—it had seemed so ordinary at the time—the last instant he or Gwen or any of them had seen her. Their last opportunity, as it seemed to him now, pressing the black stone to his lips, to have changed everything, before she lowered her arm, turned, and stepped back into her white ascetic rooms, the endless view, to die.

*H*e walked out into Gwen's garden, gone by except for sage, the thymes. Take a few deep breaths. Good night, Uncle Jack. Carrying every stuffed thing he owned. Your fucking uncle. . . . In its corner of the garden the Camperdown elm was like a fistful of twisted sticks fastened to the top of a pole. He stooped and snatched a bit of plant life from the ground, rubbed it between thumb and fingers. Lemony golden thyme.

After a day of wind, the night was still. Stillness as in 1659. Then this world—the broad common, fields— had been enclosed against dark and wilderness by a stockade fence. Hostile savages out there. Hardship of all kinds. On the other hand, there was all the chestnut, elm, oak you could ever use, river valley topsoil as fertile as anywhere on earth, the hills wild with game, the wide river so thick with salmon you could get supper with a pitchfork. New world is what you had, not that long ago. And they had it handed to them, lock, stock, and barrel, according to our guest of the day. In new snow late at night, you could feel it, what it must have been like—the rows of bare trees lining the common, silhouettes of dark houses against winter sky—same as ever in a sense. Then Wanzyck and his honchos invade the scene, roaring around in circles astride obstreperous engines, screw the old Dutchman's eyes business, bringing us right up to date. The common was a most remarkable site of historic significance, which had not been bought up for preservation by a Rockefeller, a Flynt, a Dodge. They couldn't buy it all. So you get Zabowski selling the oldest house on the street for a song and a dance thirty years ago to some clever bastard who dismantled it—priceless paneling, chestnut timbers, twenty-inch floorboards, seventeenth-century brick and hardware—and carted it off to be a museum somewhere else. The Zabowskis were cozier in the shoe box they'd built behind the old place. Two other eighteenth-century houses now stood virtually abandoned, tied up in family squabbles, sills rotting, their aged narrow clapboards still covered with the asbestos siding some entrepreneur had sold half the homeowners here forty years ago. Half the other old farmhouses had been chopped up into rents. Here come newcomers like the Fletchers to renovate or restore, plant an herb garden, various trees and shrubs, including, most recently, a Camperdown elm. Meanwhile, a neon strip of fast-food garbage, gas stations, car dealers, a new mall arose overnight in the nearby farmlands that had been cultivated to feed various peoples for a thousand years. Well, all that was just the same as it ever was, no original settler worth his salt would have turned down a snowmobile. Yet still, on a night like this, as on a winter's night, there was a fleeting thrill—past seemed present—as if a whole new future was still possible.

Coming soon: winter, old welcome excitement of the first snowfall. By the time it got here each year, you were ready for it again, even needed it. Covering the raked lawn, crowning each picket of the garden fence, changing the light, changing the air, the feeling in the air.

"It's a little cool to be sitting outside, isn't it? I saw the porch light across the way." He moved between two cars on the overgrown front lawn toward the person seated on the steps. "Lovely night."

"I thought that might be you."

"Celia? I couldn't tell who it was. You're just a dark lump from over there. I've been thinking about you."

"I saw you go walking down the common. You haven't been out walking this late in quite a while, have you?" She had a wool blanket over her shoulders, held closed at the throat from beneath, and tucked around her legs.

"You look cozy. Did you go somewhere today or did you stay home?"

"I was going to my brother's, but the car wouldn't start. I couldn't deal with that this morning, so I skipped it."

"Too bad."

"Everyone's gone, I was happy to have the place to myself, it was okay."

"They must have missed you. Especially the doctor, aren't you his favorite?"

"I talked to everyone on the phone. It was a relief to stay here. You went to Gwen's sister's, didn't you?" She added, "Sam told me."

"Quite a day, wasn't it? Very dramatic, I mean— the sky."

"You can sit down. Come on, pull up a seat."

"No, I just stepped out for a minute. It's been a long day."

"It's been a long year."

"What have you got on your feet? Are those slippers?"

She lifted a foot slightly, holding toward the porch light a big furry slipper, the toe of it a kind of cartoon head. "These are my Rudolph slippers. See the red nose. The antlers are great, aren't they? Denise gave them to me last Christmas."

Fletcher smiled. "Will you guide my sleigh tonight?"

"Sam has been coming over lately, you know. He likes to milk Gerty. It's a riot, he's so careful and serious."

"The other day he said, You know, Dad, the goat lady is nice. We only use that name affectionately, of course. If he becomes a nuisance, send him home."

"I hear all about my dad this and my dad that. He's nuts about you. I never see Kate anymore. We wave now and then. I miss her. She was so much fun when she used to come over and bake bread with me. She used to have me in stitches."

"Demanding teenage life. She's always got ten things planned."

"How's Gwen?"

"Busy. She's the director over there now. The show that's up—artists' quilts—that's her baby. It's going to travel to a half dozen places. She did a fancy catalog, the whole thing. Check it out."

"I ran into her at the market a month ago. She looked great. Sit down for five minutes. You look wiped out."

"These get-togethers, they get to you." He sat

down next to her on the wood step, elbows to knees, looking down at the funny slippers. "Still bringing babies into the world?"

"We had a delivery Tuesday. The whole family was at the foot of the bed—husband, sister, mother, husband's mother. It was beautiful, really beautiful. Everybody laughed and cried."

"So how have you been, anyway?"

"I think I've been pretty good."

"Except what?"

"I was determined to have a baby, remember? You're thirty-six, I told myself, this is it, now or never. Well, I tried it."

"You tried it?"

"I had a miscarriage in September, in the second month. I was feeling terrific, I'd scheduled an amniocentesis, then . . . Bad luck, I guess. The midwife miscarries, isn't that poetic injustice or something?"

Fletcher looked into the woman's eyes now for the first time since he'd joined her on the stoop. Deep-set, clear, candid eyes, a large straight nose, her thoroughly brave smile. He hugged her briefly with one arm, a firm squeeze. "It shouldn't have happened. I'm sorry."

"I've got a few good years left, I can always try again."

"I'm sure you can. Who's the man? You didn't get married?"

"God, no. He's been very sweet actually, but we'd already gone our separate ways. He's about ten years younger, he wants to be a physicist and develop the telescopes of the future. He reminds me of my brother when he was in med school." She rocked toward him in her blanket, bumping his shoulder. "You know it's been just about a year since you were over here. I've missed you. I thought we were friends."

"We are friends, aren't we?"

I've got something of yours, two things actually, that mossy green wool hat and a collection of poetry you came over here with once."

"I tore the house apart looking for that hat last year, I was beside myself."

"I wear it when it rains, and I've gotten to like those poems, so I'm keeping both the hat and the book."

Silence for a minute here as they looked out across the common, where bare trees cast soulful shadows under the moon. Silence as in the two, three centuries people had sat out on their stoops of a chill fall night, he considered, for all their reasons.

"Did you know all this had already been cleared by the Indians when the Europeans showed up? That work had already been done over the centuries by agrarian folk."

"Is that something you learned from Sam?" She smiled. "Of course I knew that. Oh, Gerty's for sale by the way, if you want her. I was planning to let you know. I know Sam would love it."

"Gerty? How come?"

"I'm moving. Five years around here has been plenty. To Maine. They're opening a birthing center in the boondocks. My idea is that I'm needed, I want to do good. I want to live near the ocean."

"You've got a plan. Could I become a midwife and move to Maine and live by the ocean? That sounds perfect."

"Have you spent any time there?"

"Years and years ago. I loved the whole thing, but it was summertime, when the livin' is easy."

"I'm sure it won't be as good as it sounds, nothing ever is. You want to get under this? It's warm in here." She opened the dark green blanket as she might have opened the flap of a tent—from within. Her white body, in a pale satiny nightgown, seemed almost luminous. "I was on my way to bed," she explained. She draped the blanket over his shoulder. Fletcher pulled it across his chest, returning the corner to Celia, who held the blanket closed around them.

"It is warm in here."

"It's beautiful out. So, tell me about today. What's the story? Why are you so edgy?"

"You don't want to hear about today."

"Sure I do. I love stories, remember?"

One Rudolph slipper looked out between his walking shoes. He placed his open hand on her warm stomach, then withdrew it.

"I've got a sonnet for you."

"You do?" She laughed. "A sonnet?"

"Famous. Four hundred years old or so. Ready?" With maybe one or two minor errors, he recited Shakespeare's thirtieth sonnet—"When to the sessions of sweet silent thought"—close to her pleased attentive face.

"That was beautiful, Jack." Grinning from ear to ear in that marvelous forthright way of hers. "Why do you know that, you cornball?"

"I learned it."

"Let's hear another one."

Huddled in Celia's blanket, Fletcher solemnly delivered another sonnet he had by heart—"When in disgrace with fortune and men's eyes"—fudging through small lapses, a lost phrase, with a rhythmic hum, yet stirred, inspired by his powers of the moment, the splendid words falling into place as from charmed lips. At the end of the impromptu performance, she dropped the corners of the blanket, freeing her hands to applaud, big grin, her bloomy breasts jostling in the unseasonably thin nightgown. The vapor of their breaths rose in the chill November air, their sudden laughter—you had to laugh—like to the lark at break of day arising, thought Fletcher, from sullen earth.